THE WITCH FROM THE WOODS

STEPHEN STERLING

CONTENTS

PROLOGUE

Blue and red lights dimly flashed on the road behind Detective Christie, who was grimly staring at the edge of the Blue Ridge Enchanted Forest. He could hear the sobs of kids and adults behind him as everyone was desperately trying to figure out what was going on. It had been approximately twelve hours since the disappearance of Emily Brown, a student of Cardinal Key Academy, and the evidence thus far had shown that she had entered the mysterious woods behind the school. Even at this distance, the dark woods made his stomach churn. All magi possess the innate sense to stay away from Enchanted Forests, and even normal folk tend to unconsciously steer away from them. How and why this girl entered was the mystery of the hour.

To his right, he heard a young girl crying while his junior partner, Detective Bracknell, questioned her. Her friend was lost – kidnapped maybe - and she was extremely distressed. Christie took a glance at her composure – shoulders slumped, arms shaking, heavy breaths. Her whole body was shivering in the cold. It would probably be more helpful to everyone if she went to bed. The investigation was hard enough without hysterical parents and children constantly interrupting it. Of course, sometimes they might have something helpful to add, but more likely the "information" they provided was unnecessary. *Let the professionals handle this*, he wanted to say to them, but knew that would only cause an outburst.

"I told the police everything I know already," she huffed between sobs. "I don't know what got into her! All of a sudden her eyes became like marbles and she slowed down!" She struggled to say something else, but only a cacophony of sounds muffled by her sobs came out.

"Slowed down...?" repeated Detective Bracknell.

"Yeah, we were running laps for P.E., and she was my partner. I thought she looked tired at first, but that's not like her. Usually, she's ahead of everyone else! When she stopped, Mrs. Harrison yelled at us to keep running. Then, she just sprinted into the woods! She hopped the fence in one leap! I tried to catch up to her, but Mrs. Harrison overtook me; she didn't want me to get lost in the woods, too..." The young girl was speaking rapidly and hysterically now.

"Alright," said Detective Bracknell as gently as he could. "You have been a great help today. Why don't you go get some rest so that we can go look for your friend now?"

The poor girl broke down into even larger tears, and her teeth chomped louder from her shivers. "I can't go to sleep! I can't! She was my roommate! I need to find her! And... and... what if the same thing happens to me?"

"You've already helped a lot, and you see this woman right here?" Bracknell put his hand on her shoulder and led her to a police officer nearby. "This is Officer Jenkins. She's going to take care of you and your family tonight. We have already investigated the school grounds, and you'll be safe. There are security guards and sheriffs posted everywhere, just to make sure nothing else happens. And if you think of anything else that might help us find Emily, you can let Officer Jenkins here know."

The girl seemed calmer now, and Detective Christie returned his gaze to the Enchanted Forest, lost in his own thoughts as his partner walked back towards him. If Emily Brown did manage to break out of her possession, she still needed to get out of the Enchanted Forest. And even if she did manage to find her way out (the chances for that were practically null – although there are ancient myths and legends of people traversing these primordial woods all over the globe, it has never been heard of in modern times), she could appear anywhere from Quebec to Alabama.

"I've managed to talk to all her teachers. How's the forensics team coming along?"

"You must be tired of taking in all their emotions. They haven't found anything substantial," replied Detective Christie. "Not even footprint shadows, and we double-checked that. Emily Brown was only an eighth grader who had a psychic aptitude, so it's unlikely she would have learned a spell to erase them and cast it on her own."

"Well, it definitely looks like an abduction," replied Detective Bracknell, who had bags under his eyes from overusing his magic. "This whole case reminds me of what happened a while back in Seattle. She only had one class today where they were casting any magic, and that was biology, where they were busy growing and maintaining plants. I asked her teacher, and she said that she didn't keep any mind-altering plants in her classroom. Only the medical and healing students ever study those anyway."

"Forensics combed through the school, too," answered Christie. "There aren't any traces of psychic magic that were out of the ordinary."

"Her abductor covered up their tracks, then," suggested Bracknell.

"Or they came from the forest."

Bracknell gave his partner a knowing look. *Or both*, they thought simultaneously. Dark and Enchanted Forests were extremely unpredictable. Unless the caster was especially skilled and powerful, performing spells in one was dangerous. In either scenario, whoever this must be would have to be an extremely powerful magus. Erasing all traces of magic was extremely difficult in its own right.

"The girl I was just questioning said that her friend had glazed eyes –"

"She said they were like marbles," interrupted Christie, but he knew what that meant.

"Were you any good at your psychological magic classes?" asked Bracknell. "As an empath, I was taught that psychic magic could make physical changes to the body of the victim. Do you think it's a sign of that?"

"Could be," replied Christie. "But I suspect that it's something even more nefarious."

The forest loomed darkly in the distance, its ancient trees guarding closely held secrets. The disappearance of Emily Brown was turning into a mystery that transcended the boundaries of the ordinary, and Detective Christie couldn't shake the feeling that they were dealing with forces far more powerful than they had ever imagined.

I
THE ROAD TO CARDINAL KEY

It was the first day of school for Kalina, and she was prepared to be disappointed in a thousand ways. Although her parents were very encouraging, her brother had spent all summer teasing her and telling her crazy stories of what to expect as a sixth grader. She knew of course that most of them were lies and exaggerations, but she couldn't help feeling a little bit nervous, even if she theoretically knew exactly what to expect. While she considered and searched for possibilities of hazing, bullying, and stress, she stared out the window, mesmerized by the dense woods as they drove through the winding roads of Appalachia. They still had another half-hour of driving before they arrived at Cardinal Key Academy.

Her brother Phillip sat next to her, his nose stuck in the autobiography of Aldous Norwich, a famous traveler from the seventeenth century. Phillip chose this book because he shared this rare gift. In fact, when he was being tested for his aptitude, he had accidentally teleported himself all the way to London (possibly due to the fact that he had recently watched a James Bond movie, and thus had the location on his mind). Fortunately, he was able to make his way to the Magical Court of the United Kingdom. There, he was able to find help and get in contact with an American diplomat. On the other hand, it was also fortunate for Kalina, since she got to take a vacation to England when her parents went to retrieve him.

Students normally didn't get tested for their aptitudes until the end of sixth grade, but Kalina already knew her aptitude for the most part: she was some sort of a sibyl, a clairvoyant, or a soothsayer. It's not as rare an aptitude as travelers are, but it was still a coveted and useful ability in its own right. To see and predict the future was extremely powerful, and many bad actors try to find and manipulate those with the gift. That's why Kalina felt it was important to keep her aptitude a secret. The world could be a dangerous place for magi like her.

Kalina cringed at the sensation of the minivan unpleasantly crunching over the gravel road as they approached the entrance of the school. Kalina always hated that sensation; it felt like nails on a chalkboard. Although Kalina and Philip already knew where their dormitories were, they and their parents still had to check in with the school staff. Kalina watched as her mother rolled down the window so she could speak to the young lady directing the traffic.

"Hello, Lindsey," her mother said, "same as every year?"

"That's right, Mrs. Todorova, I'm sure by now you know the way already, and can I check Phillip in for you?"

"Yes, that would be lovely, and also Kalina's starting this year!"

"Congratulations!" she exclaimed joyfully while ruffling through some papers. "Welcome, Kalina! I hope you enjoy your first year!" She finished them off by waving another car to come forwards.

After they rolled through and continued driving towards the dormitory buildings (which were only a few yards away), Phillip turned toward Kalina and said, "That's Miss Haverty, she's the homeroom teacher for the seventh graders. She also teaches English and Greek. I remember having her; I liked her a lot."

Kalina thought she looked friendly, and would probably choose Greek instead of French when she got to the upper school. Learning multiple languages was important for magi for a few reasons, primarily to open up more modes of incantation. It also gave an advantage for a magus in any sort of competition. An opponent can't block your spell properly if they don't understand what you're saying. That's why the Todorova family pushed their kids to learn Serbian.

Kalina saw many students walking and playing on the field as Mr. Todorova drove the car to a gravel lot between the boys and girl dormitories. Two kids were playing tennis while a circle of others were playing levitating ninja.

"Are we late?" asked Kalina. "It looks like a lot of other students are here already."

"No, dear," replied Catherine Todorova. "We're perfectly on time."

"A lot of students probably came here yesterday and this morning," replied Phillip.

"So we *are* late," pushed Kalina.

"No," sighed Phillip, with a hint of exasperation. "Classes don't start until Tuesday, and there's still going to be other students coming on Labor Day tomorrow."

"Well family, this is where we'll split up," declared Mr. Todorova, who parked the car and popped the trunk open.

Phillip took out his luggage from the trunk and said, "*Pratime torbe!*"

Kalina watched the bags trail behind her brother and father as they walked towards the boy's dormitory.

"Mom, can you enchant my bags, too, please?"

"No."

"Why not?"

"Not everything in life comes easy. There won't always be a spell or incantation to do the work for you. It's important for you to develop character."

"But Phillip gets to do it! It's not fair," she whined.

"Phillip put in the study hours and knows the spell. On his first day, I made him carry his own bags, too."

Kalina sighed in disappointment and frustration as she put the strap of her duffel bag over her shoulder and began towards the brick building that was the girl's dormitory. She often wondered why her parents didn't use a lot of magic at home, but she recalled her mother's voice saying, *Magic always comes with a price, especially to the practitioner. The best magi know this.* At least her father had parked slightly closer to this building she thought to herself. As they approached the tall edifice, the large, engraved wooden doors opened by themselves, and a middle-aged woman came forward to great them.

"Cat, is that you?" she exclaimed.

"Oh my goodness, Donna!" shouted her mother in reply. "This is my daughter, Kalina. Kalina, this is an old friend of mine, Mrs. Abernathy. Are you the dorm mother for the girls now?"

"Yes, I started just last year actually. How have you been?"

Kalina waited patiently as her mom caught up with her old classmate. It had been almost five years since they last held a conversation; although, they were still friends on Facebook. Apparently, Mrs. Abernathy's husband worked at the Virginia Magical Burgess as an engineer. It didn't take long for Mrs. Donna (she allowed the students to call her by her first name since she wasn't technically a teacher) to find out which dorm Kalina was in. Of course, Kalina already knew the number. Not because of her clairvoyant abilities, simply because she was informed of it when she got her new student packet earlier in the summer. Nevertheless, she knew the benefit of letting someone feel important, and gracefully let Mrs. Donna help guide her.

"You're in 714, a trio! You've got a really good sophomore mentor, too."

"What do you mean by a trio?" asked Kalina, momentarily caught off guard. A quick vision overtook her consciousness for a second, revealing a girl with curled ginger locks and another with long brown hair. *My roommates,* she guessed before suppressing anymore visions from overpowering her mind. She returned her attention to Mrs. Donna.

"There are sixteen girls, and since that isn't divisible by three, a few of the girls got duets," explained Mrs. Donna. "Now, I'll lead you upstairs myself since I think I saw Stephanie just go out with a couple of other girls – oh, speak of the devil!"

At that instant, a tall, sporty-looking, brunette girl with a pony-tail entered the lobby of the girl's dormitory. She had a clever smirk on her face and strode in with the unrivaled confidence that earned her a position as a mentor.

"Stephanie, we were just talking about you!"

"Good things, I hope!" replied the older girl charismatically, brushing her bangs out of her eyes.

"Of course! This is one of your new girls, Kalina."

"Nice to meet you! You're in 714, right? I actually just happened to take out your two roommates on a tour of the school grounds. They're out playing tennis right now."

"Accelerated tennis?"

"No just regular tennis."

"Kalina loves tennis; she's an avid player," said Mrs. Todorova proudly. "I'm her mother by the way."

"Pleased to meet you," replied Stephanie with a friendly smile. "Well, why don't I take you two up to show you your room. And we can use the leverate for your bags."

"Actually," began Mrs. Todorova, "I was thinking Donna and I could catch up for a little bit."

"That's alright," replied Stephanie. "I'll leave you to it, then. I'll help you with your bags, Kalina. *Luggage Lighten.*" She snapped her fingers and picked a bag up.

Kalina lifted her duffel and it was significantly lighter. She followed Stephanie across the room while trying to figure out how exactly the magic worked.

"How come you didn't use a spell to make my stuff follow you automatically? And how is it possible for the luggage to feel lighter?" asked Kalina.

"Well, to answer your first question: I did try coming up with one, but I had a hard time concocting an incantation for it. I asked around for one, but you'll find there are a lot of gatekeepers here – not everyone likes to share their secret tricks. Physical magic isn't my specialty anyways. As for how it works exactly... well..., it doesn't actually lighten the luggage in the sense that it has 'less mass.' That's impossible. I'm a healer, so I figured out that I can produce an anatomical illusion to give your muscles the appearance that the luggage is lighter. You might feel a little sore later. You'll learn more about that kind of theory in your classes," replied Stephanie. "Have you ever used a leverate before? They're kind of old fashioned nowadays I guess."

"No I haven't," answered Kalina, watching Stephanie open a sliding door just by waving her hand. They got into what looked like a wooden elevator platform.

"*Activate leverate!*" she shouted. "You have to be really loud and clear since the system is so old. They were supposed to do maintenance on it last year, but they never did. Apparently they ran into some technical problems."

"Is it like an elevator?" asked Kalina.

"Pretty much. A group of magi came up with it a couple hundred years before the elevator was invented. Before then, magi would just have to walk or use a levitation spell to get around. Imagine how inconvenient that was!"

Kalina wasn't sure how she felt about using a centuries old wooden box to move up and down a seven-storied building, but she didn't want to let her uncertainty show either. Kalina watched Stephanie control the leverate by slowly raising her palm upwards. They could keep track of which floor they were on by a cut-out square at the top center, which revealed a painted number of the story they were on.

"Funny story," began Stephanie, "but when they first invented the leverate, they actually had no way to tell which floor they were on, so they had to just guess."

When they got to the seventh floor, Stephanie led Kalina all the way down the hall to her room.

"Lucky you, you're right across from me," she said. "You can leave your bags in here for now. You'll have plenty of opportunities to start packing stuff away. I'll take you to the school closets now so that you can get your school uniforms."

2

ESSENTIALS FOR MAGICAL STUDY

"Do you have your supply list with you, by the way?" asked Stephanie.

"Yes, actually," replied Kalina, who foresaw that she would need it. "I brought it with me; it's in my pocket."

"Lucky for you; I can't believe I forgot to ask. In any case, the packing list is pretty much the same for all sixth graders, as you guys are coming in on a clean slate. I think I remember your roommates telling me your homeroom teacher is Ms. Dalton, right?"

"That's right," confirmed Kalina, and then paused for a moment. "Did you like her?"

"Personally, I've never had her since she only started a few years ago, but I know some others who said they loved her," replied Stephanie as she opened a door with a bronze number 18 on it. "Welcome to the school closets," she finished, motioning Kalina to enter.

Kalina entered the room and saw a young lady wearing a tawny, collared Easter dress. There were all sorts of skirts, shirts, and pants levitating around her. When she heard their footsteps, she looked up. The floating apparel put themselves away as she turned her focus to the new student. Kalina didn't necessarily find the magic impressive despite the fact that she wasn't used to it. Her mother was certainly against using mundane magic, but would probably make an exception considering that the woman probably had to get uniforms ready for hundreds of students each year... possibly multiple times a year.

"Ach, Steffi!" she exclaimed with an exaggerated German accent that reminded her of Arnold Schwarzenegger. "Wie geht's? Ich habe dich heute nicht gesehen! Who have you brought this time with you? Does she have her list?"

"Yes, and this is Kalina Todorova, she's a new sixth grader, and she's got to get her uniforms of course! Also, I did end up coming in today but there were so many people, and I got Mrs. Fowler to help my other girls."

Although Kalina was a little shy about everything being so new, Stephanie's calm and relaxed demeanor made her feel even more comfortable. She could see why she was the mentor for the sixth grade girls.

The woman was making short, quick nods in understanding. "Yes, yes, there was so much work this morning – there always is. Truth be told I stopped looking at the lists and started guessing at one point." She finally turned to Kalina and continued cheerfully, "Hello, Kalina, it's nice to meet you. I'm Miss Bauer. Let's look over your list and get you your uniforms." She spoke very efficiently and quickly. She turned around brusquely motioning Kalina to follow her into another double-doored closet. It was a standard looking closet, with half the section for boys on the right, and on the left, the girls.

"Grab a box from the back corner, Kalina, to carry your clothes." Miss Bauer pointed to where there was a stack of cardboard boxes, and Kalina walked over. They were enchanted to fold themselves up when Kalina touched one, startling her. This was one of those times when Kalina's natural gift didn't prevent her from being surprised. *Now this,* she thought to herself, *would certainly be a form of magic that my mother would appreciate.* After a second of reflection, she thought to herself again, *why do I keep thinking of my mother's taste in magical activities?*

Kalina quickly forgot about her internal dialogue and turned around to be greeted by three floating maroon polo T-shirts and two long-sleeved white V-neck dress shirts. They waved slightly in the breeze, seemingly staring at her as though they were waiting to be picked up. Each shirt sported the school crest which featured a cardinal. Kalina moved towards them, and as soon as she approached the floating shirts, they folded themselves neatly into Kalina's box. *Well this is all very convenient.*

Kalina pushed through a rack of shirts, where she found Miss Bauer and Stephanie having an intense conversation in German. She wasn't sure if they were having a debate or whether that was just the German language.

Stephanie turned towards her and asked, "What size pants do you wear? I know you filled it out on your check list, but *Miss Bauer* doesn't think it's accurate."

Before Kalina could respond, Miss Bauer interjected, "Ach! There are more accurate ways of measuring this!" She smoothly entwined her fingers together and pulled them apart, creating an ethereal string of white light. She quickly muttered some German, then whipped the string around Kalina's waist. Startled, Kalina jumped, but rather than hurting, it felt like a nice breeze of cool wind had wrapped around her torso. Nevertheless, Kalina wished she was asked first, and felt somewhat violated. Stephanie noticed her glare and offered an apologetic expression that meant something along the lines of "Sorry, this is just her modus operandi." Kalina understood: Miss Bauer had good intentions, and at this point in the day, she probably didn't have time for pleasantries.

"Hmph! As I expected!" grinned Miss Bauer smugly before snapping her fingers. Stephanie sighed as two khaki skirts, two khaki pants, and one maroon wool skirt flew towards Kalina. Like the shirts, they folded themselves neatly into her cardboard box.

Miss Bauer and Stephanie picked out the rest of her clothes, including a red beret, a brown leather belt with a brass buckle, and a pair of brown dress shoes as well as a pair of black rain boots designed with white dogwood flowers. She wondered if the boys also got florally decorated rain boots. Kalina expected to get her gym clothes here, but Stephanie told her that she would get them during P.E. on her first day.

"I'll also teach you and the other girls how to properly maintain and fold your clothes, including shining your shoes, your belt buckle, and ironing your uniforms. You can find everything you need including washers and dryers in the basement of the girls' dorm building. Next year, you'll get a handbook on simple maintenance spells. The school doesn't trust you with too much magic yet, especially since everyone is coming in with different levels of magical experience." She gave a lighthearted chuckle after the last statement.

As Kalina and Stephanie walked back to the dorms, Stephanie explained to her what she should expect on the first day of term. She also pointed out the names of all the buildings and fields that they were passing by, but Kalina only remembered Baxton Auditorium because she thought it sounded cool. Moreover, she struggled to pay attention since she was awkwardly carrying her box of clothes and was too naturally quiet to ask for Stephanie to cast the lightening spell on them.

"You'll find a packet that has a map and everything in your desk in your room," she explained. "The campus isn't too big to get lost, but it will still take you a few weeks to get used to it. I'll lead you and the other girls to your respective homerooms on Tuesday. Ms. Dalton will take it from there."

Kalina gladly listened as she felt the evening sun's golden rays pass through the bushy green cottonwoods that lined the brick walkway. Upon entering the girls' dormitory, Stephanie showed her how to check in and out – this way Mrs. Donna could keep accountability of the girls in case of an emergency. Much to Kalina's dismay Stephanie chose to lead her up seven flights of creaky wooden stairs instead of using the leverate this time. By the time they reached the seventh floor, Kalina had picked up a light sweat. She was suddenly grateful for all the conditioning her mother put her through while coaching tennis. Kalina and Stephanie strode down the hall to find room 714 already open. Inside were two girls sitting on the wooden floor playing dominoes with Mrs. Todorova.

The girl with the bright red hair jumped up first, and held out her hand. "Hi, I'm Maura; you must be Kalina – our third! I'm so excited to finally meet you." She spoke quickly, enthusiastically, and confidently. Her wide emerald eyes looked intensely into Kalina's. She spread her mouth far apart, revealing a set of ivory teeth (with one of them missing in the back). Kalina thought she looked friend-ly, and couldn't help but smile back.

"I'm excited to meet you, too," replied Kalina, as she took Maura's hand for a hearty shake. "I came in earlier, but you guys weren't here." She then turned to her left where the other girl had more deliberately stood up and walked over. "And you must be Laurelle, right? I saw your name on the door."

The girl brushed a strand of her dark chocolate hair out of her face, revealing thoughtful amber eyes behind a set of thin glasses. "Yes, nice to meet you," she said meekly.

After a few seconds of silence, Maura picked up the conversation again, "We were just playing dominoes with your mom. We showed her how to play bones. You wouldn't happen to know how to play, would you?"

"No, but I'm a quick learner. Show me how?"

"Of course! I'll teach you and Laurelle how to play the magic version later, though. My sister and I invented it ourselves! Unfor-tunately, Laurelle said they didn't use magic a lot at home, though, so that's why we're playing the normie version. What about you? Do you know any magic yet?"

"I know a little bit, but my parents have kind of an old school mentality on work ethic," responded Kalina, careful not to sound too sour.

"We try to maintain a balanced approach," specified Mrs. Todorova.

Once introductions were out of the way, the three girls sat back down in the middle of the floor, nearly forgetting about Stephanie and Mrs. Todorova, who were having a small chat.

"Well, I'll let you girls get to know each other," announced Stephanie. "Dinner starts at six, so I'll come back around that time to show you three to the mess hall. If you need anything just let me know, alright? I'm right across the hall."

The girls nodded in appreciation, and Stephanie walked out, leaving the door open.

"I'm going to leave now, too, Kalina," said Mrs. Todorova. "Do you want to say goodbye to Dad?"

"No, thank you," said Kalina, a little embarrassed. She didn't want to make the transition process any more difficult than it already was. Better to rip the band-aid off, she thought to herself. That, and she thought she was giving an impression of maturity and independence in front of her two new friends. When she saw that her mother looked a little sorrowful, though, she got up and gave her mother a quick tight hug.

"I love you."

"I love you, too. Goodbye, and remember you can call whenever you need to."

Mrs. Todorova turned around quickly to leave so that Kalina wouldn't see her eyes water. It was hard enough for her when Phillip left, but now she won't have either of her kids at home. She was glad to know that Kalina had a good set of roommates – it would make the parting process less difficult for her. She didn't think her daughter was aware how bittersweet it was for her mother to watch her kids grow up and move on.

***

Phillip walked with his best friend and roommate, Mark, down the brick path towards the mess hall. The warmth of the setting sun on his back felt pleasant, and the movements of their elongated shadows tangled before them was amusing.

He and Mark became close friends ever since they each discovered their aptitudes, which complemented each other perfectly. Mark was naturally gifted with navigational magic (not an exceptional or uncommon talent, but still useful). Wandered off the path while hiking? Ship lost at sea? Mark was who you wanted next to you or to find you. Of course, those skills only scratched the surface of navigation, a much studied field of magic, but Mark hadn't reached higher levels of navigational magic yet. Phillip, who was a traveler that definitely got lost plenty of times, certainly appreciated his friend's skill. He often wondered what he would be able to do without Mark. College was only a few years away for them, and Mark wanted to enroll as a cadet in Annapolis, an ambition which Phillip had absolutely zero interest in. What would be the point of being a sitting duck in the middle of the ocean when you could go literally anywhere you wanted in an instant?

As they were chatting, a familiar figure approached them. Her beautiful, wild hair looked like it was aflame in the sunset. She cut through the grass instead of waiting for the boys' and girls' paths to merge ahead of the main building. Mark, endearingly known as a "rules person," cringed a little bit at the blatant disrespect for the greenery. Phillip on the other hand, had seen plenty of people walk on the grass before, and it didn't even register to him that she was doing anything strange.

"Hey, Phillip! Hey, Mark!" she called out as she got closer, lightly jogging up to them.

"Hey, Aisling," replied Phillip, savoring the pronunciation in his mouth. Back in sixth grade, when they had homeroom together, their teacher kept saying *AY-sling*. It's actually pronounced *ASH-ling*. Mark merely gave her a head nod and a modest smile. "How've you been? How's Robert and your family?"

"My summer's been absolutely great! Robert and I spent a lot of time with each other. His family even invited me to go to the beach with them. It was nice to get away."

"I thought you would have spent more time on your extracurricular activities," teased Phillip, only slightly sarcastically. Aisling had notoriously earned the title of "conspiracy theorist" in their grade.

Aisling rolled her eyes, "Yes, I *have* been researching some *interesting* stories. I actually got Robert into cold cases and mysteries, too, and he's been following along."

"So which one interested you this summer?" asked Mark.

"The missing students of 1969."

"Oh?" interjected Phillip, curious about what kind of theory she came up with this time.

"Yeah, I think it might have something to do with that girl who went missing back in 2000 – Emily Brown."

Phillip and Mark stopped in their tracks and gave her a confused look. Phillip forced a calm demeanor.

"You know that's still fresh in the minds of many people. My mom knew the girl herself when she was in school."

Sensing the growing tension, Mark decided to change the subject. "So which beach did you and Robert go to?" There was a little bit of acid in his tone, but thankfully it went unnoticed. He had a small grudge against Robert, but tried not to let it show too much for the sake of friendship.

"Well, Robert's family is from New Jersey, so we went to one up there. It was nice. They also went to France this summer, but I didn't go with them. I visited my dad's family in Ireland. He didn't go with us, though, because of... well, you know." Her voice trailed off.

"Nice to get away from Maryland, huh" remarked Phillip jokingly, doing his part to keep the high vibes coming. "Got to take a break from all that Old Bay seasoning?"

"Hey! Don't slag off my state like that! We still have the best flag!"

The three continued heading to the mess hall, Mark and Phillip both debating with Aisling about whether or not Virginia was better than Maryland. It was a topic they discussed often, and usually didn't end until one side conceded to a fair point (be it cuisine, beaches, or even politics).

3
CHARMS AND ALARMS

8:30 – 8:45: Home Room

8:45 – 9:30: Language Arts

9:30 – 10:15: Mathematics

10:15 – 11:00 Magical Theory and Practice

11:00 – 11:45: Earth Science

11:45 – 12:30: Lunch

12:30 – 1:00: French (MWF) and Greek (TR)

1:00 – 1:45: Social Studies

1:45 – 2:15: Arts

2:15 – 3:00: PE & Dismissal

Kalina looked up from her agenda to the smiling face that handed it to her. "Thank you, Ms. Dalton."

"You're welcome, sugar," she replied in a sweet southern twang. "Now, why don't you go find your desk with your name tag?"

Kalina walked around looking for her desk (they were in pairs together facing the white board). She found it at the front right corner, furthest from the door where she entered, but closest to the door that led outside. To her delight, she was seated next to Laurelle, which was optimal since Laurelle seemed to be even more timid than she herself was. On the other hand, Maura was the type of girl who had no qualms immediately become friends with everyone she met. Kalina decided to put her backpack under her desk. Although all the girls were being led by Stephanie, she was the first student to come in, and she watched as the others trickled in after her.

It didn't take long before Laurelle and Maura came in; they just needed to use the restroom first, which Stephanie had also shown them. Why didn't they use their dorm bathroom first? Kalina could only guess. After they received their schedules, they joined Kalina. Laurelle was pleased to be seated next to her, and Maura was seated behind them with a girl named Alice Huddleston.

More and more students started trickling in (the boys included), and by 8:36, everyone was present. Ms. Dalton let them talk for a little bit to get to know each other, but when the clock struck 8:45, she raised her hand and cleared her throat to signal them to be quiet. Only one clueless kid kept talking, but he soon went silent when his desk partner nudged him to pay attention. Ms. Dalton smiled at them through her half-moon glasses with dark intelligent eyes. Her loose salt and pepper hair draped over her shoulders as she turned to face the windows and said, "*Windows for sight, reveal the light!*"

The blinds snapped up and the windows cracked themselves open, allowing a soft zephyr to enter the somewhat stuffy room. Kalina heard a couple of students gasp. Some were amazed, a couple amused, and the others remained untouched. Kalina came from a family that was used to a moderate amount of magic, so she was not in total awe. However, her mother would have rolled her eyes at the idea of pointlessly using magic for such a mundane task. Still, the teacher's magical finesse did put a smile on her face.

"Good morning, class," began Miss Dalton, gracefully sweeping her hair over her shoulder. "I'd say it would be a shame to waste such a lovely day indoors. I would *love* to do an activity outside to get to know all of you. What do y'all think about that?"

The students cheered, "Yes!" and lined up to go outside. Once they were on the field, Ms. Dalton had her students sit in a circle on the dewy grass. Kalina counted fifteen other students in her own class, which meant that the other sixth grade class must also have sixteen. Ms. Dalton herself sat down crisscrossed next to Kalina with a ball of cream-colored yarn in her hands. There was something off about the yarn, but Kalina wasn't sure what it could be. It felt like her subconscious was trying to tell her something, but she ignored it. *If it's important, I'll be bound to figure it out later.*

"We're going to play a game," she explained. "This is an icebreaker called 'A Tangled Web.' It requires teamwork to do this activity and the web needs to be balanced by each and every one of you for this to work. Here's how we play: I'll start first. I'll say my name and something interesting or unique that I like – to eat or to do. Then I'll toss it over to someone else – not next to me – and they'll repeat what I said as well as introduce themselves also. Then, the third person will have to repeat everything that was said so far. As we continue, we can add more rules to make this more fun. Any questions?"

Nobody said anything, which meant that either the instructions were crystal clear or they were too embarrassed to ask. Typically, Cardinal Key Academy students were bright, and Ms. Dalton was sure they would be able to figure the game out along the way.

"Alright, perfect. My name is Ms. Dalton, and I like to drink my chocolate milk with a little pinch of salt."

She tossed the ball of yarn to another student whose name was Arthur, who claimed emphatically that he could solve a Rubik's cube in less than 20 seconds. Another student heckled him, but Ms. Dalton told him to quiet down. "Remember, this icebreaker requires teamwork." The students kept passing the yarn to each other, and Kalina started to feel the passage of time differently – it was both slower *and* quicker. It was as though she were viewing time from the outside. She felt unchained from the temporal subjections of the earth.

She could start to see the pattern emerge from the chaos that the others didn't even realize existed. She saw where the ball of yarn would land three times from now, and could answer the questions about students that they themselves were yet to ask. She could see the strings of magic intertwining with the yarn and binding the students together. It looked like a primordial tapestry spun, woven, and cut by the mystical Norns themselves. Suddenly, Kalina was taken out of her trance by hysterical screaming. The world faded back to its mundane colors, and Kalina saw in the distance the figure of a woman running through the field from the Enchanted Forest behind the school.

"Help! Help!" she cried in a raspy voice, and all together, the students all turned to stare at her. Kalina thought that the unison of the motion was eerie, like they were a part of some hive mind. *That's ridiculous*, she thought to herself. *Stop being silly and start being mature.*

Kalina stood up after Miss Dalton, whose face had bleached. "Everyone get back inside!" she ordered. The honey in her voice was no longer there. Instead, it was sharp, and struck them like a blade on a whetstone. No one had the audacity to disobey, and they all headed inside. Mesmerized by the event, the students all gathered around the window, watching Ms. Dalton approach the mysterious and distressed woman brusquely. Only one student had disappeared – Maura.

As soon as she asked if anyone had seen her friend, Kalina and the other students saw her coming outside of a different exit with Dean Schulz. He was able to run faster than she could and had caught up to Ms. Dalton just as the strange woman fainted into her arms. He started talking to Ms. Dalton, and then she turned to Maura and said something. Maura turned around and ran back up the classroom, where the students were eagerly waiting for her to tell them what was happening.

Maura entered the classroom, her face flushed with a mix of excitement and trepidation. The other students crowded around her, their curiosity piqued. Kalina, Laurelle, and the others eagerly awaited her explanation.

Maura caught her breath and began, "You won't believe what just happened! So, after Ms. Dalton told us to go back inside, I ran and got Dean Schulz and another teacher who I think is the school counselor. They were both trying to talk to or wake up that lady who ran onto the field."

"What did she want?" Alice asked.

Maura shrugged, "I'm not sure. She just looked really scared... like she was running away from something."

"And what did they say to you?" Laurelle inquired.

"They asked if I'd seen anything strange or if I knew who that lady was," Maura replied. "I told them I didn't know her and hadn't seen her before. The rest of us will probably be questioned eventually, and maybe even the rest of the school!"

Kalina was puzzled by the whole situation. "Why would she run into our school like that, screaming Bloody Mary? It's so bizarre. And how did she come from those woods – they're supposed to be Enchanted Woods. She definitely came out of them right? Isn't that supposed to be impossible?"

The other students nodded and murmured in agreement, their faces reflecting various shades of wonder and concern. Ms. Dalton and Dean Schulz, still conferring with the other teacher, eventually returned to the classroom. Ms. Dalton cleared her throat and addressed the class. "Everyone, I know that was an unusual start to the day, but I want you to remember that your safety is our top priority. We have everything under control, and the situation is being handled by the authorities. Your parents will presently be notified of all the details. There is no need to worry."

Kalina noticed that Miss Dalton's confident demeanor had returned, and it reassured her. The woman's strange appearance and behavior remained a mystery, but the school staff seemed to have it in hand.

Ms. Dalton resumed the tangled web icebreaker indoors, but the atmosphere in the classroom had shifted. The students were less enthusiastic, their minds still occupied by the unusual events of the morning. Despite their efforts, they couldn't repeat the same magic from the first time.

As the day progressed, the incident on the field became the main topic of conversation among the student body. Rumors and speculations spread like wildfire, and Kalina found herself listening to various insane theories about the woman between classes, from her being an escaped mental patient to a mythological shapeshifting beast. *Probably a mixture of both*, pondered Kalina to herself, tongue in cheek.

The day's morning classes passed in a blur, and Kalina couldn't help but notice that Ms. Dalton seemed a bit distracted during their math lesson. Her dad was a mathematician, and Kalina usually enjoyed the subject, but her mind was preoccupied with the morning's events. Hopefully lunch would give her a chance to reflect and relax.

4
RUMORS AND REVELATIONS

The bell rang, signaling the beginning of fourth period. Phillip remembered how he absolutely hated that awful sound when he was a sixth grader. Eventually, he became so used to it that he barely even registered the sound anymore. One student in seventh grade had even offered him a hearing blocker after studying otology (one of the very many healing aptitudes), but Phillip didn't want to take his chances with a middle-schooler playing doctor.

Phillip was glad to have Mark at his side for Cartography, and they found seats next to each other in the back of their class. They weren't the stereotypical 'bad students,' but they had been caught a few times whispering to each other in the middle of class. There was a mix of students from various grades there, and between the two of them, they were able to give names to each of the faces that walked in.

"That's Rhodes. I know him from wrestling," said Mark to Phillip while waving at the relatively short, but muscular student.

Mr. Rumsey was the next to walk in, fashionably late by a mere 97 seconds.

Mr. Rumsey was known for being a stern, but fair teacher. He had strong countenance, but it was reserved. Phillip thought he was like a lion in that regard – quiet until being provoked into a bone-shattering roar.

Promptly, Mr. Rumsey sat on his desk and snapped his fingers, causing the door to shut. Many adult magi learn to cast magic without voicing their spells, especially the easier incantations (often said inside their heads). Phillip still couldn't get over the fact that so many of his teachers and classmates chose to waste their magic on silly chores instead of taking two seconds to do them. He kept that opinion to himself, though.

"Good morning, class. Today, we are just going to go over the syllabus and expectations for this class," he spoke with a certain low-intensity power. It was both boring and inspiring.

He whispered an incantation and a stack of papers from his desk flew to each student in the class. Mark and Phillip looked through each subject with interest.

"Because I'm assuming that you all can read, I'll go through this quickly and clearly. If for some reason you have a question, feel free to ask. Just know that you *will* be judged by me and your classmates."

Mark and Phillip exchanged smirks to each other. They had heard Mr. Rumsey could be sarcastic, and they knew that the other was silently listing a few names who could benefit from this attitude.

Keeping his promise, Mr. Rumsey finished his syllabus shortly and was able to get to the juice of the subject before the period ended. According to the syllabus, they would be starting with terrestrial based techniques, and work their way up to oceanic, and then meteorological and astronomical methods. For today, though, they were just starting with the basics.

"Who can tell me what cartography is?" asked Mr. Rumsey. Nobody raised their hands. "Anyone?" A few more slow, awkward seconds passed. "So you all chose to take a class without knowing what it was about..."

Mark spoke up, "Cartography is... the practice of drawing maps?"

"Is that a question?" replied Mr. Rumsey.

Mark hesitated to speak, and glanced at Phillip, who just shrugged.

"No," he said, with a little bit more confidence this time.

"Good," said Mr. Rumsey. "You should speak with more assertiveness. You gave me a good definition. Now, 'the practice of drawing maps.'" He wrote on the board, and all the students took out their notebooks to write it down while he continued. "This begs the question: what is a map?"

Another student who neither Mark nor Phillip had met before (a transfer student?) answered, the air having already been cleared by Mark. The class was starting to be fun, and they were discussing all different types of maps (land, ocean, space) and navigation techniques. Before they knew it, the class had unfortunately ended. When the bell eventually rang for lunch, Phillip and Mark decided to try to find Mr. Rumsey, but he had already left the class and disappeared before they could find him.

"He probably went to the teachers' lounge," suggested Mark. "They need to eat, too."

Instead they decided to head over to the mess hall where they would meet up with Aisling and her boyfriend, Robert, for lunch. After getting some sandwiches, they found the two already seated at a booth by the window.

"Did you guys hear about what happened this morning yet?" greeted Robert.

The others, who were all in the same grade, took a moment to look at each other and shake their heads. It wasn't like Robert to be the one to spread rumors and gossip, but being a telepath meant that he often knew things before the rest of them.

"I'm surprised, Phillip and Aisling, that you guys haven't heard anything, since it was your sisters' class that witnessed the *event*." His voice was dripping with suspense, and it was clear that he was luring them in.

In response, Phillip and Aisling shot each other a perplexed look, while Mark rolled his eyes. Despite the fact that Robert was probably the most popular kid in school, Mark found him to be nearly intolerable sometimes. However, he tried to keep it private for the sake of the friend group, since even Phillip didn't seem to take his side when he brought the issue up.

"Are you going to tell us what happened?" Mark asked shortly. "Or are you going to keep baiting us?"

Robert simply smiled (he was a genuinely agreeable person after all, although Mark frequently questioned whether that was a cause or effect of his popularity) and continued, "Maura's over there, Aisling. Why don't you go hear it straight from the horse's mouth?"

Robert knew Aisling loved a good mystery, and she joyfully played along with him. A telling wink from Rob. A hidden smirk from Aisling. Mark was almost jealous of their secret love language. On the other hand, Phillip was more occupied with the mystery being spoon fed to them. After Aisling got up, Phillip and Mark followed suit, while Robert stayed behind to finish his lunch. Aisling sat down next to her sister on one side of the table, while Mark and Phillip sat down on the other side next to Kalina.

"Hey, Maura. I'm just coming to check on my favorite younger sister and to see how your first day of class is going," began Aisling, interrupting the girls' conversation.

"Cut to the chase," said Maura, privy to her sister's interests. "I know why you're here; just ask."

"Apparently you guys had an exciting morning on your first day of class," prompted Aisling.

"I wondered how long it would take for you to hear about it," replied Maura, her mouth stuffed with a large bite of a club sandwich. She knew her sister would be all over the mysterious woman as soon as she heard about it.

"Don't be like that," pleaded Aisling. "Just tell us what you saw. It might be important! Kalina? Laurelle?"

"Don't ask me; I don't have the best eyesight," she replied pointing to her glasses. This was just an excuse to stay out of trouble, though.

"Come on Kalina," implored Phillip, hoping he could entice his own sister to speak.

Kalina sighed, "We hardly know anything. She appeared out of nowhere from the woods behind the school. It's a type of Enchanted Forest, isn't it? That's what was most shocking about the whole thing to be honest. She was shouting for help and was running towards us. We were told to go back inside. That's it. Maura might know more. That is, if she's willing to talk." She finished her sentence by taking a bite out of a fry, and looked at Maura.

Maura figured it wouldn't hurt if she could add on to Kalina's story. "Well, technically I was told – well, we were all told – not to tell anyone what happened or to discuss events," she said importantly, almost repeating their lecture verbatim. "Buuuut.... I reckon clarifying facts wouldn't be too harmful to the investigation. It *is* better than letting false rumors spread I suppose." She spoke in an exaggerated tone, intentionally done to irritate her sister.

"Just get on with it! Lunch is almost over," Aisling beseeched impatiently, smashing her fist on the wooden table. Phillip moved his glass over, afraid she would knock it off the edge.

"Ach, don't be so rude. Anyways, I got a pretty close look at her since I ran out with Dean Schulz," she continued. "She was dressed in rags and was pale. It looked like she hadn't seen the light of day in decades. Her feet were bare, and she looked scared. She passed out almost immediately as we caught up to Ms. Dalton who was holding on to her so she wouldn't fall and hit her head. And then I went inside and that was it."

"What did she look like? I mean like facial features?" asked Aisling.

"She had frazzled brown hair, I think, but I was told to head back inside before I could do a full physiognomic examination," she answered sarcastically. "I think they're taking her to the hospital. By the way, this is pretty much what I told the investigators who came and interviewed me."

"Interesting," murmured Aisling, and after a few seconds, the bell rang.

The three sophomores all got up and headed to their Dueling class with Mr. Campbell (often called 'the Drill Sergeant' by his students due to his commanding demeanor and also due to the fact that he was an actual Drill Sergeant in the Army).

"I have an idea," said Phillip as they were leaving the noisy cafeteria. "Mark and I will meet you and Robert in the mess hall for dinner. It's too loud and there's too many people for us to discuss right now, though."

5

THE NIGHT
TRACKERS

Later that day, Phillip and Mark met Aisling and Robert at their normal spot in the mess hall for dinner. Robert, who had just come from football practice, was still wet from his shower, but smelled fragrant. He greeted Aisling with a kiss on the cheek before sitting down with a plate piled with steak.

"So what did you guys find out?" asked Aisling without so much as a hello.

"We went to the field earlier this afternoon to do our own minor investigation," replied Mark businesslike. He savored the opportunity to show off his aptitude whenever he could, especially in front of Robert. "I discovered shades of her footprints among those of the faculty, and what I'm assuming were the investigators.

"There were seven in total. There *was* yellow tape, so we had to be careful not to be seen. Fortunately, the investigators were gone for the day it seemed, and they didn't post anyone to keep watch. Anyways, one of the footprints was obviously hers – there's a way you can tell bare feet apart from the others. One I recognized as Mr.

Wells. One looked like it belonged to Dean Schulz – we went by his office to check his footprints and compare. One seemed to be Maura's, as they were much smaller than the others. Then there were three others that I didn't recognize. I thought one might have been Miss Dalton's, but they looked too big and heavy to be a woman's footprint. Just to double-check, we went by her classroom to see if we could make a comparison, but we didn't find anything. I'm assuming the other three were from the investigators."

"Two investigators," corrected Robert. "Only two investigators were seen. Besides, Dr. Toumi had gone out with a stretcher to help Dean Schulz carry the woman to the nursing hall before an ambulance could arrive. So I know he's the third man you're talking about."

"Dr. Toumi told you all about this? Also, what do you guys think Mr. Wells was doing there?" asked Aisling, who knew that Robert mentored under Dr. Toumi and that Phillip mentored under Mr. Wells. However, the implication was that the adventure Mark and Phillip had was all in vain since Robert could have just told them what he already knew.

"No, actually he didn't. He was too busy with her today which is why I didn't get to see him. Someone else told me what was going on. Hopefully, I might be able to get a little bit more information out of him later this week, but normally he isn't supposed to talk about his other patients and their conditions. They're probably taking her to Stone Ridge."

"As for Mr. Wells," said Phillip. "He's just really close to Dean Schulz and Dr. Toumi. You know how the teachers have their own cliques, too."

"Well, that makes sense, I guess, but it is disappointing," replied Aisling, who's mind reverted back to Dr. Toumi. "Anyways, something else has been bothering me. It sounds like you couldn't find any footprints that Ms. Dalton had left behind, Mark. Does anyone else find that... *suspicious*?"

Even though everyone was used to not taking Aisling's exaggerated, conspiratorial tone seriously, it was a valid question. Phillip himself had brought it up with Mark earlier.

Mark, who felt as though his abilities were under attack, thought for a moment before answering, "Well, you know they're not physical footprints, and even if they were, it *is* possible for someone to cover them up. Or even to walk without leaving any behind – in the same way a skilled hiker or tracker knows how to not leave any traces of his whereabouts. It's true that not many people do it, as it does take time to learn *how* to do it subconsciously, but it *is* possible. Besides, Ms. Dalton *is* a teacher, and is, well, more than middle aged."

Mark, who felt like he was rambling at this point, took a moment to clear his thoughts more. They all sat down and pondered silently for a few seconds. Aisling wasn't convinced that Ms. Dalton was in the clear, but Mark was too cautious of being hastily suspicious.

"Does anyone know what Ms. Dalton's aptitude is?" asked Phillip.

Again, they returned to silence as they all looked at each other. Most teachers and adults in general try not to display their aptitudes. In the magical community it was considered rude to ask, especially since it gave that magus a disadvantage. The only exception was for doctors and other specialists who needed a public certification for their practice.

"Based on what I've heard, I just assumed she was a generalist or maybe even a pedagogue, but I guess none of us actually know. It's not necessarily something that teachers advertise to their students," replied Robert. "But I see where you're going with this. Depending on her aptitude, it's reasonable that she's naturally skilled in not leaving behind any footprints. It doesn't seem like a necessarily nefarious talent." He paused before continuing, "Did *you guys* leave footprints?"

Mark's eyes widened as the other three turned to look at them. "No..., but we probably don't have anything to worry about. I don't think the investigators are going to come back until tomorrow for more questioning since it's so late. We can head out tonight after curfew to make sure that no one sees us."

***

Phillip and Mark both stayed up late that night. Curfew for sophomores was 10:30, and lights out was at 11:00 pm. To be sure, they waited until around 1:00 am as they figured the staff would be used to catching the more amateur trouble-makers at or before midnight. Phillip teleported himself and Mark out of their dorm, safely out of sight of any faculty keeping watch on the grounds and making sure not to trigger any alarms in the process. They retraced their steps to the fringes of the wood. This time, Mark took care to consciously erase any footprints that they made.

It was a clear, cool night, and the summer sky twinkled brightly with stars. The school made sure to clear up any light pollution so that their students could chart the stars for classes like astronomy or cartography. Phillip sometimes liked to gaze in wonder at them, considering what it would be like to travel to other planets. For now, though, he had to focus on the task at hand.

Only when they reached the edge of the woods did Phillip feel comfortable enough to start talking very quietly: everyone instinctively knew to keep a safe distance from the enchanted woods. There was a lot of superstition that surrounded them, and even the faculty were hesitant to approach the boundary, especially at the witching hour.

In a low voice, he asked Mark, "Do you see any of our footprints?"

Mark had been looking seriously through a square that he made by connecting his middle and pointer fingers together – his simple but useful spell to track footprints. He didn't respond verbally to Phillip. Rather, he just shook his head in the negative while pacing around muttering to himself. Phillip just watched him patiently for a few minutes.

"They're not here," he finally said, looking up at Phillip with furrowed eyebrows. He was clearly confused and upset.

"Maybe we're in the wrong spot?" Phillip suggested.

"Don't insult my tracking abilities like that."

"Maybe they naturally disappeared?" tried Phillip again.

Mark shook his head slowly, "It would have taken at least a few days, *and* it's completely dry. Maybe if it had rained it *could* have washed them away. Besides, there are no footprints at all. There aren't even animal tracks that I can see. Somebody must have erased all the tracks – absolutely nothing is left."

Before Phillip could reply, they heard footsteps crunching on dry leaves approaching from inside the woods. The whites in Mark's eyes shone at Phillip in the moonlight, expecting him to teleport them out of there. However, Phillip instead pulled him down to the earth in a prone position and pointed to his eyes and ears. Mark understood immediately; they might be able to gain some valuable information. Instinctively, they slowed their heart rates and lowered their body temperatures – for obvious reasons, the school didn't teach things like invisibility or illusions, but students found loopholes to be able to sneak around. Fortunately, it was working because the footsteps they heard approached without hesitation, and they carried with them two female voices speaking clearly but quietly. Although Phillip and Mark could hear them, they couldn't understand the language that they were speaking. Phillip thought to himself that it might be Germanic, but he wasn't sure. The footsteps kept walking until they were about two or three yards away from where Mark and Phillip were lying down on the very edge of the dense brush. One of the women then held up her hand and whispered, "shhh." Her hooded head turned toward the two boys, clearly sensing their presence. Phillip didn't wait to be discovered, so he quickly reached over to Mark and teleported them back into the safety of their dorm.

Their adrenaline was rushing. Those two women were clearly *not* faculty. It was practically unheard of for your average magus to be able to hike through an Enchanted Forest, let alone casually sauntering through at night while having a serious conversation. Were these women monsters in disguise? Perhaps they were some sort of satyr, dryad, or other non-human entity? These kinds of beings were considered to be found only in ancient myths and legends.

"Who... or what... do you think they were?" asked Phillip.

"I don't know, but as soon as they turned towards us, I felt an impending sense of doom," replied Mark, whose heart was still racing.

"Same," said Phillip. "Like my stomach was dropping into a deep, black pit, but I'm pretty tired now. I'm going to head to sleep."

Phillip climbed into bed and closed his eyes, but it took his body a while to be able to relax. The adrenaline was still pumping in his veins. Above him, Mark's breathing had slowed down to the steady rhythm of a soft slumber. It was an uncanny ability that he possessed. Phillip closed his eyes, cleared his mind, and tried to achieve the same.

6

FAMILY WEEKEND

Kalina watched from her window as a scarlet sun rose over the pine trees bordering the campus. Behind her, Maura and Laurelle were still sound asleep. Kalina didn't care about waking them up, though. She was far too excited for her parents to come this Saturday – she had so much to tell them about her first week. Her mother was insistent on homeschooling her, so all these experiences were very new to her. She wanted to tell them everything about her classes (her favorite at the moment was Language Arts), her friends (especially about the fact that Laurelle cried the first few nights), and the crazy woman (the one that her brother and his friends were asking about).

It didn't take long for both Laurelle and Maura to both wake up, as they were also eager to see their parents for family weekend. Since breakfast didn't start until 8:30 on Saturdays, they played Go Fish and gossiped until then. Apparently, Maura already had a crush on a boy in their class named William. Laurelle, more comfortable with her roommates now, pointed out that it was ridiculous to have a crush on somebody within a week of meeting him. Kalina didn't voice her own opinion; the boy had seemed nice enough to her, but they hadn't spoken much yet. She didn't want to be too harsh with her judgments until she had gotten to know him better. Occasionally when they imagined they heard a car outside, they would look out the window, but they knew most of the parents wouldn't start coming until at least 10:00 am.

Breakfast was Kalina's favorite meal of the day, and she certainly took advantage of it at school – there was plenty of everything! Amber-colored eggs – scrambled, fried, and poached. There was bacon, sausages (of all varieties, her favorite being the bratwurst), thick pancakes, and thin crêpes. Waffles shone with butter and sweet, aromatic maple syrup. Salty and greasy hash browns were available and ketchup to go with them. There was also the classic southern biscuits and gravy, which Kalina had never tried. She always wanted to get everything available, and she tried to. Unfortunately, she discovered that her eyes tended to be bigger than her stomach, and she learned to exercise more self-control in her eating habits. Today, she shared half of a waffle with Maura, ate some bacon, some scrambled eggs, and took a glass of milk.

The girls had some trouble deciding what to do after breakfast. They hadn't been given any homework on their first week, but they stuffed their stomachs far too much to go play tennis, which was what they originally told their dorm mom. They ended up settling to return to their room. By providence, they ran into Kalina's mom at the entrance of the girls' dormitory building. After a little bit of chit-chat, Catherine Todorova led her daughter back to where her husband had parked. They had come a little bit early, so there weren't too many other cars yet. Mr. Todorova, ever so practical, wanted to head out before there was too much traffic.

To her surprise, Kalina found Mark along with her brother and father. Although he had visited a couple of times before, nobody told her that he was joining them this weekend. After giving her dad a large hug, they all got in the car and headed off towards Prince William. The Todorova's were very lucky to live relatively close, only a little over an hour's drive, so they could use mundane means of transportation without it being a hassle. A few kids' parents had flying carriages or Pegasuses. A couple families even had flying cars, which were still expensive and thus unaffordable for the average magical family. It took almost eight decades after the invention of the car for the magical community to figure out the aerodynamic spells and runes to work with the mechanical parts of an automobile. The Magical Union of North America had spent billions of dollars to subsidize the research. In any case, Kalina and her family arrived home safely by normie means of transportation.

Phillip and Mark retreated upstairs to Phillip's bedroom, excluding Kalina to her chagrin – she really wanted to know what they were up to and be a part of it. In the meantime, her mom decided to treat her to a day of shopping and fun. Their favorite place to go to was Old Town Manassas, where they had Ekaterina's for lunch. There was also a used bookstore nearby, with a niche section on magical subjects. Kalina chose a book on divination and, in the normie section, found an Agatha Christie. She found four of them actually.

Before it closed, they stopped at the farmers' market. Kalina and her mom loved to cook, and they were planning on making an elaborate dinner that evening. Kalina told her mom that she wanted grilled steaks, served with loaded baked potatoes and roasted broccoli. For dessert, they would have chocolate chip cookies.

Since neither Phillip nor Mark had any culinary talent of interest, they were in the living room playing a board game called Elementafl. It emerged in Holland in the late Renaissance and resembled a chess board with pieces representing earth, water, air, and electricity (after the ban on pyromancy in the early 1900s, electricity replaced fire as the fourth element). Mr. Todorova enjoyed watching it and was known to be a passionate player. However, when Phillip and Mark started shouting incantations at each other, he had to ask them to quiet down.

When they sat down for dinner, Ivan Todorova said grace. Almost immediately afterwards, he bluntly brought up the subject that seemed to be hanging in the back of every one's mind.

"So was it your class, Kalina, that saw the mysterious woman?" he asked in a slightly Slavic accent. "You do have Mrs. Dalton, yes?"

Kalina opened her mouth to respond, but her mother cut her off. "Ivan! I'm sure she doesn't want to talk about that! It must have been traumatizing!"

"Don't be like that, Catherine, it's probably all the students have been talking about for the past week," he countered. "Well, Kalina?"

"As a matter of fact, that's true. In fact, I believe that Phillip, Mark, and Aisling have been investigating the matter. They came to us at lunch one day and started asking us a bunch of questions. I wonder what else they've found out."

Kalina was bitter about the fact that Phillip had excluded her from the days' activities, otherwise she wouldn't have bothered to put him on the spot like that. Catherine raised her eyebrows at her son. Mark gulped his food loudly, while Phillip stuffed his face with a large chunk of steak. He hated when Kalina threw him under the bus, and she always seemed to know how to choose the worst moments for it. Rumors had already been spreading that the woman might have been Emily Brown, who was a year younger than Catherine. It was clear that Mrs. Todorova was uncomfortable with the topic. After a few seconds, Catherine feigned nonchalance and changed the topic.

"So," she began, making an effort to recover the awkward silence. "Isn't Aisling that girl you have a crush on, Mark?"

Mark, who had been recently practicing (and currently failing) at exercising extreme control of his emotions, began uncontrollably blushing. Next to him, Phillip pinched the bridge of his nose in second-hand embarrassment. *Why would she ask something like that?* he wondered as Mark struggled to get the words out.

"Actually, Mrs. Todorova, she has a boyfriend now. They started dating at the end of last year."

"Really?" she continued, trying to save her mistake. "Who in the school could be a better match than you?" She thought she was trying to lift his spirits, but in fact she did the opposite.

"Robert Nelson, the quarterback of the football team. He has a dual aptitude, also. Telepath. Telekinetic," he replied in a monotone voice, while staring down at his plate. He thought he was being stoic, but everyone could tell that the difference in his demeanor meant that he was uncomfortable.

There was no need for Mark to further explain who exactly Robert was, most of the academy and the parents already knew him by virtue of his football talents. Beyond that, he was said to be one of the most powerful telepaths in a century, something that intimidated Mark often. *Robert must know how I feel about him,* reminded Mark to himself, another blow to his self-esteem.

Kalina had officially tuned out. She didn't bring up the conversation, and it certainly wasn't her responsibility to handle it. Apart from that, she personally didn't care about the tragic, romantic love-triangles of her brother's friends. The drama of middle-school had already become tiresome enough, and it had only been the first week! As far as her opinion on Robert Nelson went, well, she didn't have much of one. She knew that her brother was okay with him, but really they were only friends because of Aisling. *Whatever...* Frankly, there were plenty of other items on her personal agenda that she cared about more.

***

They all woke up early Sunday morning to prepare to go to church. The girls wore sharp matching dresses that they had picked out yesterday at the mall, and the guys were each dressed up in a suit. Mark had brought with him a fashionable navy suit, and was excited to join the Todorova's at an Orthodox Church for the first time.

They all entered the church together. Phillip led Mark to a seat on the right of the nave while his mother and father lit candles for their friends and loved ones. Upon entering, Kalina herself venerated an icon of the Theotokos and found a place on the left side of the aisle across from her brother. The service had already started a few minutes prior, but there were only a couple of people there yet. The sweet smell of incense permeated the air where Kalina stood.

She closed her eyes and listened to the chanters. She knew most of the English, Slavonic, and Greek passages by heart. When she opened her eyes again, it looked as though the morning sun had gilded the whole church. The icons on walls seemed to be shining and moving – growing and shrinking, and she thought she heard the voices of angels speaking in the language of heaven. It was as if she herself was alone in the presence of God.

Her eyes closed once again, and she drifted into a deep trance. She started seeing images of a beautiful mansion that she was being enticed to follow. Surrounding the path were rows of orange trees. She was aware that she wasn't alone, either. Four other girls flanked her – two on each side. They were all dressed in nineteenth century autumnal petticoats. Down the path she could see a woman, but she couldn't quite make out her features. As she began to approach, her vision was cut off by the authoritative voice of the deacon.

"The doors! The doors of wisdom! Let us attend!"

Kalina looked up with surprise. *Has it been an hour and a half already? When did all the people arrive?* All these questions clouded her mind as she prepared herself to take communion.

After the service was over, she hung out with her family at coffee hour. She realized that this would be the last time she would see her normie friends from church for a while, and it disheartened her a little. She wished she could talk to them about Cardinal Key Academy, but knew that she would be breaking the law if she did. As far as she was aware, hers was the only family that was involved in the magical community at this parish. Not even their priest knew about it, and Catherine Todorova regularly visited a trusted convent for confession.

At a young age, all magi were taught about AIMM, the International Agreement for Magical Mystery. It made for some awkward moments at church, since Kalina wasn't sure how to understand the Church's intolerance towards "magic."

"It's not the same," Catherine had explained to her daughter. If Christianity had taken off in England instead of Greece, we might be calling a priest a wizard or wiseman instead. Even in the Roman Catholic Church, they refer to their teaching authority as the *Magisterium*. Your average person isn't given the gifts God has given us. Those who try to steal that power for themselves are called witches and warlocks, especially if they're using against the will of God (which is pretty much always). There are even some 'magi' who really shouldn't be practicing magic since they're tempted to use it against God and His work. *Always* stay away from those people and those disgusting, profane forms of 'magic.'"

The response didn't completely satisfy Kalina, but it made some sense. Her mother's stern warning frightened her at the time, since she could see glimpses of what that kind of nigromantia (the academic term for black magic) would look like. It certainly had prepared her to be cautious of abusing her abilities, especially around her normie friends.

After a while of playing and talking, Mrs. Todorova told her daughter that it was time to start their drive back to Cardinal Key. Instead of stopping at their house, they immediately drove to the academy. Phillip begged his parents to just let him teleport them back, but they refused. It was frustrating for him, and he often complained to his parents that their approach to magic was too conservative and old-school.

"It's a family ordeal," said Mr. Todorova. "Besides, are you absolutely confident that you could teleport one, two, three, four people *plus* yourself back?"

"Yes," asserted Phillip with false confidence – it was more people than he had ever taken before. On a good day, his maximum was three, including himself.

"Well until Mr. Wells gives his approval, the answer is *niet*."

"I don't mind the drive, Mr. Todorova. I thought it was a lot of fun with you guys," claimed Mark. Phillip scoffed at his friend trying to butter up his dad.

"Thank you," replied Mr. Todorova. "I hope my son gets more sense out of you. Out of all his friends, you are my favorite at the moment."

Before his son could argue with him anymore, Mr. Todorova walked straight to the car, and Phillip dejectedly followed him.

"Suck up," he muttered at Mark (he was just teasing of course).

Mark shrugged. "What am I supposed to do? Argue with *your dad*?"

They walked shoulder to shoulder, taking off their blazers and loosening their ties. Phillip hated long car rides (according to him, that was anything that took longer than a half-hour), but Mark loved them. He liked to try to use his aptitude to conjure faster routes, which Mr. Todorova appreciated.

7
UNDER THE STADIUM STARS

It was finally Friday evening, and Kalina, Maura, and Laurelle sat in their dorm, studying for their class on Magical Theory and Practice while they waited for Stephanie to show up to take them to the football game.

"Can you guys think of anything besides incantations that can cast magic?" asked Laurelle, who was significantly less familiar with the use of magic.

"Well there are certain rituals," replied Kalina, looking over.

"Yeah, but that's not really specific. What kinds of rituals? I tried finding it in the book, but I can't."

"I think I saw it on..." replied Kalina flipping through her textbook. "... page twenty. What question is this for?"

"It's for number fifteen on the worksheet. We need five examples."

Maura jolted around. "How are you on number fifteen already?" she nearly shouted in shock. "I'm only on eight. What are you on Kalina?"

"I'm on ten, but I skipped eight because I got stuck. And to answer your question, Laurelle, I can think of hand movements, using plants or other materials, like gems or certain metals. So I guess that counts as three so far..." she tapered her voice trying to think of some other examples she had seen in her experience.

"My sister Aisling is a scribe," began Maura. "She does writing and makes drawings to cast spells. Sometimes she makes her own magic cards."

"Doesn't writing words count as an incantation?" asked Kalina, unsure of the difference between the colloquial and the scholastic use of the term.

"I think it has to be spoken aloud for it to count as a true incantation," replied Laurelle. "Plus, you don't necessarily have to write words. It can be runes or symbols. I suppose that's where geometry comes in."

As soon as she had finished her explanation, they heard a knock on the door. Maura was the first to get up and answer it, revealing their sophomore mentor behind it. Stephanie leaned against the door frame with her face painted in red, white, and gold, the school colors.

"You girls ready to go to the first game of the season?" she asked, always a never ending spring of zeal. "We're up against our mortal enemies: The New England Terriers!"

Her question was obviously rhetorical; her charisma galvanized the people around her without fail. Kalina had recently been wondering if that was part of their mentor's aptitude but thought it would be impolite to ask. Her tricolor-haired dorm girls were already sporting matching T-shirts and shorts with the school name and mascot – the Cardinals, obviously. The girls were excited for their first home football game, and they walked quickly with Stephanie towards the football field.

Before they left, they gathered all the other girls in the dorm. This was the perfect time to get to know some of the girls in the other sixth grade class, since last week they couldn't due to family weekend.

They talked about their classes that week, and how they performed on the diagnostic tests. Laurelle herself was rather behind on the Practical Magic, but she was clearly smart and a hard worker. It was obvious that she felt insecure about her lack of magical knowledge, and was trying to give it her all to catch up with her classmates. Kalina pitied her a little bit, but didn't voice it. *What kind of parents don't teach their children anything about magic? Even my mom, conservative with her casting, taught me the fundamentals.*

They arrived at the football field early enough to see staff members and some older students putting up the wards to prevent magic from being used unfairly during the game. Kalina watched as more and more people trickled into the bleachers. The New England team's silver and blue uniforms contrasted starkly with red and gold of Cardinal Key. Each shone under the bright white lights of the football stadium. Kalina wanted to see if she could foresee who would win, but after a few minutes of strenuous effort she gave up. *Those wards must be really detailed.*

"Ladies and Gentlemen," announced a loud voice (obviously amplified by magic). "Please rise for the national anthem."

The noisy crowd silenced, and the student choir sang perfectly. At the end, they cast small magic fireworks from the tips of their fingers. The air sparkled red, white and blue, and then the teams burst out.

"How are they doing that if pyromancy is illegal?" asked Laurelle. Kalina herself probably would have asked the same if she didn't already have the experience to discern illusory spells.

"They're not really fireworks," answered Maura. "It's actually a fairly simple illusion – that's why they don't make any noise. Believe me, I had the same question the first game I ever went to."

Kalina watched the game while chewing on a hotdog and a bag of popcorn. She knew nothing of football, and relied on Maura to understand what was going on. Maura happily obliged her position as her friends' personal sports narrator. Having already come to many games to see her sister cheerlead, Maura was in the perfect position to teach her friends what they needed to know. Even quiet Laurelle cheered enthusiastically when the Cardinals were performing well. Kalina, on the other hand, got bored relatively quickly. *No wonder Phillip never invited me to one of these. He was actually being a nice brother.* The band's half-time show, however, was rather entertaining. When she brought it up to Maura, she simply responded that the band kids had awful reputations of being arrogant and nasty to each other.

"You know your brother's friend, Mark?"

"Yeah, he spent last weekend with us."

"Well, he was actually in the band last year; he played the trombone, but he doesn't play anymore. Apparently, the band director has a temper and a rude way of getting his students to turn on each other. Now, Mark just does wrestling and track. If you want to avoid drama, avoid the band."

The buzzer for the third quarter went off.

"How do you know all these things?" asked Laurelle, who had been sitting on Maura's left.

"Ach," she replied, "my sister is like a gossip magnet. I'm pretty sure I'm like the only one she vents these things to. Oh look! We just advanced the ball thirty yards. We're winning – "

The collective gasp of the spectators cut her off, followed by whispers and muttering. The whole crowd had sat down, and the girls followed suit. Kalina had just barely seen what happened, but it looked like Robert Nelson got tackled and was laying on the ground, unmoving.

Laurelle leaned over to Maura and Kalina and whispered, "Is he okay? What's happening?"

Kalina felt the oracle inside her pushed to speak, as though all her effort of prediction earlier was only just now flooding into her system. Never before had a prophecy felt so important to her. Unable to control herself, Kalina stood up and recited an answer:

In twilight's trance, on the gridiron's embrace,

A warrior rests, in the moon's soft grace.

In the cocoon of slumber, he'll quietly roam,

Through winter's chill, to the whispers of home.

A lamb's sacrifice, in spring's gentle stream,

He'll awaken, reborn, from the devil's dream.

On bleachers she waits, the prophetess unseen,

For the cosmic dance to unfold in the sleeper's sheen

That was all she had to say, and she fought back any other words that started to bubble up in her throat. Her voice was plain and articulate, with a slight echo that a more observant listener would recognize as the voice of prophecy. She did not mean to prophecy, but it happened anyway. Maura and Laurelle both looked surprised, and their mouths were agape. Other people around them looked at her and glared, seemingly offended. It must have sounded like a black spell, with mentions of the devil and sacrifice. Some looked confused, but before anyone could comment, she walked away, ignoring the mutters and rumors of people behind her. Maura and Laurelle hastened to follow suit.

"What was *that*, Kalina?" Maura cried out to her once they left the stadium. Kalina thought she heard a slight indignation in her voice and hesitated for a half-second. The night sky was clear and the full moon shone brightly. Its unobstructed silver rays revealed everything that was normally invisible in the night. A soft breeze came over Kalina, giving her goosebumps; she could see and feel everything and everyone. For a brief second, she was tempted to succumb to the bliss of foresight. It was like there was an influx of magic in the atmosphere. Where it came from, she didn't know. What she did know was that she had the power to speak words that could either crush her friends – catalyze her roommates – even weave destiny at the realest level. Alas, at the last second she turned away, fighting inwardly. She knew she had to maintain control of the prophecy. She was in control. Not the gift. Her. Almost in tears, she raced back to her dorm without any utterance or acknowledgment to her friends.

8
THE HOSPITAL'S SECRETS

Saturday morning, Phillip and Mark stepped out of their Uber and walked into Saint Luke's hospital in Stone Ridge. They both woke up to a text in their group chat that Aisling had sent around 2:00 am. *EMERGENCY EMERGENCY EMERGENCY COME TO SAINT LUKE ASAP. EMERGENCY!!!!!!*

The vague but extreme message confused and worried them at first, but news traveled fast at Cardinal Key Academy. It wasn't long before they found out the details of what had happened at the football game last night. Naturally, Aisling followed her boyfriend all the way to Stone Ridge and had spent the night with him and his parents. The back of her fuzzy, fiery hair greeted them when they stepped into the lobby.

"Aisling!" called Phillip, and she briskly turned around. There were heavy bags under her sleepless eyes, and she was still in her cheerleader uniform. "How's Robert? Is he okay?"

Almost immediately, Aisling began to scold them. "I've been waiting for you guys forever! Where have you been?"

Phillip wanted to defend himself and Mark, but Aisling started to tear up. Instead of making excuses, Phillip just reached over and gave her a hug. "I know I'm sorry. I wish we came sooner to help." Mark came over and joined in, deeply resonating with Aisling's pain despite his bias against Robert.

After a few moments, Aisling heaved a deep sigh and stepped back. She rubbed her red eyes with her fists and said softly, "Robert's still unconscious. He hasn't woken up yet. He's being treated by Dr. Toumi."

"His mentor?" asked Mark. Dr. Toumi was also the school physician and acted as a counselor to some of the students. Naturally, he went to every sports game in case of an accident. An ambulance was also kept nearby for the same reason.

"No, Dr. Toumi's wife. She works at this hospital."

Phillip and Mark both nodded their heads, even though neither of them had known that Dr. Toumi's wife was also a doctor.

"Well anyways," she continued with a raspy voice. "I didn't exactly call you guys here to see Robert. He's bound to have a lot of visitors from the football team today anyways. His parents are having a rough go of it. He's their only child, you know." She closed her eyes and took another deep breath. Phillip was afraid that she was about to pass out. "I called you guys here because this is where they checked in that mysterious woman; she's in one of the rooms on Robert's floor."

Mark and Phillip exchanged glances. Mark didn't like to casually and recklessly break laws, and although Phillip didn't consider himself to be a particular "rules person," entering a vulnerable and unconscious woman's hospital room was a little bit too far for him, both ethically and morally. Nevertheless, he had to give credit to Aisling – even though she got no sleep and her boyfriend was seriously injured, she stayed focused on her self-given mission. Phillip was certainly impressed, but it was unclear whether his impression was positive or negative. *Maybe it's not such a good idea*, he declared to himself.

"So, what?" he replied, just a bit too caustically. "We're just going to sneak into another patient's room and steal her medical records or something? Do you need to take a nap, Aisling?"

Aisling didn't appreciate Phillip's patronizing and condescending tone, but she was too tired and too serious to be bothered about it. She led them outside and pointed to the third floor. "There, that room. Third window from the left. Teleport us there."

Phillip didn't appreciate Aisling's demanding tone, either. He didn't like to be commanded to do anything, and he sometimes felt that his friends treated him like their own personal taxicab. Maybe he should start charging them, he thought to himself.

"I can't just teleport in there," he hissed at her. "I don't know what kind of wards they have! School is one thing – I'm familiar with that - but a hospital is completely different!"

"I've been studying it all night," replied Aisling calmly. "There's a security guard outside her room, but the blinds are closed. As for the wards, they're super basic, take a look for yourself." Aisling handed him a rose-tinted piece of quartz glass used by students to "see" magic. Mark himself took his own out, which was more translucent and of a higher quality.

"No offense, but you might be crossing the line here, Aisling. We could get in serious trouble for this," said Mark, always sensitive about Aisling's feelings. "Someone might see us. They might even have cameras in her room."

Aisling rolled her eyes, "Don't be ridiculous, Mark. That would be an invasion of her privacy. That's like... illegal... I think."

"I'm in," declared Phillip boldly after a short examination of the floor. Although he had qualms at first, his courage was bolstered by his curiosity. Besides, he justified to himself, they might be able to help solve the investigation and bring her justice. "Are you coming with us, Mark?"

Mark brushed his sandy hair back before making a decision. He simply sighed and acquiesced to peer pressure. The trio formed a solid balance between boldness, caution, and rationalism. They found a small corner hidden from the general public and security cameras where they could do magic without being seen. When they were in the clear, Phillip teleported them up. After about three years of practice, his accuracy for short distances was virtually perfect. They landed directly in front of the bed of the woman. There, Aisling found her medical charts and started skimming through them.

"Samantha Hastings," she whispered. She pulled out her cell phone and started taking pictures of the file while Mark and Phillip kept watch. Mark felt guilty because it seemed like they were taking advantage of the situation, but he went along anyway. Not wanting to risk staying too long, the trio left immediately after Aisling was finished, which only took about a minute.

"There," she said. "Too easy. A minute in and out. No trouble."

"No trouble, yet," Mark grumbled.

"What'd you find out?" asked Phillip.

"Her name is Samantha Hastings, mid to late 30's, which is disappointing. They ordered a DNA test to confirm who she was."

"Why is that disappointing?" questioned Mark.

"Because she thought it might have been Emily Brown, the girl who went missing back in 2000. That's what the rumor is supposed to be, right Aisling?" answered Phillip.

"Yes, and it would have made things easier, but I had doubts – Emily Brown was a blonde, but that *could* have changed. We still need to figure this whole thing out; I've never heard of a Samantha Hastings before today. There's something else I need to tell you guys now before I forget," she hesitated before continuing. "Robert had been working with Dr. Toumi and his wife this past week on trying to use his telepathic abilities to wake up Samantha Hastings. The conspiratorial part of me suspects that he might have been sabotaged."

Even though Aisling had a tendency to connect apples to oranges, this actually made sense to Phillip. *Maybe her analytical abilities really have matured since sixth grade.*

"I think you might actually be onto something there," said Phillip. "As far as I know, there's never been an incident with the security wards before. What do you think, Mark?" Phillip wanted to get his friend's opinion because Mark was very careful to not jump to conclusions too quickly.

"I agree that this is a possibility worth considering, and I'm sure the staff are already doing an investigation. Between this and the footprints mysteriously disappearing, I'm willing to go further and say there might even be someone on the inside working to keep this whole mystery under wraps."

"Hold on," said Aisling, who for the first time in her life might not actually be in the know. "Are you saying that there's proof that the wards actually have been tampered with? That's how Robert got taken out?"

"That's what we heard at least," replied Phillip. "I don't know if it's just a rumor, but the kid who tackled him was apparently an advanced kinesthetic. Rumor has it that he's been kicking himself with guilt."

"I know," replied Aisling. "He... actually came to visit last night. He was sobbing by Robert's bedside, asking for forgiveness. Of course we didn't blame him. These accidents are rare, but they do happen."

Ultimately, Aisling appreciated her friends' opinions, especially since she had enough self-awareness and honesty to tell that she could take things too far sometimes. It was good to be grounded by these two.

Phillip wanted to see Robert before he teleported himself and Mark back to Cardinal Key Academy. They had to break the bank with the Uber because Phillip didn't feel comfortable teleporting to places he wasn't familiar with yet and they weren't sure hiring one was technically allowed at school (a potential AIMM violation in hindsight). Aisling led him up, and he saw the handsome football star asleep on a hospital bed. There were a few members from the football team there, and his parents were at his side talking to them.

Phillip felt awkward, especially since he wasn't really a close friend or teammate of Roberts. He made a short prayer for his recovery and returned to Mark.

9

THE LIBRARY INCIDENT

"Alright class, for homework, I want you to work on questions two through forty, evens only. I also want you to write a short paragraph about the four different elements and how they relate to different aptitudes, both physical and psychic. You only need to give a couple examples for each one."

Kalina hadn't been paying attention to the lesson at all; her mind was preoccupied with the strange events of the football game and the mysterious woman. All day and all night she had been haunted by deep, penetrating thoughts, visions, and dreams that she couldn't control. *What else were you expecting? The atmosphere here is saturated with magic.* It was like her abilities were slowly burning her up. She was roused from her daydream with the sound of zips and shuffling of her classmates preparing to go to lunch.

This nearly sudden change in behavior wasn't lost on her roommates either. Ever since the football game last Friday, she had become nearly silent in the dorm, during class, and at meals (if she were even present at them). She was a lot less social. She would sometimes go out for a run by herself, study by herself, or just lay in bed.

Today, Kalina didn't want to deal with her friends prodding her, so she went to the library instead. She was looking through a section on dream interpretation when she saw three students huddled together in a corner whispering to each other. She felt compelled to talk to her brother and see what kind of progress he and his friends had made on the mysterious woman.

"What have you guys found out so far?" she asked in a quiet voice – it was a library after all.

Phillip straightened up in surprise and looked at his sister. "It's kind of private, Kalina. Why don't you go hang out with your friends?"

"I want to hang out with you," she replied.

Aisling and Mark both knew better than to get involved between siblings, as they themselves had their own personal bonds and dynamics with their brothers and sister.

"Well..., we don't want you to hang out with us," replied Phillip, accidentally making his words harsher than he intended them to be.

In any case, Kalina ignored him and investigated their table, which was full of newspaper articles. Aisling had her laptop open in front of her and Kalina saw that they were indeed researching the mysterious woman. *Of course I'm right. I'm always right.*

"So I was right that you guys were investigating her," she said. "So her name's Samantha Hastings? I can help, you know."

"Okay, that's it. You have to leave. Go away. Now!" scolded Phillip.

Kalina, upset, turned around and walked away from the trio. Her brother had never spoken to her like this before, and she was fuming. She was there when the woman was found. She could help. She knew things. All these thoughts and ideas started to cloud her brain and her whole body started to twitch. Suddenly, dark spots clouded her vision, and she collapsed to the ground.

IO

THE DANGERS OF KNOWLEDGE

The library was normally empty during lunchtime (especially at the beginning of the year), so Aisling, Phillip, and Mark decided to head over to do some research away from eavesdroppers and prying eyes. Aisling had been taking the lead the past couple of days, and Mark and Phillip were pretty much her helpers in "solving the case" of Samantha Hastings.

"So, what do we know so far?" asked Aisling, who despite having a knack for finding things out, tended to be very disorganized with her collection of information. Mark took charge of organizing everything while Phillip aided with both tasks.

"Let's start at the beginning," began Mark. "Our mysterious woman's name is Samantha Hastings, and she went missing at the age of fourteen in 1994 in Washington state. She was a student at the Cascadia School in Washington with an aptitude in cellular regeneration. She was an eighth grader, and this was six years before the disappearance of Emily Brown. The same investigator, Detective Christie, who was here when she showed up, was also there when she disappeared. He's a federal detective employed by the Grand Magistrate of North America. Besides these two cases, he has a successful streak, and was able to quickly move up the ranks. When Emily Brown went missing six years later, he was contacted since the case was eerily similar to that of Samantha Hastings. Unfortunately, neither were ever found... until a couple weeks ago at least. They both were last seen or heard entering their local enchanted woods."

Aisling kept nodding her head. "Right, right. So, I've had an idea about something that we should start doing. I had a feeling that these two cases are connected, and Detective Christie probably does, too. There's a lot of similarities between them. Not only were they last seen entering enchanted or dark woods, but they were the same age, same gender, and the disappearances occurred from midwinter to early spring."

Phillip and Mark were intently listening to her. All these similarities were circumstances that they were taught to be aware of when casting magic. It was almost certain that there was a magus – or even a witch or warlock who was behind these disappearances – abductions, rather.

Aisling continued, "Most of the reports on these claim that they were abducted, so I think that's a safe assumption. Last night, I started looking up other missing girls on the internet - the ones who were never retrieved, and I found a couple. I started filtering them all by criteria, but I didn't really have to. They pretty much followed the same pattern tracing back to 1982 with the disappearance – I mean abduction – of Deirdre Walsh. I have the names and articles that I printed out, but I think we might be able to go deeper. We should see if we can find out if there were any more."

Aisling took out a folder and her laptop from her backpack. Mark and Phillip did the same, following her lead. It didn't take them long to start throwing down more names on a sheet of paper, and they divided up the regions of North America. Phillip took the east coast. Aisling took the west coast and Quebec since she studied French. Mark took the Midwest and Central America.

Mark kept repeating to them, "Remember: female, pubescent, mid-winter to early spring, and by an enchanted forest."

"Should we count normies?" asked Phillip.

"I think for now it would be useful to count them, and then later on we might leave them out," said Aisling. "But I guess if they fit all the criteria *and* disappeared by a known enchanted forest, it's worth marking them down. Just remember that if they were found and the mystery was solved, then it's not a mystery anymore... obviously."

On that note, they kept taking notes on a sheet of paper. Once in a while, they would compare names and dates to see if they could find another pattern. They only had Samantha Hastings and Emily Brown to work off of, but they wanted to cover all their bases. So far, they had found six other girls in the 1900s, including the ones that Aisling had previously mentioned.

The names were the following:

- 1982: Deirdre Walsh, magus, homeschooled, went missing at the Sequoia Enchanted Grove at the age of 15

- 1970: Marine l'Etoile: magus, student at Academie de Champlain in Quebec, went missing in the Enchanted

Laurentian Forest range at the age of 12

- 1952: Peggy Olson: normie, student at Riverside High School in Michigan went missing by (not in) the Manistee Enchanted Forest at the age of 14

- 1928: Saoirse and Siobhan O'Brian: magi, twin sisters at the New England school, went missing in the New England Enchanted Woods, part of the greater Appalachian Enchanted Forests

- 1904: Edith Anderson: magus, student at the Southern School in Georgia, went missing in the Piedmont Dark Forest, part of the greater Appalachian Enchanted Forests

"I wonder why they're spaced out the way they are," pondered Phillip out loud. "Do you think there might be an astrological reason for it? I don't know if I see a pattern, but they are all even."

"So they are," replied Aisling.

"What are you guys talking about?" asked a girl who seemed to appear out of nowhere.

Phillip jerked his head up and was startled to see his sister sneak up on them like that. He didn't want her to get involved with what they were researching. Honestly, some of the cases he read were pretty brutal, and he couldn't bear if something like that happened to her. As an older brother, he felt that it was his responsibility to protect his sister.

She didn't back down of course, but the thought of Kalina in the shoes of one of those kids who had had awful things done to them set him off. Eventually, he snapped at her to leave them alone. He was wondering if his protective instinct had turned too harsh with her when he saw her suddenly collapse as she was walking away.

"Kalina!" he shouted as he got up and rushed towards her. Her whole body was twitching as she lay on the ground. "HELP! She's having a seizure."

Mark, who was next to him, cried out the words for summoning assistance that they were all taught in sixth grade. "*Medical emergency! Library!*"

Dr. Toumi had arrived in less than two minutes, with Dean Schulz on his heels. By that time Kalina's seizure had subsided, and she was regaining consciousness. Even though she was feeling better, Dr. Toumi wanted to take her back to the nursing room so that he could run some tests on her and make sure that she'll be alright.

"I'll make sure that Ms. Dalton is aware of her situation," said Dean Schulz. "Aisling and Mark, you two should start heading back to class. Lunch is almost over. Phillip, you can come with us since it's your sister, and I'll call your parents to let them know what's going on."

II
A CALCULATED WHISK

Phillip was sitting by himself in the mess hall waiting for Aisling to show up. Mark had decided to stay in tonight since he was feeling extremely fatigued from their dueling class – Mr. Campbell had been especially tough on him today. Phillip wasn't in an excellent mood either, with what happened to his sister earlier. He was hoping that Aisling could get some news out of her sister since Maura was Kalina's roommate.

"Hey, Phillip," said Aisling with a bowl of salad. Clearly, she wasn't too hungry either. "How's Kalina doing?"

"She claims to be doing better, but I'm still worried about her."

"Yeah, so is Maura. Apparently, Kalina has been acting pretty anti-social lately. According to Maura, all she does is stay in her room. She thinks it has to do with something that happened at the football game. According to Maura, she had some sort of an outburst, but I don't really understand what happened. Maura didn't remember the whole thing, but she was talking about the devil and sacrifice or something?"

Phillip stuck his fork into a roasted potato. This didn't sound like his sister. Normally she was pretty social, even if she did lean on the introverted side. Typically, she was significantly more active with people she was friends with. As far as he knew, she was fairly popular in her junior tennis team back at home.

"Maybe she's just having trouble adjusting," said Phillip, thinking out loud, trying to rationalize his sister's actions.

"You would know better than me," replied Aisling with a shrug. "My sister is quite the extrovert, though, and she's pretty good at reading people. However, she can't really place what's going on with Kalina. It's like she's blocking her and everyone else out. Do you think the stress could have caused her to have a seizure like that? What did Dr. Toumi say?"

"Actually, he said that he couldn't get a good read on her either. I think his exact words were that she was 'blocking' him out also, but he's such a talented empath. I don't understand the mental aptitudes sometimes."

"Maybe your sister's also a psychic," suggested Aisling. "If she's half as talented as Robert, that could explain a lot. It could even explain why she had her seizure. Robert once told me that when he was a kid, he would sometimes pass out from these massive migraines because he couldn't stop hearing other peoples' thoughts."

Phillip made a thoughtful look. "That would actually make a lot of sense, and apparently my grandfather was a psychic, too. He was gifted with bilocation, you see. Anyways, I should probably go call my dad. We were texting earlier about Kalina because the school called him, and I promised I would call him after dinner."

"Cool," said Aisling. "I'll see you tomorrow, then."

Phillip placed his tray into the bussing-slot by his booth, where an sophisticated magical system of disposal organized trash from dishes and sent them back to the kitchen.

The sun had set beneath the horizon, but it wasn't completely dark outside. Phillip enjoyed these liminal spaces he often found himself in and took a second to breathe in the fresh country air. He wanted to make the phone call with his dad private, so he teleported himself to the rooftop of the boys' dormitory, which was inaccessible to the average student. The phone rang for a while before his father picked up.

"Hello? Phillip?"

"Hi, Dad," responded Phillip. "How are you? How's Mom?"

"We're good, she's right here. Let me put you on speakerphone."

Phillip was happy to speak to his parents. Although he lived a semi-independent life at school, he found that he still required their advice. He made small talk to them about his classes before the subject of Kalina came up.

"That being said," he began. "I did ask Aisling, whose sister is Kalina's roommate, and she said that Kalina has been acting anti-social. Should I try to talk to her? I was pretty harsh last time I spoke to her at the library, and she was pretty short with me at Dr. Toumi's office, which I guess is fair."

He explained the events that led up to Kalina's seizure (tactfully leaving out the subject of their research), and although he blamed himself a little, his parents made him realize that he couldn't possibly have been the cause of her seizure. Dr. Toumi wasn't exactly sure *what* could have caused it, but his best guess was that it was induced by the stress of a change in environment. His recommendation was that they regularly talk to Kalina to make sure that she's okay.

"I was considering setting therapeutic appointments with Dr. Toumi, which is something he suggested, but the only problem is that she thinks she's perfectly fine," said Mrs. Todorova. "In fact, the more we try to make sure she's okay, the more determined she is to act like nothing is bothering her. Ultimately, Dr. Toumi said that if she doesn't want to talk, then it's best not to force it out of her."

"Maybe it's best if we give her some space to figure it all out," stated Mr. Todorova. "Although, it would be a great help to us if you went to talk to her Phillip. You might be able to figure out what's going on."

Although Phillip generally agreed with his father's sentiment, he wasn't sure how to approach Kalina, especially if she was taking every action to avoid him. He *could* just teleport into her room, but that would be unethical. Besides the fact that it's not just her dorm, boys were strictly forbidden from entering the girls' dormitories and vice versa. What if her roommates were getting dressed? That would be an extremely inappropriate position to be in.

He rested for a while on the rooftop, staring at the night sky. He wished he paid more attention in astrology, but it was an extremely elusive subject to him. *Perhaps Kalina is a clairvoyant*, he thought to himself. Never before had she expressed any specific magical aptitude, but to be fair neither did he. If she were able to predict the future, then it would be near impossible for him to find the right time to get to her... unless she didn't have a choice.

A plan began to emerge in Phillip's mind's eye to, well, not kidnap his sister. He would just be... "whisking her away." He didn't want to get in trouble for skipping class, so he would do it after fourth period – before lunch. He knew the school like the back of his hand, so Kalina wouldn't be able to hide. *This is pretty dark*, he thought to himself again, but it didn't matter. His sister's well-being was his top priority.

***

Mark and Phillip were hunched over at their desks working on interpreting a contour map for Mr. Rumsey's cartography class. Part of the class included the study of magic-altering conditions – things like elevation, the angle of the terrain. Even things like nearby water sources have a lot of impact on casting since they add noise and humidity to the environment.

Mr. Rumsey approached Mark and Phillip's desk silently to scrutinize their work. He raised an eyebrow and said, "Interesting" before walking away to look at the other students' work.

"What does that mean?" whispered Phillip to Mark, who just shrugged.

"I don't know, but I don't think he said that to any of the other students."

Mark and Phillip spent the rest of class scrutinizing their work, trying to figure out what Mr. Rumsey was talking about. Before they knew it, the bell rang.

"I've got to go get Kalina," reminded Phillip.

"Alright, let me know how it goes," replied Mark.

Phillip had thought of eight different routes that Kalina could take on her way out of class. Only three of them would matter if she was going to the mess hall for lunch. If she was avoiding him, though, she would try to stay away from the mess hall.

Phillip teleported himself into the hallway on the middle-school side to find his sister among her classmates, but he couldn't see her. He teleported around the corner, but still couldn't find her. His third option was to see if she was headed to the library. Lo and behold, on the staircase he teleported directly in front of his sister.

Kalina sighed, "Well, I guess we're doing this."

Before she could say or do anything else, Phillip whisked the two of them away to the rooftop of the boys' dormitory.

"We need to talk," he informed her.

"About what?" she asked disingenuously.

"About what happened at the library and the way you've been acting. It's not normal."

"So, you kidnapped me to tell me that I'm not normal. Great brother you are, Phillip," she responded facetiously.

"Don't do that. You know what I mean. This isn't normal *for you.*"

Kalina just shrugged her shoulders and kept up the act. "I don't know what you mean. I'm doing fine in all my classes. I'm eating. I'm exercising."

"That's not what I've heard."

"So, you have people spying on me now? How very UDBA of you."

Phillip knew that she was going to make this difficult. Her manipulative tactics weren't going to work on him, though.

"Look, I'm just trying to look after you. That seizure was a big deal, and... I'm sorry that I spoke that way to you at the library. It's just that we were trying to have a private conversation. I'm sure you feel that way sometimes with your friends."

Kalina didn't give an emotive response at all; she just took a deep breath and said, "It doesn't really matter. I'm not bothered by it, and I'm fine now."

"Well, you're going to need to convince Mom and Dad because they're coming tomorrow."

Phillip was getting frustrated, and it started to show in his voice. However, he certainly got Kalina's attention. He wasn't sure how she would handle it, but she might be able to fake one weekend for her parents.

"Great, but for now can you let me go get lunch please?"

Phillip relented and teleported them back to the mess hall. After he got food, he went to sit by Mark and Aisling.

"How'd it go?" asked Mark.

"Awful," said Phillip, who didn't feel like talking about it. He knew exactly what would happen. Mom and Dad would come, Kalina would act cute and friendly, and everything would go back to the status quo.

I2

TEMPTATION VS TRUTH

Phillip's prediction came true, but his parents had advised him that it might have been best to back off Kalina for a little bit since that seemed to be what she genuinely wanted. They spoke to Dr. Toumi, who wasn't totally convinced of their plan, but let them pursue it while still receiving updates. Although Kalina was a lot less social, she was doing well academically, and the year was continuing without any major hiccups for her.

Tonight, she was planning on pursuing the project her brother and his friends started by testing the limits of her abilities. Months of research into divination and projection gave her an idea that she wanted to try out. For her, the only problem at this point was her roommates constantly bothering her and making noise in the room. For her experiment to work, she needed total darkness and quiet.

"Hey, Kalina, do you want to come study with us in the library tonight?" asked Maura, even though she knew that Kalina would probably decline the offer.

"No, thanks. I've got some research to do," replied Kalina almost a little too shortly.

"Kalina, you've been obsessed with this random woman – "

"First of all, her name is Samantha Hastings. Second of all, I never said that it was *her* I was researching." Of course she didn't 'say' it, but yes, it was the direction of her thoughts at the moment.

"You've been obsessed with Samantha Hastings for several weeks now! You've been acting weird ever since that football game and now it's almost Thanksgiving break! You haven't been studying at all! How are you keeping your grades up?"

"I'm not cheating if that's what you're implying," snapped Kalina back at Maura.

"That's not what I –ugh, never mind. Be alone. Whatever." At this point Maura was too exhausted to argue with her roommate. She knew that silence would be better in the long run in order to keep the peace in the dorms. Something was off with Kalina; this wasn't the same girl she had gotten to know during the first few weeks of school.

Maura turned around and left her dormitory. Presumably she was headed to the library to do homework with Laurelle and some other students from their class (probably also taking some time to flirt with William, too). That was alright with Kalina, who was able to achieve top marks even just doing the bare minimum. She didn't have to study since her aptitude allowed her to see the answers to the test before she even saw the questions. She felt slightly guilty about it. In the past it was a policy of hers to achieve good grades the more "honest" way – without using prophecy as a crutch. That's exactly what it was: a crutch to give her answers that she can later forget about.

She didn't have to worry about any of that right now, though. Her parents were coming on Saturday (two days' time) to take her and Phillip home for Thanksgiving break. Then, she would have more time to work on her abilities and to do more research. So far, she'd been able to master remote viewing Samantha Hastings by using binaural beats she found on YouTube. *It wasn't technically stalking*, she justified to herself. *It's an observation.* There wasn't much to observe anyway, as Samantha Hastings was still in her coma. Her parents were able to find her, but they decided not to move her body all the way to Washington. Fortunately, she has an uncle who works in D.C., so her mother has been staying with him.

Kalina decided to put on her headphones and listen to her favorite beats by Passerelle. She found these to be the best for inducing a trance in which she felt she could see above the known universe. The physical world slipped away. Her body was asleep, but her mind surpassed being awake to a state of cosmic awareness.

Instead of traversing the celestial plane, she found herself in a familiar field. She looked down at the ground, realizing she was taller. Instead of her usual clothes, she was in an antebellum dress. She could even feel the corset, which fit snugly around her torso. *This isn't as horrible as Hollywood claims it to be.* She followed a path through a dense maritime forest. The trees eventually opened up to a meadow. Across from her was a beautiful plantation mansion. Rather than heading towards it, though, she diverged onto a small bunny trail and sauntered down a hill towards a stream. There she found a shed where a black boy was peeling an orange. When he noticed her, he immediately stood up and held out his hand to present her an fresh orange.

"Have you made a decision yet?" he asked, offering her the naked fruit.

She could feel the girl inside her hesitate. The fruit was tempting, but she felt that she shouldn't take it. After a long pause, she reached for the fruit. Before she was able to touch it, Kalina was woken up. The binaural beats had reached its end, and Kalina was startled by the bothersome YouTube ads that followed it.

***

Saturday had finally come, and Kalina looked forward to a week's vacation in which she could freely isolate herself to meditate in private. However, she soon found out her plans were to be thwarted. When she got into the car, her parents had her cornered. *Great, am I going to have to deal with an hour of this?*

"So, Kalina," her mother began. "Your father and I have been talking to some of your teachers, and they seem to be worried about you. Do you know why?"

Kalina hated being asked leading questions, so she prompted her mother to continue with a snide remark. "Why ask questions you already know the answer to?"

"Don't talk back to your mother, Kalina," scolded Mr. Todorova.

"It's okay, Ivan. I want to hear Kalina's side of the story; that's all."

Catherine Todorova's 'leniency' was clearly a pretense, and there was a hint of innocent accusation in it. Kalina hated when her parents played good-cop & bad-cop. When she stubbornly remained silent, Catherine Todorova decided to continue anyways.

"Apparently, you've been acting anti-social and distant from your classmates, which I know doesn't sound like you. Is everything alright? Are you depressed? According to your classmates, you haven't been studying at all!"

"So," retorted Kalina defensively. "I'm still earning good grades and doing my homework."

"Watch your tone," chimed her father. "And that's not the point!"

"Your father's right, Kalina. That isn't the point," she began a little more harshly. "We're worried about you. That's why I've decided to set up a meeting with Sister Maryam at Saint Nina's Convent on Monday. Don't worry she was also raised in the magical community and her abbess is aware of her 'expertise', so don't feel like you can't talk to her."

Kalina realized that Phillip, who normally had his nose stuck in a book while they were driving, was awkwardly listening to their conversation. She returned a glance at him that in sibling language meant, "what are you looking at?"

Phillip leaned over and whispered, "Is this about your seizure?"

Kalina shook her head, further irked that her brother had joined the interrogation

"Is it about the woman?" he asked again.

Kalina hardened her face and gritted her teeth. *Why can't everyone just shut up and leave me alone!!!*

"Are you having visions?" he asked one more time.

Startled, Kalina widened her eyes and stared directly into Phillip's. She shouldn't have been so taken aback. If anyone were to guess her aptitude first, it would have logically been her brother. Nevertheless, a sudden realization hit her: she had been so obsessed with inducing visions and discovering the mystery of Samantha Hastings, that she had been too careless about letting other people become aware of her abilities. How did her brother find out? Rumors, maybe? If he knows, maybe her friends (if they still are her friends) know? Do her teachers know? Her parents? *Careless. That's what you were. This is what happens when you abuse your gift.*

Her reaction was all Phillip needed as an answer. For the rest of the trip, no one uttered another word; they just listened to the radio. Apparently, the Magical Union of North America was facing a constitutional crisis, but Kalina wasn't paying attention; her thoughts on school, her family, and her abilities were racing in her head. She knew she had messed up – potentially big time.

***

"Christ is in our midst," greeted a sweet and gentle voice behind them.

"He is and ever shall be, Sister Hannah" replied Catherine, turning around. "Is Sister Maryam in her cell? I've set up an appointment with her for Kalina."

Catherine would regularly come to the convent for confession and spiritual advice. Sometimes she came just to help the sisters out or attend a service with them. Since all her baby birds had flown away from the nest, she found that she had more time on her hands and decided to spend it here. By now, she was familiar with almost all of the sisters who lived the monastic life at St. Nina's.

The nun's face smiled warmly at Mrs. Todorova. "No, but Sister Maryam and Abbess Aemiliane told me that you were coming today. I think she'll see you outside."

"Will we be seeing the Reverend Mother?" asked Catherine.

"If you would like to. I can take you to her before you see Sister Maryam. Oh! Here they are right now!"

"Christ is in our midst," greeted the abbess. "It's good to see you again."

Catherine made a respectful bow before embracing Abbess Aemiliane and giving each other a kiss on the cheek. Kalina copied her mother in formally greeting the abbess, and they made introductions.

"I'll let you speak to Sister Maryam now, as I've got a lot of work to do preparing for the feast day of your namesake, Saint Catherine of Alexandria herself later this week."

"Thank you, Abbess," replied Catherine Todorova.

Catherine, Kalina, and Sister Maryam walked outside to a bench in the garden so that they might speak in private. Since it was late fall, most of the plants had died already. However, Catherine and Kalina had been there in the spring before, and they knew it was a beautiful place to be.

"So, how have you been, Kalina?" asked Sister Maryam.

"I'm doing well. I'm getting really good grades in all of my classes."

"Be honest with Sister Maryam," interjected Catherine Todorova. "There's obviously something wrong."

Seeing Kalina make a hardened face at her mother's prompting, Sister Maryam suggested, "Do you wish to speak to me alone, Kalina?"

Before making a response, Kalina pursed her lips in thought, then glanced at her mom. She was considering how to politely ask her mom to leave. In understanding, Catherine nodded her head.

"Well, alright. I'll just be over there," she said, pointing at another part in the garden before walking off in that direction.

Still, they sat in silence for a few moments before Sister Maryam spoke up.

"I know why you've been bothered recently. You've been getting visions haven't you?" she asked.

Kalina, surprised, responded, "How do you know? Does my mom know?"

"I don't know if she knows per se, but this isn't my first rodeo. I was able to come to my own conclusions based on what your mother has told me. It sounds like you haven't been acting with precaution, either. I wouldn't be surprised if others have started to guess."

"My brother knows. I trust him, though."

"It's good that you trust him, but you have to be very careful with your abilities. It isn't safe sometimes for psychics who can see the future, and I can tell that your talents are beyond what even you are aware of."

"What does that mean?"

"With power as great as yours– "

"Comes a great responsibility," interrupted Kalina, remembering the cliché from Spider-Man.

"No," said Sister Maryam grimly. "With great power comes great danger – and temptation, especially for psychics. And I don't just mean by people who want to abuse your power, which there are plenty of. You don't think that the evil one and the princes of darkness want to tempt you to their side? You could be a valuable asset to them. By the nature of your power alone, you'll be more tempted to fall into the hands of evil!"

"I'm just using it because I'm trying to help someone," replied Kalina, scared and uncertain of what exactly Sister Maryam was trying to say. She suddenly felt the need to give an excuse for her actions.

"Is that true?" asked Sister Maryam, who reached down to the dry pathway to pick up a struggling earthworm and return him to the moist grass. "Is that why you're using powers to shortcut your way into earning good grades? 'The road to hell is paved with good intentions.'"

"Are you a psychic?" questioned Kalina, surprised at how much Sister Maryam was able to discern about her. She felt like a book being read.

"No, I actually never learned my aptitude. For all I know, I don't have one," she answered while placing the earthworm into a bed of grass.

"I thought everyone had an aptitude… Are you a generalist?" asked Kalina.

"No, my aptitude is undetermined. Only about a half of magi receive a specific aptitude, the rest being what you might call 'generalist.' You'll see at the end of the year when you all get tested. Only about fifty percent of you will actually test into a specific aptitude by the end of your first year. More the second year, then the third. I don't know whether or not I'm a generalist because I was home-schooled, which many magi in North America are. You have to think about us, too. Sometimes homeschooled magi will get tested if they want to get a job in a magical government, but often there's no need to. Anyways, that's not what we're here to discuss."

"What do you suggest I do, Sister Maryam?" asked Kalina, who felt more ashamed the more she spoke to the sister.

"It really isn't that hard, Kalina. You just have to be normal."

"How can I be normal when I've learned and experienced all these things? When there's this woman who I could help?"

"She's not your responsibility. You need to learn to control your gift. I'm assuming you've been inducing it somehow? Not drugs, I hope."

"No, I've been using something called binaural beats."

Kalina was shocked when Sister Maryam snapped her head towards up with grim wide eyes.

"I would be very, very careful using that method," she said sternly. "I've heard of binaural beats before, and it's a quick way to attract demons. I've heard many stories of people falling into possessions due to subliminal messages in the undertones of these sounds. You must also be careful about stealing the gifts of higher intellect before you earn it. God does not look kindly on thieves."

"I haven't seen any demons... or angels, I swear," gasped Kalina, again not sure if she was comprehending what exactly she was being told.

"Alright, but in the future I want you to try reciting the Jesus Prayer –"

"Like hesychasm?" asked Kalina.

"No, hesychasm is reserved only for those most experienced in prayer and always should be practiced with the blessing of a spiritual elder. You are far too young to begin. Perhaps, one day, you will be able to achieve not only prayer from your lips, but also noetic prayer from the heart. For now, start with a few at a time. I trust you have a prayer rope?"

"Yes," replied Kalina, nodding her head sincerely

"Good, you can even do some other short form prayers like Saint John Cassian directs us to do.""

"Yes, Sister Maryam. Is there anything else I should do?"

"Do you have a rule of prayer?"

"I have one of those small red prayer books from St. Tikhon's," replied Kalina.

"Good, I want you as a minimum to do the morning and evening prayers in there. Besides that, make sure that you're social and study hard. You don't want to use your gifts as a handicap. Also, don't waste your time and ruin your friendships by obsessing over things that don't concern you. Trust in God."

Kalina nodded her head in understanding. After that serious conversation, Kalina asked Sister Maryam some more questions about aptitudes and the monastic life, which she was happy to answer. Soon, they headed back to Catherine Todorova, who was patiently enjoying the late autumn weather as she waited. Her hand was gracefully feeling through her prayer rope, repeatedly asking for the intercessions of the Theotokos. By the time they finished their talk, the bells were ringing, signaling it was time for sixth hour prayers.

13
THANKSGIVING'S HUNT

Mark and his older brother, Peter, were belly to the ground in the middle of the woods (regular woods this time). They were disciplined enough to ignore the critters and the cool dampness of the autumn forest floor. Each held a rifle in hand. It was Poitier family tradition to go hunting for their own turkeys for Thanksgiving dinner. Since they had to spend all day waiting, Mark determined that it was an optimal time to ask his older brother about his knowledge on Primordial and Enchanted Forests and Groves. He considered his brother to be the perfect person to ask about this because they shared aptitudes. Peter himself worked for the Virginia Magical Burgess as a professional navigator and cartographer. Of all his older brothers, Mark felt closest and most admiring of Peter.

"I don't know too much about them. Nobody does quite frankly. The VMB was thinking of restarting research a couple of years ago, but the idea got shut down. For now, they're still a complete mystery. Why do you want to know?"

"I'm curious about exploring the one behind school," answered Mark in partial truth.

"Didn't some woman who went missing a couple decades ago pop out of there a few months ago? The news sent everyone reeling in the Department of Navigation. We have absolutely no ideas on how she did it. Is that what this is about?"

Mark didn't hesitate. He decided to be truthful to his older brother. If he couldn't trust his own blood, then who could he trust?

"Yes, my friends and I are trying to solve the mystery of Samantha Hastings – that's her name. We believe that there were others like her that may have been kidnapped. We want to find out what happened, and I have an idea that we should try retracing her steps."

"That could be a smart idea if we knew more about Dark Forests, but they're an enigma. She's the first person I've ever heard of – that anyone has ever heard of in the past thousand years – to be able to navigate themselves out of one. Like I said, no one has any idea how."

They laid in the prone position for a while since they thought they heard a noise. A doe jumped out in the open, and Mark shifted his rifle towards her. She was beautiful, but not what they were hunting for. *Death for death's sake was in poor taste*, he thought to himself. He didn't want unnecessary blood on his hands, even if the creature wasn't human. He fired a shot to scare her off, hoping that she wouldn't come across any other hunters on her way home.

Afterwards, he continued the conversation. "You work for the VMB, right? Don't you do navigation and cartography for them?"

"Yeah, but not terrestrial. Recently, I've been helping out the astrological division to chart out the stars. There's a lot of strange things happening recently, and it looks like it's going to get even crazier out here. There might even be a war coming based on one of the astrological interpreters."

"Among the normies or the magi? Never mind you probably aren't allowed to talk about it. Anyways, do you have any ideas on how I might be able to chart out or navigate through the Blue Ridge Enchanted Forest? Hasn't there been any sort of substantial or successful research?"

"Not since the 80s. I know because like I said, the topic came up a couple years ago. It's too dangerous in America at least. Most of the research is European. You can probably find a few papers in Finnish and German, but that's about it. We're not going to be able to tame this beast anytime soon."

Mark and Peter laid silently in the prone position for a while; Mark was lost in thought. His soul almost jumped out of his body when his brother fired a shot next to him.

Peter stood up and said, "I think we got one! Hopefully Dad and Matt got one. In any case we can always just pick up another bird at the supermarket."

Mark was one of six, and one turkey simply wasn't enough for a family of eight. However, his older brothers Andrew and John became vegetarian in their teenage years due to their aptitudes. Andrew was an augur (worked with birds a lot, but still ate beef for some reason), and John was a zoolinguist (wasn't comfortable eating creatures he could communicate with). Still, the rest of the brothers could definitely eat their share of protein.

Mark had to carry the turkey by himself back to the car since Peter was the one who hit it (fortunately it was a skinnier one). As they headed back to the truck, Peter talked to their Dad and brother on the walkie-talkie to let them know they caught a bird. They hadn't caught one themselves, but were already headed back since it was starting to get late.

14
THE GAME OF AIR AND EARTH

Kalina took a deep breath. A week of sobering reflection made her realize that she had been treating her roommates and other classmates worse than chopped liver. Her heart was pounding in her chest at the fear of rejection, but she knew delaying the inevitable would only make the situation worse. Fortunately, she wouldn't actually have to initiate the conversation.

"Kalina? What are you doing staring at our door?"

Kalina turned around to see Maura's freckled face making a questioning look at her. Next to her were Laurelle's furtive amber eyes looking kindly at her.

"We've been watching you since we came in at the end of the hall. Are you alright? Did you get locked out?" asked Maura again.

Kalina took a deep breath and humbled herself before she began, "Look, I know I've been really distant the past couple of months, and I know I've been treating you and everyone else poorly. I'm really sorry about that, and I hope that you can forgive me and that we can be friends again."

"Oh, Kalina! Of course! We've all been so worried," replied Maura, beaming. "To be honest, I really thought that it might have been something I said or did that made you upset at me. I kept replaying that football game in my head."

"Oh no! It wasn't that. I've just had a lot on my mind; that's... umm... that's all. We don't need to talk about it..."

"Okay," said Maura, and Laurelle simply nodded her head. "Well, we were just hanging out with Alice. If you want, we can all go to the stoikee court if you want to play? We were just talking about how we needed a fourth person actually."

Kalina agreed and was extremely appreciative of Maura's and Laurelle's understanding. She actually enjoyed stoickee, and thought it was a fun replacement since there weren't any (good) tennis players in her grade.

Stoickee was a game that all sixth graders were taught in their Magical Theory class. It was invented in the early 20th century by a teacher in Canada to teach students about elemental magic. It involves only two of the four elements: air and earth. In some advanced three-man variations, water is also included (more typically played in Quebec and some parts of the north). It is typically played by four or more players.

There are two sets of two "balls" used by each team. Each team has their own set. One of the "balls" is actually an octahedron (colloquially called the octo) and carried around using a lacrosse-like net-stick. The other "ball" is actually a puck-like cube and is passed around on the ground with stoickee sticks. The octo may not leave the air (that is, touch the ground), and the cube may not leave the ground completely. The surface stoickee is played on is typically smooth and wooden or marble.

Each team has its own goal, represented by a tree trunk. At the top of the trunk is a ring in which the opposing team has to get their own octo through to score. At the bottom of a trunk is another ring, where the cube goes through. Each team is responsible for getting their own octos and cubes back. For octos, this is particularly tricky, because they must stay in the air, so magic is often used. A player will typically cast a boomerang charge.

Players may sabotage efforts of another team to retrieve their balls or to give them penalties. When a penalty for a ball occurs, the ball "vanishes" (they're enchanted to become invisible) for two minutes, meaning the team will be unable to play offense and will have to play defense.

The players may not use their hands or feet to manipulate the balls. If a limb intentionally touches a cube or octo, there is an enchantment that causes that limb to go numb for 15 seconds.

Maura stopped by one of the dorms to get Alice, while Kalina and Laurelle headed downstairs to let Mrs. Donna know where they were headed. They also needed to check out the equipment for stoickee – two air-nets, two earth-sticks, and a octo and cube each. In a normal game of stoickee there would be two sets of octos and cubes (four total, one of each type for each team.). However, since there were only four of them, they played the modified version.

By the time Laurelle and Kalina got all the equipment set up, Alice and Maura were ready to head to the stoickee field. The game of stoickee required a separate field from the football field (where students also liked to play normie sports such as soccer, lacrosse, and field hockey). There were a few stoickee fields in case multiple teams wanted to play, but fortunately they were all empty. In the magical community, stoickee was an esteemed sport, and schools often encouraged their students to practice. Three years ago, Cardinal Key Academy won the North American championship, and it was repeatedly brought up whenever the game was discussed.

The girls chose the first field on the left and set up teams. Alice and Maura would be one team, with Alice taking charge of earth, and Maura, air. Kalina herself would be playing air, and Laurelle would be responsible for earth. Each team went to their own trunk (a trunk has a ring through the top and bottom which count as the goals).

They flipped a coin to see who would start with each ball. Kalina earned the octo, which meant that Alice would start with the cube. The game began. Kalina was a decent player, and she got some practice in. Maura was on another level, though. Even with her prophetic abilities to help her perform against her opponent, it took a lot of effort to get past Maura's net, but eventually she did get the ball through the ring – just barely.

This meant that the burden of aeriality lay with Maura, who quickly incanted, *"Tardus cassus!"* before the octo hit the ground. The octo was still pulled down by gravity, but the spell made the process significantly slower. Kalina herself was impressed; she didn't think she would have been able to cast that spell as well as Maura, who got the octo to fall at nearly a quarter of the rate of gravity.

Kalina hesitated to catch up to Maura, who had already caught the octo in her net and was cradling it side-to-side towards Kalina's trunk. In front of her, she saw Laurelle dribbling the cube towards Alice's trunk. That's good at least, she thought to herself as she was trying to stop Maura from scoring a point.

Eventually, the girls tired out and started getting hungry. When they got to the scoreboard, it showed in glowing numerals that Maura got an air point over Kalina 3-2. Below that, Alice also had an earth point over Laurelle, 5-4.

"Getting better, Laurelle!" exclaimed Alice. "Do you play often, Kalina? Maura is one of the best players in our class."

"She doesn't play as much as me," answered Maura on her behalf (which was true). "She's just naturally gifted at everything."

Kalina shook her head, smiling at Maura teasing her. "Not everything. I play tennis with my family and at home. That's where I get my athleticism from. Besides, I've learned to play in class, remember?"

After the game, all four girls decided to head back to the dormitories to return their equipment before heading to the mess hall to get dinner. Alice said she was going to invite her roommates, Michelle and Zara, but they probably had already eaten. Kalina was glad that she had an excellent start to her first day back at school – she even made a new friend. Nonetheless, in the back of her head, she was still concerned with what her brother and his friends were up to.

15

PLOTTING THE FORBIDDEN PATH

"I was wondering when you were going to arrive," said Mark to Phillip immediately as he walked into their dorm. "Settle down and then we can talk about our plan of action."

"Well that sounds peculiar. You've definitely piqued my interest," retorted Phillip. "Is this something that involves our good friend Aisling? Is she back yet?"

"Yeah, I texted her earlier. We've already planned to meet for dinner and then hit the library. She was a little upset yesterday that she had to wait for you to come first before I started talking. You know how impatient she can be."

Phillip merely shrugged. "My family is serious about going to church on Sundays."

After dinner, Mark led his friends to the library. He had scheduled in advance for the trio to have one of the private rooms so that they could talk about his plans. Ever since the incident with Kalina, all three had become a lot more careful about making their plans and conducting research out of sight.

"You know how that mysterious woman came from the woods? And how we witnessed those two... *'people'* (or whatever they were) emerge from the woods?" began Mark. Aisling and Phillip nodded their heads, understanding where the conversation was headed. "So over Thanksgiving, I asked my brother, who's a navigator for the VMB, about archetypal Enchanted Woods and what we know about them. There are other countries across the pond that are more interested in researching them, but in the 80s, the Magical Union of North America shut down all the projects because the forests here are so much more dangerous and violent than those in Europe. Which brings me to my next point. I have written an essay on why we should restart exploration, and how given our collective aptitudes, especially yours Phillip, we would be less in harm's way."

"Wait, so it's been illegal to enter the woods this whole time?" asked Aisling, confused. The students knew they were supposed to stay on campus grounds, and there were patches of fence that surrounded it (there were a lot of holes, too).

"No, not at all. Most magi and even normies actually have an intuition to stay away from them according to some of the 70s research," answered Mark. "It's just that MUNA was losing a lot of money and personnel. There have been a couple more fruitless attempts by private researchers and companies since then, but they didn't really discover anything new. We just haven't been interested in the topic as much in America. However, we now have an ace up our sleeves – a teleporter. If we're in danger or we get lost, you can just teleport us back."

"I'm not sure about that. In any case, we're still going to have to get permission from Dean Schulz if we want to do this. And who would be our sponsor?" questioned Phillip.

"Well there's only one natural answer to that, my friend," replied Mark, grinning. "Mr. Wells, who does your private teleportation classes, is the perfect candidate."

Phillip thought for a moment but was pleased with Mark's idea. It seemed as though he spent a lot of time, research, and effort coming up with this plan, and it sounded like a feasible plan of action.

"It definitely seems like you've got something," said Phillip. "How are we going to get this to the dean, though?"

"And what if Mr. Wells doesn't want to be our sponsor?" asked Aisling.

Mark sighed, "You two have such little faith in me. I've already talked to Mr. Wells about it, and he was excited about the idea. I think he actually likes having me around to help you, Phillip – like when we get lost. As for the dean, I've already set up a meeting with him during our cartography class tomorrow. Mr. Rumsey probably won't be too happy, though, huh?"

"Is that fourth period?" asked Aisling. "I have Enchantments at that time. It's actually my favorite class, but that's okay. I think this is more important."

***

"Your essay was very impressive, Mr. Poitier," began Dean Schulz. He was dressed in a plaid suit. He took his reading glasses off, allowing the students to gaze into his intense sky-blue eyes. He skillfully raised one of his eyebrows. "What made you interested in Enchanted Forest exploration?"

"My brother works in this field. He has the same aptitude as me."

"Really? Are you sure that's it?"

"No, actually," Mark boldly decided to be direct and honest. Hopefully, the dean would respect that. "The appearance of Samantha Hastings triggered my interest in this subject. As far as we know for certain, she's the only person who has been able to come out of there."

Mark intentionally left out the details of the two women he and Phillip had witnessed. He wasn't sure how the dean would react to *that*. First and foremost, it would incriminate him and Phillip for being out past curfew. Second, going that far into the Blue Ridge Enchanted Forest would have been considered dangerous enough for potential suspension. Third, they might possibly be considered as withholding information from the detectives, and Mark wasn't sure what the consequences for that would be.

"Yes," replied the dean. "And look at the cost she had to pay. You're going to need to do better to convince me."

Mark was expecting this kind of push back from the dean. He wasn't known for playing easy with his students. However, the trio were aware of his philosophy to motivate his students towards achieving their full potential and were hoping to appeal to that sentiment.

"First of all," responded Aisling. "She was abducted. We don't *know* that the forest did that to her. There have been *so many* abductions and disappearances that happened by a Dark or Enchanted Forest. Our research could help save lives! Look at all the other cases and disappearances that preceded this. Second of all, we would be in a team. We would have a talented teacher" she pointed to Mr. Wells "a talented navigator, and our secret ace... a teleporter!"

Aisling presented with a lot of charisma and energy, and even the dean looked enthralled in the moment.

"And where do you fit in all of this, Miss Donovan?"

Aisling stumbled on this question; she had just assumed she would be a part of the team. She quickly tried to come up with an answer, and unfortunately stumbled over her words.

"W-well, I uhh... I-I make... magic cards. I can make beacons, or, or something else – anything that we might need in case of an emergency. Ummm... maybe some healing cards, yeah. I also did a lot of help with the research."

Dean Schulz sighed, "I'll have to think about it. Now go to class; I want to talk to Mr. Wells in private."

The trio left the dean's office neither with high hopes nor in despair. The dean was usually known for making an immediate and precise decision, so they were perplexed by his answer (or lack thereof rather). They decided it would be best to focus on the rest of the semester for now, and they each headed back to their respective classes.

16

FINAL EXAMS WEEK

<u>Phillip's Schedule:</u>

   1: Language Arts w/ Mrs. Cervantes

   2: Calculus 1 w/ Mr. Van Rijn

   3: Geography w/ Mr. Mackenzie

   4: Cartography w/ Mr. Rumsey

   5: Dueling w/ Mr. Campbell

   6: Greek w/ Miss Haverty

   7: Private Teleportation Tutoring w/ Mr. Wells

<u>Mark's Schedule:</u>

   1: Language Arts w/ Mrs. Fowler

   2: Precalculus w/ Mr. Clark

   3: Geography w/ Mr. Mackenzie

   4: Cartography w/ Mr. Rumsey

   5: Dueling w/ Mr. Campbell

   6: French w/ Mme. Stephens

   7: Private Teleportation Tutoring w/ Mr. Wells

<u>Aisling's Schedule:</u>
1: Language Arts w/ Mrs. Cervantes
2: Precalculus w/ Mr. Clark
3: 2D Art w/ Fraulein Bauer
4: Enchantments w/ Mrs. Cervantes
5: Dueling w/ Mr. Campbell
6: French w/ Mme. Stephens
7: Legal Studies w/ Mrs. Fowler

Aisling found Mark casually laying against a tree with his textbook open on his lap. He wasn't reading it. He just seemed to be sitting there, waiting. The trio had agreed to meet up for a study session since they were determined to do well on their final exams. They still had hope for approval and didn't want Dean Schulz to reject their research proposition based on poor grades.

"Hey Aisling," he said as he saw her approaching. "You got the stuff for Language Arts?"

"Yeah, where's Phillip? I thought he was going to be studying with us."

"We were practicing navigation techniques and teleportation. If we did our calculations correctly, he should be somewhere in the Manassas Battlefield. He's gotten a lot better at traveling to places further than he can see."

Just as he finished, Phillip popped back right next to Aisling. His sudden appearance caught her off guard, and she jumped so hard that she threw her textbooks all over the place.

"Our math was slightly off, but close enough. I accidentally teleported back in front of the dormitories first," he said to Mark, almost robotically. "Oh hey, Aisling. Sorry to startle you like that. Are you guys ready to start studying for Language Arts? That's the subject I'm most worried about."

Phillip bent down and helped Aisling pick up her books. They all sat down on the grass and got out their Language Arts textbooks: *Mastering English for Junior Magi, Grade 10*. They decided to study outside instead of the library since it would be packed with other students studying for their finals as well – mostly middle-schoolers. Mark brought a blanket since the ground could be cold and wet during the fall.

"Mrs. Fowler said that both tenth grade Language Arts classes will have similar tests," informed Mark, who knew that Aisling and Phillip had Language Arts with Mrs. Cervantes. "She told us that we should focus on composing and interpreting magical prose," he continued. "Also, do you guys have to write an essay on medieval symbolism in *Tristan & Iseult*?"

"Yeah, it's due the week before Christmas break," answered Aisling. "Well, let's start on interpreting spells because that's slightly more difficult than composing them – for me at least." Aisling had more experience with casting magic in her enchantment classes, so she was able to build up a lot of magical stamina and creativity.

The trio spent their Saturday morning practicing for their Language Arts test by interpreting and casting incantations to double check their work (casting wouldn't be allowed to check answers in the classroom during the test unfortunately).

"Okay, one more. Do you guys want to do the challenge problem?" asked Aisling. "It's on the next page."

"Sure," replied Mark.

Phillip was secretly hoping that they would stop there because he was so tired, and it was his turn next in the rotation to cast the spell. Nevertheless, he didn't want to be the weak link in the chain and flipped the page only to read a spell in a language he was unfamiliar with.

Escrit en piere, la plume esclere!

"This looks like French," commented Aisling. "But a little different."

"Maybe it's an alternative version," suggested Mark, whose father was a linguist. "*Escrit* could be like *ecrit*. That is, to write. Pierre is a French name. And la plume is self-explanatory. I'm confused with *esclere*, though."

"Well, if *escrit* is actually *ecrit*, then *esclere* would be *eclaire*!" exclaimed Aisling excitedly.

Phillip listened to the two French students figure out the problem for him, hoping that eventually he would be able to help out.

"Well, that doesn't make sense," said Mark. "Write on Peter, the light plume?"

"Well, a plume is a sort of pen," informed Aisling. "Like for calligraphy. Sometimes scribes use them for specific cases. I wonder if this is some sort of notarizing spell. That would make sense with the name Peter. But why is the pen light?"

Phillip found an opportunity to give his two cents. "Well, *esclere* could be to clarify. And obviously, Peter refers to a rock or a stone."

Mark smacked his forehead with the palm of his hand. "Of course! *Eclaire* can mean to enlighten. *Write in stone, the enlightening pen!*"

"Still not exactly clear what it does, though," said Phillip, who was racking his brain.

Fortunately, they had Aisling, a dedicated scribe. "It's probably a kind of copying spell. You write or draw whatever you want on a piece of parchment, and it etches itself onto the surface of an object. Geez, I can think of multiple times when an incantation like this would have come in handy!"

"Alright, let's see if it works," said Phillip, who tore out a piece of paper with doodles and placed it on a grassless patch of earth.

"Are you sure you want to do this one? You're looking a bit pale," remarked Aisling.

"Don't worry, I've got this. *Escrit en piere, la plume esclere!*"

Phillip took his palm off the paper and removed it. However, only traces of drawing copied itself onto the hard ground. The other two huddled over him to examine the results.

"I don't think you were pronouncing it correctly," offered Mark. "Maybe Aisling should do it since she takes French and is also a scribe.

Phillip sighed and handed her the paper. She copied the spell, and when they removed the sheet, an almost perfect replica of the drawing was etched into the earth.

"Great job, and now I'm hungry," said Mark tersely. Clearly, he had been waiting to go eat for quite some time.

It was finally lunch time, and they had used so much energy casting magic that they were both fatigued and starved. By the looks of the cafeteria, many other students were feeling the same way. The mess hall was always busiest this time of year due to finals, and salivating meals were prepared as a special treat for the stressed students.

Phillip looked longingly at Aisling's country-fried steak and fries. She always commented that the school needed to purchase some Old Bay seasoning to go on top. Mark chose an equally delicious fried chicken and waffles (he had a bit of a sweet tooth this morning after all that casting).

"Why didn't you get some steak yourself?" asked Mark. "It's not Wednesday or Friday."

Phillip looked up from his veggie plate. "It's the Nativity Fast," he replied. "I just have to eat extra carbs to catch up with you. Hence the extra French fries."

"How long is the fast?" inquired Mark again.

"Forty days, like Easter."

Mark sighed, "That's rough. I don't know if I could do that and still cast magic."

"Some spells actually require an ascetic state, and it's good for self-mastery," chimed in Aisling, who was slightly more familiar with it due to her Catholic upbringing. "Besides, even without fasting, there are a bunch of students who end up fatiguing themselves. I heard that last year, three eighth graders passed out while trying to perform an advanced level spell!"

As if on cue, Phillip started seeing black spots and fell out of his chair. Mark, who was sitting next to him, rushed to his side.

"Phillip! Are you alright?"

"Yeah, I'm okay. I'm just tired," he answered, gaining consciousness relatively quickly.

"You have to see Dr. Toumi!" exclaimed Aisling.

"I said I'm fine. Besides, we still have so many topics to study."

"Phillip," demanded Aisling. "You need to see Dr. Toumi. You won't be taking a test if you're unconscious – or worse, if you burn yourself out!"

"People self-combusting from too much magic use is just a myth that parents tell their children to scare them," slurred Phillip, trying to act like he was stable enough to keep going. Neither Mark nor Aisling were convinced.

"Come on, Phillip," encouraged Mark. "Aisling and I will take you to Dr. Toumi. Best case scenario, he'll give you the clear. If not, then we'll be forced to call for a medical emergency."

"Fine," said Phillip, bitter at his friends' ultimatum.

His pride wouldn't let him admit that he needed help walking, but Mark and Aisling flanked him especially close since they could tell he had vertigo. Fortunately, Dr. Toumi wasn't seeing any other patients at the moment and was sitting in his office eating lunch – some hummus and pita bread.

"Hi, Dr. Toumi," said Phillip, still trying to maintain a steady composure, but he was mumbling his words.

"Phillip, what happened to you?" asked Dr. Toumi, who could immediately tell something was wrong.

"He fainted," said Aisling.

"Yes, yes," said Dr. Toumi, who got out a stethoscope. "Too much exhaustion from magic – I can see it. You need to lay off the teleportation for a while. Did this happen while you guys were studying?"

"No," answered Mark. "We were at lunch."

Dr. Toumi was checking Phillip's eyes as he was talking. "What have you eaten today, Phillip."

"I had some tea and a veggie plate and some fries."

"Is that it?"

"I can't have meat for the fast. Aren't you fasting, too?"

"Yes, but Phillip, you are not a monk. You can have breakfast, and if you need to, ask for some fish. Eat a lot of chickpeas, beans. They have a lot of calories and protein. Maybe even eat a little cheese if you have to. You need to keep up - especially if you are practicing magic at your level. I will give you some multivitamins to take with you as well."

Dr. Toumi was now checking his heartbeat and his breathing. He was casting spells that three weren't familiar with by making quick motions with his hands. This certainly wasn't the first time that a student had visited him in this condition, and with much repetition and practice, the spells became almost automatic.

"Okay, Phillip. I want you to eat a lot more food. Maybe even have a plant-based protein shake. The students and chefs at this school are very talented. I'm sure if you ask, they can get something compliant for the fast for you. But remember, it is about the *spirit* of the fast. You need to abstain from casting anything for the rest of the day probably, but you can still study. Do you need some aspirin?"

"No, I should be okay, Doctor, thank you."

Afterwards the trio decided to split off. Phillip and Mark would study for their cartography class in their dorm, while Aisling had some other classes (French, Enchantments, and 2D Art) that she had to study for.

17

A CHRISTMAS TERROR

Although Kalina was desperate to sleep in after a long week of finals, she woke up to the noise of her mother running errands downstairs. *Did she go to MagiMart without me?* With a small rush of adrenaline, she ran downstairs to check what her mom was doing.

"You *did* go without me!" she exclaimed, as her mother was putting groceries away.

"Of course I did," replied Catherine without remorse. "There's a lot of work to be done, and I can't wait for you and Phillip to sleep your days away before doing it. Now are you going to help, or are you just going to stand there like a deer in the headlights?"

"Well, I just woke up."

"Then go back upstairs and stay out of my way!"

Kalina understood that her mom was in one of her moods. She was clearly stressed about the fact that she would be the one hosting Christmas this year for her family. In this case, the wisest thing to do would be to return upstairs and do some light reading before coming back down again. She picked up the book on divination that she purchased earlier that year and laid down on her bed to read it. Before she was able to get comfortable, however, Phillip decided to make an intrusion into her room.

"Don't you know how to knock?"

"Don't care. I woke up to mom yelling at you just now. Is she stressed about the family coming? I heard she invited Uncle Kenneth."

Kalina sat up on her bed to talk to her brother.

"Yeah, you know how she can get. It'll wear off soon. Probably when she wants to make cookies with us. In the meantime, I'm just going to sit back, relax, and do a little bit of reading. So, if you wouldn't mind..." Kalina finished her thought by waving her brother away from her.

Phillip, as any dutiful older sibling would do, took this as a cue to bother his sister further. "Whatchya got there?" he asked, snatching the book from Kalina's hands. "He opened up the table of contents and started reading the chapters: 1: *Introduction to Divination*; 2: *Beans, Bones, and More*; 3: *Water Watching*.... Is this even real magic?"

"Yes, and I'd like it back please!" Kalina raised her voice just enough with the threat of their mother hearing them.

"Fine," replied Phillip, and handed the book back to her. "You want to go get breakfast?"

"Sure," said Kalina, admitting that she was hungry for breakfast.

Phillip instantly teleported them just outside of Psomira Bakery & Café where there was a niche spot in a small grove of trees that he was used to teleporting to. He let Kalina order first (always the same thing: a breakfast sandwich) before he ordered a latte and bagel. They found a place to sit, delaying their return to the belly of the beast.

"So, how do you think this year is going to go?" asked Phillip sarcastically.

"Well, mom's hosting and she's the most level-headed of all the siblings. She knows how to keep the peace and won't tolerate pettiness."

"Yeah..."

Phillip and Kalina took their time eating and chit-chatting about school. They really just wanted to keep the conversation going before they had to head back.

BUZZ... BUZZ... BUZZ...

"Who is it?" asked Kalina.

"It's mom," said Phillip. "She's saying that – hold on, she's calling now. Hello? We're at Psomira. Do you want us to... Okay, we're coming now. Bye. Mom's freaking out about something. She wants us to head home now."

They both got up and found a secluded place to teleport back home. They landed in the living room, where Mrs. Todorova was glued to the TV. It looked like she was watching the Magi Channel.

"Mom?"

"Oh my God!" she shouted and rushed over to give them a hug.

"Mom, what's going on?"

There were tears streaming down her cheek, and she walked back over to the TV. Phillip heard the sound of sirens and a reporter talking over a film of fire.

"There was an explosion at the Magical Christmas Market. You know the one in DC? I hope your father's okay; he's working in the magical district today."

"Do you want me to go get him? I've been to his office before."

"No! I want you to stay home safe and sound today, okay? I'm going to try to call your father again. You two just keep yourselves company."

Phillip and Kalina were both nervous and decided to head downstairs to the basement. Kalina suggested they play a board game, but neither really felt up for it.

"I wonder if it was an attack," said Phillip. "Dad would know. Do you think you could... you know?"

"I'm not using my abilities like that anymore," replied Kalina. "Sister Maryam advised against it until I become further matured in my studies."

She added the last part because she didn't want Phillip to keep pushing her on the subject anymore, and she knew that he would respect the opinions of a spiritual authority.

Kalina, as curious as Phillip, added, "If it *was* an attack, why would they do it during a weekday in broad daylight? Shouldn't they wait until nighttime when it's closer to Christmas?"

"Unless the purpose was to send a message," said Phillip. "The Christmas Market usually has more security when there's more people. It wasn't about the people, then. It was about the psychological, maybe even spiritual aspect of it."

"Nothing's ever happened like this before," said Kalina, who was at a loss for words.

"At least not in the magical community," added Phillip.

After a few moments of silence, they heard the doorbell ring. They wanted to see who it was, so they headed upstairs. Their mom had already opened the door and was greeting Gramma Nelson with a hug.

"I came as soon as I heard the news. Have you heard anything from Ivan?"

"I just got off the phone with him. He says he's twenty minutes away. They sent everyone home early, and he'll probably be tele-working for the rest of the week."

"Hi, Gramma Nelson," said Phillip, giving his grandmother a hug. Kalina followed suit.

"Well, why don't we do something to take our minds off this for now and thank God that everyone in our family is safe."

"The death toll is twenty-three," responded Kalina. *Shoot, I just made another prediction. Must be the emotions running high.*

"How do you know?"

"I... uh... think I heard it on TV when Phillip and I came in. Is there something you had planned that you want to do, Gramma?" Kalina could have more smoothly transitioned the topic, but in the end it worked.

"Well, why don't we help your mother make some Christmas preparations while she gives her siblings a call. Have you guys started making the cookies yet?"

It was family tradition to make all sorts of cookies every year for Christmas: chocolate chip, Russian teacakes, Hello Dollies. They switched up the menu every year for diversity, but they always turned out delicious. Even Phillip, the one with no culinary talent, took part in making the sweet treats (one of his Achilles' heels). While they were busying themselves in the kitchen preparing the baked goods, Mrs. Todorova headed upstairs to call her siblings. Presumably, she didn't want her children to hear what she was talking about.

"Gramma Nelson," began Phillip. "Uncle Clyde is taking off on a Skyship cruise tomorrow to get here. Do you think whoever did this will target any of the airlines?"

"I don't know," replied Gramma, implicitly confirming that the incident *was* an attack.

Catherine Todorova had finally come downstairs to give everyone the news on what happened. She was really only addressing her mother, but Kalina and Phillip listened intently.

"Clyde just woke up. He doesn't know whether or not he'll be taking the Skyship or if he'll do something else. He doesn't want to take any chances with his family."

Grandma Nelson nodded, "And Nicole?"

"Apparently New Amsterdam (the magical bureau of New York) is on high alert and is sending everyone home for the rest of the week. She pretty much confirmed to me that it was an attack, but nobody knows who's responsible or what's going on yet. She says she'll start driving down tomorrow since she doesn't really feel safe by herself up there."

Mr. Todorova had just walked in while she was finishing her sentence, and the two siblings rushed to greet their father. He embraced them both before walking into the kitchen to give his wife a kiss and say hi to his mother-in-law.

"I'm going to go change. I will come back down to do some more actuarial work. Have you spoken to Clyde yet?"

"Yes," responded Mrs. Todorova. "He's not sure if he'll be able to make it because of the attack."

"Yes, yes. I'll look into the probabilities for that."

Ivan Todorova placed his stuff down before heading upstairs to change out of his suit. As a magus with an aptitude for mathematics, he was hired by many companies to do actuarial work, data science, and even checking engineering calculations. His favorite thing to do was risk management as an actuary: statistics, probability, and analysis. As a trained magus (or mađiòničār, as they're called in Serbia), he was in a unique position to not be restrained only to economic or financial fields of predictions.

They made the most of the rest of the day with what they had. No one was in a particularly jolly mood because of the attack (the fatalities were in fact twenty-three), but they dutifully finished the Christmas decorations and offered prayers for the victims. Phillip returned to his room (*probably sulking or talking to Mark* thought Kalina) while everyone else was cooking dinner. Unexpectedly, the doorbell rang.

"Are you expecting anyone?" asked Grandma Nelson.

"No, I don't know who it is," replied Catherine, who put the knife down to open the door. Kalina peered over the corner to see who it was.

"Aunty Nicole!" she exclaimed loudly and ran over to give her aunt a hug. "Mom said that you were going to come tomorrow!"

"Well, I didn't have anything else to do, and I didn't want to stay in New Amsterdam by myself."

Everyone gathered in the living room to welcome Nicole and help her with her luggage. She was fortunate to come just in time for dinner, since she was hungry after the long drive.

"Save room for dessert," said Catherine. "We made a bunch of Christmas cookies earlier today, plus those Pylebridge ones that light up. By the way, Ivan, did you ever end up doing the math for the Skyship?"

"Yes, I entered all the data into the calculations, and it looks like there's a very small chance that there will be an attack. However, they're going to be shutting down all the airways for the next week, so it doesn't really matter. He'll either have to purchase an airplane ticket or use his new flying car."

Catherine Todorova shook her head. "It'll have to be an airplane then."

For the average person this would have been expensive, but Clyde Nelson was a respected entrepreneur known in both the magical and non-magical fields of business. Similar to Mr. Todorova, his aptitude as a statistician allowed him to purchase the stocks most likely to win big.

"What about Kenneth have you spoken to him?" asked Nicole without thinking.

"You invited Kenneth? What for? To ruin Christmas?" sneered Grandma Nelson.

"He's still my brother, mom."

"Barely."

"I'm not getting into this with you tonight. Let's just finish dinner and have a jolly holiday."

***

The rest of the week went by smoothly without any mention of Uncle Kenneth, at least not while Phillip was present. Uncle Clyde was able to get a flight to Dulles, and they went to pick him up on Thursday. While Aunty Nicole and Gramma Nelson went to their traditional Anglican service, Phillip and his family went to their own Orthodox Church. Across the aisle, he could see his mom and his sister huddled close together. It was Baltic inside the church since the heating had malfunctioned over the weekend. *Is this how Mary felt when she gave birth to Christ in the manger?* pondered Phillip, staring intensely at the icon of the Nativity.

Phillip was excited to return home after the service since all his maternal cousins would be coming to visit. They were there yesterday to help put up the tree, and they shared new spells that they learned at their respective schools. They wouldn't be able to do any magic when Grace and Matthew (Uncle Kenneth's children) came over. He privately hoped they wouldn't; those two always seemed so spiteful towards the rest of their family. Everybody could see that Kenneth's kids were jealous because they didn't have magic. They couldn't even keep up academically with their cousins.

"Mom?" prompted Phillip, unsure of how this would end for him.

"Yes, Phillip."

"Since we're in the car and Gramma isn't here. I wanted to ask why Uncle Kenneth married a normie – a non-magical woman if he knew that it would only cause problems with the rest of the family. Even his kids seem bitter about it."

Catherine Todorova gave a deep sigh. It was a deep question, and she wasn't sure what the best way to answer it was.

"They were in love, and they thought that they could make it work. There's a chance that his kids could have been gifted a little bit of magic, but they didn't. As far as his kids know, they were robbed of their inheritance, their family, their culture. I'm not sure whether they're more bitter towards him or towards their mother. Although I supported him in the falling out, I ended up wishing that I hadn't because their marriage became such a disaster."

Ivan Todorova silently kept driving, while Kalina intently listened. She didn't want to ask any of her own questions, but let Phillip do the talking. *It's an absolute mess, and I'm not sure whether I pity Uncle Kenneth or think that he got what he deserved.*

18
PREPARATIONS AND PROPOSALS

When Phillip returned to his dormitory, he was delighted to find two pieces of paper that had been slipped under his doorway. They were two new schedules for him and Mark, and presumably Aisling got one, too. At the bottom, there was a new class: Enchanted Forest Research w/ Mr. Wells. Phillip took out his phone and texted a picture to Mark and Aisling, knowing that they wouldn't be arriving until after New Year's Day. He could have let them find out when they came, but he was too elated not to share the news.

When Tuesday rolled around, Aisling, Phillip, and Mark all went to the library to hang out and discuss their next plan of action. Aisling proudly showed off her new magic cards and a new contract with a fairy she encountered in Ireland over winter break. After overcoming the disbelief of her friends, she convinced them that she discovered the fae while exploring a cave by the sea in the Irish countryside.

"I didn't summon her or anything," she explained. "I just happened to find her! Unfortunately, I'm not really supposed to talk about the details of the contract with anyone else – that's part of the deal. Anyways, I've made some magic cards."

Although Aisling had clearly put in a lot of effort into making them, they weren't the same quality that someone might get at a magical shop – those ones were sturdier and MQS (Magical Quality and Safety) approved. Still, Phillip admired the advanced design and painting on the laminated cardstock – a magical card this niche would be extremely hard to find in your average shop. He looked back up at Aisling, who was clearly pleased with the respect her two friends had shown for her craftsmanship.

"Most of them are charged already. You just need to trigger them with a little bit of raw magic," she informed them, even though everyone already knew how they worked. Most adult magi didn't use them because they saw them as a crutch – a novelty item for kids to play with or for emergencies. "Unfortunately, they're one shots only. I've also made some combat magic cards in case we run into any trouble in the forest."

Phillip and Mark exchanged looks of surprise at how carried away their friend got. They had not suspected Aisling could break such an important law, even though her enthusiasm had led her to be a little bit reckless in the past. Aisling's face darkened in anxiety as she saw fear shadow over Mark's and Phillip's faces. Their visages became grim at the thought they could all be implicit in an act that might land them in iron chains.

"You should probably get rid of those," whispered Phillip nervously. "How did you even find out how to make those?"

"Somebody blew the whistle on combat spells used by USDM federal agents," she responded. "You're right, though; this was stupid of me." She slapped her palm on her forehead. "I didn't think this through. I need to figure out the right way to dispose of them. Besides, they could be dangerous to any of us if they're not cast properly. Anyways, have *you guys* made any preparations for our new class?"

"Actually," began Phillip. "I was reading up on the teleportation anchor. Apparently, lots of wandering magi and wizards used to use them in the past, especially for traveling to sites of importance or if there's a pilgrimage site. In theory, that would allow me to automatically travel to whatever location I set up the anchor without having to concentrate or make any calculations. Well, that's the short version at least – it's a bit more complicated. What about you, Mark?"

Mark heaved a deep sigh. "Honestly, I've learned more about what we *can't* do than what we *can*. There was a point in time when I considered using astronomical observation as a foundation for navigation, but it's too inconsistent. The stars will change position on the observer, or the forest will get misty. One thing that has been tried in a lot of the declassified reports that I've read is the *Clue*, like in the story of the labyrinth and the minotaur. It's not just a hint; it's more like a ball of yarn. A couple of laboratories have made attempts at reconstructing the original one. In the research, it always seems to end up getting cut or frayed, but it's worth a try. There are some new strengthening enchantments that I started looking into."

Although Mark hadn't come up with anything promising like advanced magical cards or an anchor to teleport them to safety, Phillip and Aisling both knew that he was going to be one of the most valuable assets for their new class. This was his idea in the first place, and he would be their navigational expert. Phillip had gotten to know Mark pretty well and was impressed to see how well his best friend could tackle any problem. Phillip found that whenever he himself came face-to-face with an obstruction that gave him the slightest inconvenience, he got frustrated far too quickly. That being said, Mark did seem pretty demoralized about how little he was able to discover over break. Aisling seemed to have caught on, too, so they decided to help him out while they went to get some supper from the hall.

Before they left the library, they found a couple of books they all thought would be helpful in terms of fortifying a Clue, including the original myth of the labyrinth.

"The problem with the Clue," began Aisling as they all headed to the mess hall. "... is that it was designed to be used for an area built by a man – a powerful magus no doubt – but still a man. For all we know, the Enchanted Forests were designed by God Himself.

"Another point of interest from the myth was that although it was Ariadne who used the Clue, it originally came from Daedalus. Again, this might imply that the source of navigation of the Enchanted Forest must come from whoever made them. Does that make sense?"

"I hope not," sighed Mark, as he opened the doors to the mess hall. "If it does, that doesn't bode well for us. It also raises too many philosophical and theological queries as God would be the one who made the forests."

"Don't worry, Mark. We'll figure it out," assured Aisling.

This didn't exactly have the intended effect. Mark tried to be stoic, but his friends knew that the more "stoic" he got meant that he was more upset. Mark furrowed his brows in thought.

"I don't really know if I want to fight with this one right now," he stated. "I've been doing that for the past two weeks. Let's just get dinner."

Aisling on the other hand wasn't ready to let this one go. Although her personality was intense, the advantage was that she was able to think outside the box – concepts that her friends wouldn't have ever considered approaching.

"That's an excellent idea, Mark," replied Aisling. "We'll eat some food and *then* we can start practicing enchantments!"

Before either Mark or Phillip could reply, Aisling sprinted back to the library, presumably to check out more books. Normally students were only allowed to check out three at a time, but Aisling had built such a report with the school librarians that they typically let her leave with a few extra. Her reading speed certainly aided their research.

Mark sighed and Phillip smiled. "That's Aisling for you; she'll probably have read half the library by the time we graduate!"

Mark grabbed two large turkey legs and a loaded baked sweet potato. Phillip, who normally ate a more balanced meal, copied Mark's carnivorous taste.

"That's unlike you," he remarked.

Phillip felt obligated to cheer up his friends and family whenever they were in a poor mood, so he spent dinner trying to make Mark laugh a little. Normally, Mark was rather stubborn with his moods compared to most, but Phillip got him to lighten up a little with some freshly procured magical memes (the lingua franca of their generation).

After they left the hall, they decided to head back to their dorm to relax, forgetting about Aisling. Aisling, on the other hand, didn't forget them, and she nearly knocked them over as she pushed open the door to the mess hall. Mark smoothly dodged the juggernaut, but Phillip, surprised, teleported himself immediately out of there. Aisling, who was unused to Phillip's teleporting habits, just stood there for a moment in shock. Mark, on the other hand, laughed heartily. Of all the events of the day, this was the funniest for him.

"This happens whenever he gets frightened," Mark chuckled. "I like to do it to him sometimes."

Phillip teleported back and said, "Sorry, Aisling. You caught me off guard, there."

Aisling didn't care, though, she was more concerned with their new class, and presented them some of the literature she found while at the library. Mark and Phillip recomposed themselves and followed her upstairs to a practice space (it was too cold outside) while she explained things like modern materials science and enchanting. They spent the rest of the day studying, determined to impress Mr. Wells.

19
THE PRIVATE STUDY

Sixty degrees, six inches, minus sixty degrees, one point five inches...

Kalina's train of thought was interrupted by Ms. Dalton hovering over her desk. She bent over and said quietly, "Kalina, please stay and talk to me after dismissal. Don't worry you're not in trouble."

The last sentence was a relief to Kalina. It was only the first day back from break, so she didn't know *what* she would have been in trouble for, but it eased her mind nevertheless. She returned to the Nordic design she was drawing for Art class. Laurelle, next to her, chose a simpler Nordic Rune to practice, but it wasn't Kalina's place to judge her.

After P.E., Kalina ran back up the field to Ms. Dalton's classroom to find her on the floor drawing arcane symbols with white chalk. The desks were all pushed up against the walls to make room for the large circle in the center of the wooden floor.

"Well, you look like you're all outta breath," said Ms. Dalton in her sweet-tea southern accent. "Why don't you take a seat while I finish this up? Do you know why I asked you to come?"

"Am I in trouble?" asked Kalina, even though Ms. Dalton had already assured her she wasn't.

"No, not at all. I wanted you to come because I think that you could benefit from some private lessons with me. I know about your precognitive abilities, by the way, and I can help you master them."

"How did you find out?" asked Kalina, surprised.

"Oh dear, you don't keep them very well hidden, and for good reason. You're strong. Your power *radiates* out of you. I'm actually rather impressed that you're able to keep it under control as much as you have! You've demonstrated much self-mastery."

"How long have you known?" asked Kalina, confused but also flattered with the remarks.

"Oh, I first had my suspicions on the first day of class, believe it or not. I have a knack for finding out what a magus' aptitude is. One of the reasons I love being a teacher. Now, I know you have swimming on Mondays, Tuesdays, and Thursdays, so why don't we meet on Wednesdays and Fridays? Does that sound good?"

"Yeah, that's perfect, but what are we doing?"

Ms. Dalton stood up and motioned Kalina to stand next to her. "You see these runes; do you know what they mean?"

Kalina walked over and examined the symbols. Despite learning about all sorts of runes, symbols, and how to draw them in art class, she had no idea what any of these were. "Honestly, I have no idea," she admitted. "I'm guessing the circle is a sort of boundary, but you've done it with chalk instead of salt or flour."

"It's okay that you don't know, but at least you got the circle correct. Looks like someone was paying attention," she said to Kalina, who appreciated her encouraging style of mentorship. "Many of these symbols are far more ancient than what you'll encounter in any book at your level. This is a meditation ritual to help you understand your precognitive abilities. You see, many modern academics will tell you that your powers are 'psychic.' That is, merely psychological, and only comes from the fact that your aptitude allows you to perceive things that others cannot. However, there's much more to your abilities than that. If you wanted to, you could access higher, metaphysical realms of existence."

Kalina, as a Christian, was used to the idea of spirituality and didn't ignore its existence. "How do we start?"

Ms. Dalton directed her to lay down on her back inside the chalk circle. There was a blanket and a pillow for comfort.

"In the future, I'll teach you how to sit properly. For today, though, you can just lay down since it's your first time. Now, while I light the candles and set the ambiance, make sure you get yourself into a comfortable position."

Even though the sky had started to darken, Ms. Dalton closed the blinds in order to block off any distractions. She lit twelve candles and placed them outside the circle around Kalina. Afterwards, she sprinkled what Kalina thought was lavender-scented water. It reminded her of being sprinkled with holy water at church, and wondered if it was similar. *Is it always going to be as elaborate as this?* she wondered. She was used to the more minimalist aspects of just listening to binaural beats. However, she removed these opinions so that she could continue to focus on the meditation.

After a few minutes, she could no longer hear Ms. Dalton's footsteps, assuming that she must be finished with all the preparations. Now, she heard a soft, comforting hum emanate from her teacher. It felt tender, and she tried to match it. Although Ms. Dalton didn't tell her to, it felt like the right thing to do at the moment. The tone resonated throughout her body, which soon reached a state of slumber and rest. Her mind was awake, though, and without the distractions of the material world, she felt her mind transcend to a different plane of existence. In the past, when she had tried the binaural beats, she found success in seeing different parts of the world. This was different. This wasn't the earth she was observing, or even the material cosmos, but something above it.

This must be the spiritual plane she said to herself.

She took a moment to explore her surroundings, but the mechanics were difficult since there was no way walk. The faint outlines of a tunnel appeared and she willed herself to go through it, wondering what answers lay on the other side. There are no words in any language to describe what Kalina sensed. She found herself in a world of fractals, expanding and shrinking, and she felt an outside conscience approach. Closer and closer and closer. Kalina was anxious, but she could neither feel her heart race nor could she run away.

"Don't be afraid," said a soft voice echoing all around her. "You are welcome in this house."

Kalina willed herself to look around, but that's not the way perception works on the astral plane. As if sensing her desire to see him, a bodiless figure emerged seemingly out of nowhere. It wasn't the same way as seeing Phillip teleporting out of nowhere. The approach was a mix of the atmospheric glitches being formed into a body that resembled a human. He had a pale blue complexion and glowed softly. Kalina tried to open her mouth to speak, wanting to ask who this being was, but she couldn't.

"I am simply a being, come to help you find your way. I believe this is your first time here?"

Apparently the figure could read her thoughts, and Kalina understood this. She also took note that she would have to be careful of what she was thinking at all times.

Are you an angel?

This time, the being answered in the same super-consciousness way as Kalina.

I suppose one could say that. Why don't you tell me why you've come?

Kalina was able to share all her thoughts in an instance – her aptitude, her class, Ms. Dalton, the ritual, and more. Not all of it was intentional, but she was still getting used to controlling her thoughts.

It is good of you to come, then. I am familiar with this woman who you know as Ms. Dalton, and if she has sent you here, then I know I can trust you to do what is right with your abilities.

And what is it that I must do? wondered Kalina.

Do not force revelation immediately. For now, you must learn from Ms. Dalton on how to control and use your aptitude.

In any other state, Kalina would have had a hundred more questions to ask the incorporeal being, but her mind wouldn't let her. All those thoughts were held in a little box in her subconscious. Now that the conversation was decidedly over, she found herself being pulled back to her physical body. Kalina sprung up gasping for air. She had swum deeper into the waters of the cosmos then she had ever ventured before. Ms. Dalton, upon seeing Kalina awake, licked her thumb and her pointer finger to start putting out candles.

"How was your journey?" she asked.

Kalina hesitated, thinking of the right words to describe her experience, if it was even possible to describe with words.

"It was incredible. I think I even met an angel – he said he knew you!"

Ms. Dalton's eyes brightened and she smiled with enthusiasm.

"That's excellent, Kalina! I'm impressed that you've made so much progress so quickly. You must have met Heibion. What did he say to you?"

"He told me that it was important that I keep learning how to control and use my gift rightly, and that you would help me."

"Well, that's what the plan was in the first place, and I'm glad we've found success on our first try."

"What else should I learn? Should I try this on my own?"

Ms. Dalton had gotten up and started putting her materials away.

"No," she answered. "It's important that you put yourself under the guidance of someone more experienced. That's what I'm here for. Eventually, you'll learn how to do this by yourself, though. Don't worry."

Kalina asked Ms. Dalton a few more questions before she went to dinner. When they were finished in the classroom. Ms. Dalton cast a spell in a language Kalina wasn't familiar with (it wasn't Slavic, but had similar harsh fricatives), and all the desks returned to their normal positions.

20

AN UNEXPECTED DETOUR

Phillip was on his knees panting. Aisling laid flat on her back, eyes closed, dripping in sweat. Mark was the only one left standing against Mr. Wells, who had beaten the other two into submission already. In Phillip's defense, Mr. Wells was significantly more familiar with his magical habits and could anticipate his maneuvers.

"If the three of you guys can't even beat little old me, then how are you expecting to survive in the Enchanted Forest?" he taunted.

"*Viasynitou Anemou!*" incanted Mark, sending a rush of wind at Mr. Wells.

Mr. Wells simply merely raised a hand to block Mark's attack, although he did slide back a little bit.

"Really? A soft breeze? A middle-school stoickee player could produce a stronger gust of wind," scoffed Mr. Wells, making a face of disappointment. "What has Mr. Campbell been teaching you kids?" Before Mark could think of another attack, Mr. Wells raised his hands and incanted, *"Vines, find. Wind. Grind."*

Mark thought the incantation sounded silly, but his mind changed when ivy shot from the ground beneath him and tightly wrapped his legs. The prickly stems pulled him to the ground and started enclosing his body. Phillip was up now and was helping Aisling back to her feet. She brushed her hair aside and took out her handmade cards out of her pocket. She picked the first one out of her deck and only looked at it for a half second to make sure that it was usable. She held up the card in the air and cried, *"Spiorad an Morrígan, cuirim glaoch ort!" (Spirit of the Morrigan, I summon you!)*

Mr. Wells now turned his attention to Aisling with a surprised look on his face. He wasn't familiar with either Irish or Gaelic and wasn't sure what to expect. Soon, his face was covered in shadows. Startled, he turned his head upwards to see a flock of ravens clouding the sky. They suddenly and sharply descended towards him to attack him. Taking a card out of Mark's playbook, he shouted, *"Viasynitou Anemou!"* A much stronger and more concentrated burst of air came forth from his mouth, sending a shockwave among the birds. The birds didn't seem to mind because they were soon able to regain position and continued their attack on Mr. Wells. In response, he raised his hands up and whispered something that Phillip and Aisling couldn't hear. Usually when a magus does that, it means they want to keep a spell secret. The birds then went limp and started collapsing all around them and training was over.

"What was that?" Mr. Wells shouted angrily at Aisling. He quickly paced towards where she stood, snapping his fingers as he passed Mark to release him from the vines. "Why are you calling on ancient, pagan death goddesses to fight me on your behalf? Do you know how *dangerous* and *illegal* that is?"

Aisling shuttered under the pressure of Mr. Wells' choleric questioning. "So, I made some cards for the forest to protect us..." her voice trailed off meekly.

"Show me," he demanded, and Aisling reached into her pockets to show him some of the cards she made. After looking through her deck, he continued, "Almost half of these are illegal in the United States! Not just dangerous but actually left-handed, black magic, nigromantia illegal! You could go to prison for these *or worse*. Where did you even learn how to make them?"

"Well, I, um..." Aisling began, not sure how to tell Mr. Wells about her adventure in Ireland. "Well, actually I made some based on MagiLeaks, and I uhh... also made a contract with a fairy in Ireland, and she taught me how to make some of these, the healing ones. She even made some for me herself, so I know that *those ones* are probably safe."

"None of these are safe!" he shouted, angrily, but Mr. Wells clearly did not expect that answer. "An *actual* fairy?" he asked with wide eyes. "Well, I wasn't expecting that someone as young as yourself would get a contract from one. You need to be more careful, Aisling. There's a thin line between bravery and recklessness. The fairy probably got one over you." He continued to look and examine the cards.

"I didn't mean to hurt you," muttered Aisling apologetically.

Mr. Wells replied with a scoff. "I'm more worried about you, but some of these do look like they could be useful, especially the healing ones. I can tell which ones you made and which ones you didn't." He paused for a moment to calm down, thinking. "How about this, I will hold onto this deck and let you use the ones that are legal *and* safe. The other ones, I'll teach you how to safely dispose of them. You may use the ones that are legal *only* when we go into the forest. I don't want you wasting some high quality cards just for training purposes. Furthermore, if you want to use your own cards and not ones from the store, you must have permission from your enchantment and art teachers –both of them – if you want to be able to use them. Understood?"

"Yes, Mr. Wells. Thank you."

"A few more things: how long does your contract last? Can you give me a copy? And what is the name of the fairy you met?"

"So..." began Aisling sheepishly. "The fairy *did* give me a name to call her, but not her real name. I can't give you a copy because it was a part of the contract that only I could see it. And as for how long the contract lasts... it's indefinite for the next decade. Either one of us can break it at any time, but it comes with consequences."

Mr. Wells pinched between his eyebrows took a deep exasperated sigh. "I can't help you if you can't give me any information. I know a thing or two about these sorts of folk, and I need to make sure you're safe."

"I can do my best to write down what I remember from my contract, but I don't know whether or not I should. Also, the physical copy is all the way in Ireland."

"Alright, training for today is over. Go do whatever it is you guys do after class," he commanded bitterly and walked off. He was clearly more unsettled than Phillip had ever seen him to be.

The trio was left to talk about their training and come up with a plan for the next class.

"I'm not going to lie, I feel pretty beat," said Mark.

"Me, too," agreed Aisling. "Why don't we go meet at the library, and then head to dinner. There's something I discovered that I wanted to discuss with you guys anyways and see if you can help me research it."

***

When Mark finished his shower, Phillip told him that he could head down to the library before him, since he liked to take his time getting washed up. Furthermore, he wanted to have some privacy to make a short prayer.

After Phillip got dressed and made his devotions, he headed downstairs and towards the main building. It didn't take him long to reach the library, but when he pushed open the door, he found himself surrounded by a very different library than the one he was used to. He turned around to leave, but he discovered that the door behind him had vanished. In its place were rows of shelves stacked with books. In front of him was a librarian's desk, and he walked over to it to see if he could get some help or information. On the wooden desk was a silver bell, but as soon as Phillip raised a hand to ring it, a voice stopped him.

"I wouldn't do that if I were you," advised a young girl's voice. He couldn't place her accent, but it sounded Italic. She was about Kalina's age, but was wearing what looked like a Roman stola. Without looking at him directly, she walked past Phillip and placed a stack of books on the desk in front of a sign that said 'RETURN.'

"Why not?" asked Phillip, still dazed by his sudden transition.

"Why do you want to?" she replied. Phillip wasn't sure whether she was being sarcastic or genuine.

"To get help from a librarian," he replied.

"Do you know who he is?" she asked.

"No," replied Phillip, confused.

"Then how do you know he's going to help you?"

"How do you know he won't?" he retorted

"I've spent a lot of time here, and I've never heard anyone ring that bell. I've never seen any librarian or whoever the caretaker is or are. It's probably best to keep it that way. You can't unring a bell," she finished mysteriously, and then turned around to walk away.

"Hold on," said Phillip after her. "Where exactly is 'here'?"

The young girl turned around again and merely shrugged her shoulders. "I don't really know, to be honest. The best theory is that it's nowhere. Is this your first time at the Archives? That's what I like to call this non-place."

"I thought this was a library?"

"It is... among other things."

"Well how do I get out?"

The girl gave him a perplexed look. "The same way you came in of course. Are you not a traveler?"

"Yes, how did you know?"

"Well, you couldn't have gotten here unless you were one or you knew one. I know one; that's how I got here. He saved me from being burned alive. Follow me. I'm about to meet up with someone who could be able to help you."

Phillip was taken back at how she nonchalantly mentioned an almost horrible death, but obediently listened to her. The girl turned around once more and headed directly towards a bookshelf. Instead of stopping in front of it though, the bookshelf rearranged itself to let her through. She cut through piles of books that seemed to move willingly out of her way. What was strange was that the girl didn't look like she was casting magic, it was almost as if the books were sentient. Before long, they squeezed through a narrow hallway and entered into a circular room. In the center sat an elderly man on a short stool, with his eyes closed.

"Peace unto you, Lucia, did you return all those books I gave you?"

"Yes, and I found something else."

The man opened friendly eyes and looked directly at Phillip, who tried his best to return the warm gaze.

"Salutations, my friend." The gray-haired man stood up and walked over to Phillip. "My name is Septimus, and you?"

"I'm Phillip, it's nice to meet you," responded Phillip, amused by the strange way the man spoke. He had the same Italic accent that he noticed with the girl, Lucia.

"Now, let me guess. Certainly post-Renaissance. Probably post-Victorian. I'm going to go with the twentieth century. Am I right?"

Phillip became more and more confused. First he had been told he had traveled to 'nowhere,' and now someone is asking him 'when' he was from. His best guess was that this was a nexus of some sort, and would explain the ancient Roman fashion they were both wearing. Best to think about it later; he just wanted to find a way out.

"No, actually, I'm from 2023," he stuttered. "When are you from?"

"Lucia and I are from what I believe you would call two hundred years after the incarnation of our Lord."

"That would make you thousands of years old, though!"

"Time doesn't pass here, and as a fellow traveler, you have the ability to soon find how to delay your aging process, but that will be much later in your education."

The implications in this statement were massive to Phillip.

"You mean I could be immortal?"

"No, there is no such thing. Just that you could age much more slowly – live longer."

"I've never met another traveler before. Is it possible for us to time travel? Is that how this place works?"

Septimus patiently answered his question. "No, as far as I know there haven't been any 'time-travelers.' There have been people who tried it, but the problem is that you cannot transmute your matter to a time that already has your matter. It creates a paradox; you see? As for where we are... this place is one of the wonders of the cosmos, if it even exists inside it. It contains all the history of the universe except for itself."

What the elderly man stated sounded like he was referring to the Law of Conservation of Mass. Even still, Phillip struggled to comprehend what the old man was saying, but it didn't seem like he really knew either. *Perhaps this library is like an Enchanted Forest. It might even contain information on the Enchanted Forests,* thought Phillip.

"Is it possible for me to explore the library? Say there was a topic that I was interested in," suggested Phillip.

"I'm afraid you're not ready for that. This is a largely banal place – hard to physically die in, but easy to get lost in. You are still very new even to your own aptitude. It's safer for you to head back home now."

"How will I be able to get back home?" asked Phillip.

"You just need to go back the way you came," replied Septimus kindly. "That's the first lesson if you want to have a chance for further exploration."

"That's what Lucia said, but the door disappeared when I looked back."

"What do you mean? It's been behind you this whole time, hasn't it?" Septimus pointed behind Phillip, who turned around and recognized the doors to his school's library.

"Before you go," said Septimus. "Take this." He held out a hand with a carved wooden fish. Phillip brought it close to his face to study it, and when he looked up to ask what it was, he found himself back in the halls of Cardinal Key Academy. Septimus and Lucia were nowhere to be seen.

21

THE MEMORY STORE

"Sorry I'm so late," whispered Phillip as he approached the table where Aisling and Mark were sitting.

"What do you mean?" asked Aisling. "Mark just got here about five minutes ago. We haven't started at all yet, but now that you're here we can begin."

Aisling took out a book titled *Encyclopedia of Psychic Techniques,* and began flipping through the pages. Meanwhile, Phillip was torn on whether or not he should tell his friends about his small adventure. *Best save it for later.*

"You realize none of us here are psychics, right?" asked Mark facetiously.

"Yeah, but we might be able to find one to help us," she replied.

"Speaking of which," began Phillip, "how has Robert been doing? Any progress?"

"Dr. Toumi, the wife, has been seeing lots of brain activity in MRI scans and through psychic scans. Unfortunately, he's not actually conscious, so they don't know for sure what is going on, but they think it has something to do with his telepathic abilities. There have been some telepaths trying to reach into his mind, but they're being blocked out. They keep commenting that he's remarkably powerful."

Phillip thought she looked downhearted as she spoke. Perhaps all this intense research and studying she'd been doing had been a way to cope with her boyfriend's traumatic injury. He decided that it would be a better idea not to bring up Robert too often if that was the case.

"Here," she finally said, and pointed to an article in the large reference book. "There's something called 'memory stores' that certain psychics can make. I was thinking about that time you two saw those mysterious women in the woods but couldn't understand what they were saying. What if we find a psychic to get the stores and a linguist to help translate what you heard?"

"Those are a lot of ifs," replied Mark pensively.

"He's right," admitted Phillip. "But I don't have any other ideas so far. We've pretty much hit a dead end except for the forest research."

Mark sat back and sighed, "Well, do you have any psychics that you have in mind to ask, Aisling?"

"Well," she began, "There are a couple of students in our class – "

"No," interrupted Mark sharply. "We don't know who we can trust. Someone might tell Dean Schulz, and who knows what he'll say. He was already on the fence about letting us do a research class on the Blue Ridge Enchanted Forest, and I don't want to test him further. We better not open the gates too much."

"What about Dr. Toumi or Mr. Wells then," she asked.

"I don't think Mr. Wells is a psychic," replied Phillip. "I don't actually know what his aptitude is."

"Oh... I just assumed..." Aisling trailed off. "Well, that leaves Dr. Toumi, then."

"Our Dr. Toumi or his wife?" suggested Phillip.

"His wife," decided Mark assertively. "She's not as meshed in with the school, and she'll be less likely to say anything to anyone. Doctor-patient privilege and all that."

"Well it's decided, then," said Aisling. "We'll go back to Saint Luke's this weekend, and we can also visit Robert while we're there."

***

Phillip was always shocked at the amount of food that Mark could consume and yet stay so fit. He knew Mark was a beast when it came to physical fitness (he was on the wrestling team), but he still looked in awe as his best friend piled his plate with scrambled eggs, bacon, and sausage for breakfast.

"Aren't you afraid you're going to have a heart attack?" he asked.

"Nope. Gotta get that protein in," he said tersely.

After they were finished getting their food from the line, they walked over to the booth where the trio normally sat and waited for Aisling to come. It didn't take long for her to show up with just a scone and a cup of tea (she seemed to try so hard to stick to her Irish heritage). Tired, they sat in silence as they ate their food until they were finished.

"Are we ready to go?" asked Phillip.

"Yeah, I'm done," replied Mark.

"Are you sure it's not too far for you to teleport us?" asked Aisling.

"I can do it. Besides, we don't really have any other options. Last time, Dean Schulz told us that we weren't allowed to use Uber again – for safety reasons and the like. We nearly got suspended for that actually. You know... with the International Agreement of Magical Mystery and all that."

The trio headed to the back field to give Phillip some space to focus. Suddenly, they found themselves in the parking lot of Saint Luke's Hospital. Mark bent over and Aisling sank to her knees.

"It's the immediate change in environment. Temperature, pressure, light, and all that. Your body gets used to it after a while," reassured Phillip. "It didn't happen last time because we didn't travel too far. The environment was virtually the same."

After Mark and Aisling recovered, the trio headed towards the entrance of the hospital. After they checked in, Aisling led the way to where Robert was. They stood quietly as Aisling went up to brush his cheek. She only stood close to him for a few moments before brusquely turning around and walking out of the room, passing Mark and Phillip, who could see tears in her eyes.

Phillip was the first to emerge from the room. He laid a hand on Aisling's shoulder and asked, "Are you alright?"

Aisling sniffed and cleared her voice. "Yes, sorry, let's go find Dr. Toumi."

It didn't take long for them to find her either as she had just happened to be walking down the hallway.

"Dr. Toumi," called Aisling. "Are you busy right now?"

Her dark straight hair swished as she turned abruptly to face Aisling. "Oh, hello Aisling, are you here to see Robert?" she asked in a light Syrian accent.

"Hi, Dr. Toumi. We actually just visited him. We wanted to see if you had some time to talk. We want to ask you a question that's kind of related to him."

"Okay, well, right now I have to go visit each of my patients and make sure they are okay. Can you wait for a couple of hours until I'm finished? I take a coffee break around 10:30."

The trio nodded, and headed back to Robert's room, where they sat in silence and scrolled through their phones. After a couple of hours, they went to find Dr. Toumi.

"Oh, there you guys are," she said to them as they were walking down the hall. "You've caught me on a good day. Nothing too serious is going on. What can I do for you?"

"We were wondering if you could help us create a memory store," requested Aisling on behalf of the group.

Dr. Toumi looked surprised at the request. "Why didn't you just ask my husband? He could have helped you do that."

"Well, it's because we didn't want to bother him, and because of the whole situation at school with that woman and Robert, and we're just worried." Aisling knew she was grasping at straws, and she couldn't remember why they thought Dr. Toumi would be willing to help them.

Dr. Toumi sighed. "You guys are very lucky to ask me today. I've actually recently been researching memory stores as a way to help comatose patients. Do you have something you want to store the memory in?"

Aisling pulled out a red USB drive and handed it to Dr. Toumi.

"Who's memory am I storing?"

"Ours," responded Mark and Phillip simultaneously.

"The two of you? Hmm, that could work," replied Dr. Toumi, nodding to herself. "Normally, it's just one psychic who does it to himself or to another person, but it's been known on occasion that more than one party may be involved for clarification of events. This would sometimes happen in a trial if there were conflicting witness accounts."

They all sat down and closed their eyes. While Mark and Phillip concentrated on the night at the edge of the woods. Dr. Toumi silently mouthed some words and focused her energy on connecting the three of them. Mark and Phillip soon detected their presence in each other, and Dr. Toumi's in theirs. Although she was highly talented, this was not a spell she practiced often. It took her a while before she could download the memory into the USB.

"I don't know what you two were doing at the edge of the woods where the woman appeared from, but if I were you, I would take this to one of your teachers or to Dean Schulz. It could be very helpful for the investigation."

"Of course, Dr. Toumi, that's what our plan was," lied Aisling. "Thank you so much."

Out of politeness, Phillip asked if he could teleport the trio back to school from Dr. Toumi's office, and she agreed. He wondered if as a result, she might have some wards put up around the hospital.

22

IN SEARCH OF WORDS

The following week seemed to fly by in a whirlwind of excitement as the trio eagerly counted down the days until their much-anticipated visit to Mark's house over the upcoming weekend. Mark, well aware of the likelihood of his father's reluctance, opted for a different approach and decided to discuss their plans with his mother first. To his delight, she readily agreed to their weekend excursion, and he began making arrangements to approach his father for assistance in translating the mysterious conversation they had overheard.

Their training for their upcoming journey into the mystical Blue Ridge Enchanted Forest was progressing exceptionally well. Aisling, Mark, and Phillip dedicated themselves to honing their defensive skills and spending countless hours brainstorming innovative navigation techniques tailored to the challenges of the Enchanted Forest. Furthermore, Phillip and Mark, with their innate gift for geographical spells, delved into crafting the anchor. Naturally, Aisling helped with the design, runes, and enchantments. This spell would serve as a lifeline to a designated spot, ensuring that Phillip could teleport instantly to safety should the group ever become disoriented or find themselves in danger within the forest. First, they had to use their knowledge of cartography to map out where the spell should be placed (altitude, moistness, etc.). Then, they needed to get permission from Dean Schulz to actually dedicate that patch of land for the anchor. The dean, who was very interested in the spell, agreed instantly.

Finally, the long-awaited weekend arrived, and it was a breeze for Phillip, who had become a frequent guest at Mark's house during school breaks, to teleport the trio to the Poitier residence in Charlottesville. Upon their arrival, Mrs. Poitier was bustling about in the kitchen, preparing coffee and laying out the ingredients for a delectable lunch. Mr. Poitier had apparently just gone out for a run, but would be back in time to join them. In the meantime, the trio stumbled upon a deck of Uno cards and decided to engage in a friendly game to pass the time. Aisling playfully suggested enchanting the cards to change colors randomly, but Mark, cautious to do anything funky at home, decided to decline her offer.

Approximately twenty minutes later, Mr. Poitier returned home, offering a warm and brief greeting to the trio before heading upstairs to freshen up. Meanwhile, the magical dining room table, a cherished heirloom passed down through Mrs. Poitier's family, seamlessly set itself for lunch, complete with plates, cutlery, and glasses. It was a unique inheritance from her great-grandfather, a renowned and accomplished magical carpenter. Mr. Poitier's shower was notably swift, and they all gathered around the table, ready to discuss the progress of their investigative efforts.

After an in-depth explanation, the trio were pleasantly surprised to find that Mr. Poitier was not at all upset at their adventure. Mark himself earlier was anxious that his father would demand that they be cautious – or demand that they stop altogether. However, Mr. Poitier, a man who favored action over empty words, had been impressed by the determination and dedication displayed by his son and his friends. Rather than trying to dissuade them from their personal quest, he wholeheartedly supported their efforts and praised the information they had gathered thus far.

"So, you require my assistance in translating this 'mysterious' conversation you overheard a few months ago?" he inquired, with a hint of curiosity.

"Yes, sir," responded Phillip with as much sincerity and respect as possible. "However, we're not even sure which language or language family it might belong to."

Mr. Poitier chuckled and remarked, "And how do you expect me to read your minds to discern it?"

"We have a memory store," Aisling explained, reaching into her small purse to retrieve the USB drive and handing it to Mr. Poitier. He commended their preparation and creativity.

"I hope this will work. Let's head over to the computer right now," he suggested.

Mr. Poitier led the trio to his office, where he plugged the USB drive into his desktop computer. The screen momentarily went black before displaying the memory, though it appeared somewhat blurred due to the merging of two memories. Nevertheless, the audio was clear, and they all huddled around the computer to listen attentively. Mr. Poitier replayed the audio several times before offering his insights.

"I've never encountered this language before. It doesn't appear to be a fabricated language, judging from the fluency and tone of their voices. Based on the variations in accents, it's unquestionably the first woman's native language, though it doesn't match the second woman's accent. It's not African, American, or Sino-Tibetan. Perhaps Semitic, but it's unlikely. I doubt it's a form of Berber either. Most probably European – Indo-European. If I had to make an educated guess, I'd lean toward it being a Celtic language. It's one of the few language families that I have scant experience with. May I retain a copy of this?"

"Certainly, sir, please go ahead," Aisling replied. "Thank you for your invaluable help. And, by the way, I do speak Irish, but I can assure you that I couldn't make sense of anything they were saying. That rules out the Goidelic branch, at the very least. It might be Welsh or Breton, though, I suppose. There is one more thing, the second woman, the non-native speaker, sounds upset with the first one."

"Your observation is astute. The hissing sounds typical of the Welsh language are present in the audio, and I agree that there might be a disagreement. Nonetheless, I'll need to conduct further research and potentially seek input from a colleague," Mr. Poitier responded thoughtfully. "On a different note, would you all like to stay for dinner?"

The trio exchanged glances, silently gauging their thoughts on the invitation. Mr. Poitier, observing their hesitation, kindly spoke on their behalf, "Why don't you stay? I'll inform my wife."

23
LIFTING OFF

Maura brusquely walked ahead of two roommates, frustration evident in her voice as she complained, "I just don't understand *why* she doesn't like me! The *rest* of my teachers do!"

"I don't think she necessarily *dislikes* you," answered Kalina, who tried to reassure her roommate.

"Well that's easy for you to say," remarked Laurelle, who had become significantly more vocal with her opinions since they first met her. "You're her favorite by far."

Kalina was a little embarrassed by the observation and blushed, even though she knew what Laurelle said was true. She tried to downplay the comment and save face. "I wouldn't say I'm her favorite," she lied, "And I definitely don't think she dislikes *you*, Laurelle."

"Oh, no, I think she likes me just fine," replied Laurelle casually. "And she's mostly nice to the class as a whole, but you *are* a bit of a teacher's pet."

"How?" asked Kalina defensively.

Laurelle folded her arms and continued, "Well, lately she's been talking to you more; she pays more attention to you. She asks you to help her with the classroom and no one else. Also, what exactly have you two been doing for the past several weeks after dismissal?"

Kalina was mortified by Laurelle's insight. She hesitated for a moment, then truthfully admitted, "She's been giving me some private instruction – it's specifically related to my aptitude. Remember when I had my seizure? It's related to that, and she's helped me be able to prevent cases like that. I'm not supposed to say anything more than that." *Most* of what she said was true, but she wanted to speak as briefly as possible about it. She was starting to feel desperate to move on from this topic.

Neither of the other girls gave a verbal response. Even though they weren't supposed to learn about their aptitudes until the end of the year, they just nodded their heads in feigned understanding. In was considered proper etiquette in the magical community not to pry too deeply into another magus' aptitude.

After a few seconds of awkward silence, Kalina spoke up again. "Well, I should get going to see her now anyways. I'll meet you guys at dinner."

Since Kalina arrived early, she got to catch Ms. Dalton in the midst of completing the intricate circle in which Kalina entered her trances. While Ms. Dalton delicately painted the floor in strange ruins and shapes, the two engaged in some light conversation concerning Kalina's schoolwork.

After having a break and undergoing an intervention from her family, Kalina was able to place unwavering attention towards her courses, swiftly ascending to the top of her class without utilizing foretelling as a crutch. She was able to harmonize her aptitude and natural intelligence to orchestrate her achievements now – relying on neither alone. Among her subjects, Earth Science held a special place in her heart. She liked the hands-on aspect to it, and she especially enjoyed the astrology section since it resonated with her own divining aptitude. (She also savored the times when the class got to wake up to clear midnight skies to observe the sparkling celestial bodies from the astronomy balcony.)

When Miss Dalton had finally finished the intricate work, Kalina began the ritual to enter the deep trance. Outside the boundary of the circle, Ms. Dalton hummed in a deep, low tone. Kalina had been trained to match it, and she quickly harmonized with the vibrations in the air. She could feel the resonant note reverberate throughout her bones and into the very core of her body. She wasn't quite beyond the material plane of existence, but the barrier of the liminal realm started to open up. This had become her favorite experience of the ritual.

Ms. Dalton summoned each candle to life one by one. Although Kalina's eyes were closed, she could see their flickers and dance joining in the mesmerizing choreography of the enchantment. The air permeated with the aroma of burning spice, whose smoky tendrils tantalized Kalina's nose. It wasn't the same as the incense used at church, but Kalina put those intruding thoughts into the back of her head.

The atmosphere was set, and Kalina transcended into the dreamlike realm within the astral plane. As she drifted through the obsidian expanse, the angel who she encountered several weeks ago on her first journey finally reappeared. His figure initially seemed to emanate from an infinitesimal space, but expanded in stature until he loomed twice the size as Kalina.

Beneath the entity, Kalina tried to bow down reverently before the angel, but she was unable to translate such customary earthly gestures into the ethereal dimension. The angel read her intentions, and her effort seemed to amuse the shining entity whose warmth and radiance touched and comforted Kalina.

"Hello, it is a joy to finally see you here again," spoke the angel in a graceful cadence. "I have been closely observing your progress, and the time has come for you to embark on to the next phase of your mission. For this endeavor, you will require the guidance and aid of Ms. Dalton.

"As I promised, I will lead you to discover the origins of Samantha Hastings so that you might save her. For this, you must enter the very place whence she came."

"Do you mean the Blue Ridge Enchanted Forest," inquired Kalina meekly.

"Precisely. Ms. Dalton will serve as your protector and guide while you use the map I have provided for you."

"What map?" questioned Kalina.

The radiant entity merely offered a benevolent smile and directed his gaze towards Kalina's hands. She followed his gaze to discover that she was holding a cupcake that was frosted with an otherworldly essence. Confusion etched over her heart as she returned her focus back towards the angel.

"Eat it," he instructed. "And it shall lead you to the path you are destined to follow."

Kalina, curious and trusting the angel Heibion, stuffed her face with a large bite and savored the exquisite flavor. She marveled at the taste. Never before had she tasted anything so delicious and palatable in her whole life. It was like consuming the dawn, sweetened by the honeysuckle dew, and it was as soft and moist as a nebula. Her own baking could never compare, and never was she able to recreate it. After swallowing, the darkness around her faded, revealing a different more mundane and dull darkness.

The sun had already set, which meant that Kalina had been in the astral plane for at least a couple of hours (she had gotten used to the difference between the feeling and passing of time). Miss Dalton was sitting deep in her own meditation across from Kalina as she waited for her protégé to return. The only light was from the candles that circled Kalina, who sat for a moment in silence, unsure of what to say to catch her mentor's attention. Fortunately, she was saved from having to ponder any longer. Miss Dalton slowly opened her eyes and looked penetratingly at Kalina.

"You're finally back. Is there anything you want to share or ask me about this time?"

She asked this same question every time, but normally Kalina didn't have too much to say because very little ever happened.

""The angel has graced me with his benevolent presence once more," Kalina spoke, her voice resonating with a steely resolve. "He has conveyed that the time has come for us to embark on the next phase of our sacred mission. We must venture into the heart of the Enchanted Forest."

Kalina tried to sound calm, noble, and heroic, but deep down she felt a boiling of excitement at her quest. She thought she saw the same infernal hunger for adventure in her mentor's eyes.

24
BATTLING THE BEAST

Phillip, Mark, and Aisling had been ferociously preparing for their first time entering the forest. After several weeks of training, Mr. Wells was finally satisfied enough with their progress to secure approval from the dean to embark on a preliminary expedition of the Blue Ridge Enchanted Forest under his own supervision. It wasn't meant to be a long adventure – only up to one mere hour in total. The time stamp was not only a safety feature but would also serve to determine the forest's peculiar impact on the passage of time.

While they were waiting for Mr. Wells to arrive, Phillip and Aisling were double-checking the teleportation anchor. Although Mark was better suited for the precise coordination of the anchor, Aisling would more easily be able to tie down the extra enchantments. Furthermore, Mark was busy a few yards away from them tying down the Clue, the precious ball of yarn that would theoretically lead them back whence they came. Over the past few weeks, Mark and Aisling had been working with Mrs. Cervantes (the enchantments teacher) to fortify the Clue's endurance. They also received advice from the chemistry teacher on which materials would hold up best in the forest.

The three considered bringing their cell phones with them as back up in case anyone got lost, but they ultimately decided against it. First of all, the chance of receiving any sort of cellular signal in the enchanted woods was a remote prospect. Additionally, none wanted to risk losing their phones and never being able to find them again. Their parents would be livid.

Mr. Wells soon arrived in rugged gear fit for a winter hike. After thoroughly double-checking his students' preparations (the anchor, their clothes, their enchantments, etc.), he confirmed that it was time to cross the threshold and explore the forest.

Mr. Wells positioned Phillip and Aisling at the head of the group. Phillip's keen intuition and teleportation abilities made him the best sentinel to spot and react to any potential danger, his duty being to whisk the group to the safety of the anchor at the slightest hint of peril. Mr. Wells and Mark would follow behind. Mark would be responsible for unraveling the Clue, and Mr. Wells would be able to make sure that none of his students would get left behind accidentally.

Phillip and Aisling walked ahead, shoulder to shoulder. After what felt like hours of hiking monotonously through the dense and dry brush, they stumbled upon a rocky clearing. Excited at their discovery, they turned around to ask Mr. Wells for advice. Instead, they made another horrifying discovery – that Mr. Wells and Mark were no longer behind them. In the first moments of their realization that they were completely alone, a subtle feeling of panic crawled down their backs. The comfort and reliance they had placed in Mr. Wells' guidance vanished, leaving them feeling disoriented and vulnerable – they were two lost souls in an uncharted realm.

Courageously, Phillip decided to take command of the situation. He forced his voice to remain calm as he spoke. "We knew this was a possibility," he declared, his words carrying a reassuring weight meant to bolster their spirits. "We had to train for this circumstance, remember? We have to continue the mission. Hopefully Mr. Wells and Mark are still together, and they have the Clue."

Aisling resolutely nodded her head in agreement. "Let's stay close and keep going; I don't think we're in the Enchanted Forest anymore."

Phillip and Aisling approached a steep cliff, aware that if they had Mark with them, he would be able to locate where they had stumbled into. They followed the rocky wall until they found a crevice that led upward. Before they climbed up, they decided to take a break. The two adventurers were tired, hungry, and thirsty. Aisling sat down to eat a granola bar, while Phillip leaned against the stony surface of the cliff.

"It's still sunlight," he commented. "But it looks like it's starting to get late." Phillip looked down at his stopwatch to see how much time had passed: it claimed only twenty-four minutes. *That doesn't feel right,* he thought to himself. *It felt longer.*

Aisling turned to look down at her shadow, and then the other way to squint towards the horizon. The sun's golden rays cast an amber atmosphere around them as it began its gradual descent. "We should keep going," she said. "It's probably not a good idea to stay out here too late. Besides, I don't want Mr. Wells thinking that we've gone missing – or worse, dead."

Phillip and Aisling picked up their gear and braced themselves for the steep path up ahead. They ascended to the top swiftly, and when they did reach it, their thighs and calves were sweaty and burning. Upon reaching the summit, the two were amazed to see before them vast piles of gleaming gold, interspersed with precious metals and a glittering array of gemstones. The sight was nothing short of a surreal treasure trove, shimmering in the waning daylight. The sight beckoned them to explore further.

Phillip's jaw dropped in awe. "Where do you think this came from? We're going to be rich!" he exclaimed. His eyes gleamed at the allure of the untold wealth, and he was already imagining all that he could do with it.

Aisling, on the other hand, was more suspicious. Phillip leaned down to pick up a single gold coin, and Aisling rushed to stop him. "We shouldn't take it," she cautioned severely. "It could be cursed."

Phillip pursed his lips. "You read too many fairy tales," he retorted condescendingly.

Nevertheless, Aisling was unyielding, despite the exasperation from her hike. "Might I remind you that I have met and made a contract with an *actual* fairy. Maybe if you read more fairy tales, you would know about what happens to people who steal random treasure that they find."

Phillip considered the weight of wisdom in Aisling's voice. She was right of course. Greed, he remembered, is a treacherous companion. Although it was tempting to take the riches, caution and honor prevailed over his desire. Silently, he withdrew his hand from the piles of treasure.

His thoughts were interrupted when the world became darker and a cool breeze passed over him and Aisling, sending a shiver down their spines. At first they locked eyes with each other – both had felt the cold presence. They then turned around in unison to face what lay behind them, only to discover the colossal and malevolent beast. They stood completely beneath the silhouette of an enormous dragon, its massive wings unfurled, and its slit eyes burning into their bodies.

"What do we have here?" the dragon menacingly hissed. "A tasty snack for dinner?"

Before Phillip could teleport them away, Aisling bravely stepped forward to address the beast.

"Oh, great and powerful dragon!" she began with wavering conviction. "*I* am Aisling Donovan, scribe of the century, enchantress of the age, and a daughter of Erin. I come before you with bravery and humility to propose a contract that could mutually benefit us."

Aisling tried to sound powerful and important, but the dragon seemed to be merely amused. Smoke puffed out of his nostrils, indicating that he was scoffing at Aisling's gesture. The large beast then transformed into a tall and strikingly handsome man with his scales thinning into golden hair. He seemed to want to speak to Aisling. He approached her closely and leaned down, his face almost touching hers. His presence was imposing and uncomfortable for the poor girl. Despite her efforts to stand her ground, Aisling submissively bent her head. Her heart was racing nervously as she failed to keep herself from trembling.

"A contract?" the dragon whispered into her ear. "I'm not sure you could offer anything substantial to me, but I have always wanted a pet. And you are such a cute thing. What would you desire in return?"

Aisling hesitated, her thoughts racing. The dragon, undeterred, continued to speak, his voice growing louder as he offered increasingly enticing temptations. "I can shower you with riches, I can bestow upon you boundless love, or I can even make you a queen."

Aisling's heart was beating even faster now. They were all lies she knew, but she couldn't control her thoughts. They raced from one scene to another, like the dragon was forcing them on her. There was trauma and triumph. Despair and desire. Calamity and tranquility. She was burdened with the memories of her home life, and she couldn't bear to maintain these troubles anymore – that was the danger of the beast.

Phillip, watching the scene unfold from a short distance away, could no longer contain his unease. He spoke up urgently, his concern evident in his voice. "Aisling, we should go," he whispered loudly, recognizing the potential dangers of bargaining with the beast.

Pleased with his work, the dragon slowly turned his attention towards Phillip. He slithered as he deliberately walked towards the other student. Behind him Aisling had collapsed to her knees. Her forehead touched the ground in what looked like a prostration.

Phillip could hear her faintly whisper something – a prayer perhaps, but it was drowned out by the dragon's scalding voice.

"What about you? What do you... desire?" he asked in a seductive tone.

Phillip didn't want to back down, and he looked directly into the eyes of the humanoid dragon. He was expecting to fight against fear, but the eyes looked beautiful to him. They were oceans of blue fire surrounding an island of coal. He couldn't help but be attracted to them, like a moth to a flame. Their warmth was alluring, but the longer he looked into them, the more he felt something stir within, a smoldering ember that kindled and grew. Despite the growing pain, he couldn't tear his gaze away from those mesmerizing eyes.

"It's okay," the dragon purred, as if reading his thoughts. "You can look as long as you would like to." His touch gentle and soothing as he rested a hand comfortingly on Phillip's shoulder. The contact left Phillip feeling strangely weak, and he thought he could hear his name being called from a distant place, but it felt far removed from his immediate reality.

His eyes blurred in pain, and he started seeing black spots as he lost consciousness. His physical reality became a metaphysical fight – and the worst part was that the dragon had found someone else to team up with. Phillip's vision cleared, and he found himself confronted by his own distorted reflection.

The dragon's teasing voice simmered around in Phillip's head, speaking unnatural and horrible things. This is the way they feast before devouring the fresh bodies of their prey. It's not just about a corporeal conquest but spiritual submission as well.

"Oh my," the dragon whispered. "You are such a filthy transgressor, aren't you? You think I'm evil? Take a deeper look within yourself!"

Phillip tried to close his eyes, but he couldn't. He was forced to confront the dragon's challenge.

"You can't hide from your own thoughts," giggled the dragon playfully. "Gorge on them!"

The air shimmered around Phillip to reveal his worldly passions that he worked so hard to bottle deeply inside himself. His jealousy surged at the attention Kalina was given by their parents. Mark was there, too, another facet of his complex feelings. The memories of certain family members and cousins stirred a tempest of disgust and simmering hatred, emotions he had fought to suppress but were now bubbling to the surface.

He struggled to remember his faith. He observed the fasts and his rule of prayer, but those only led to his pride to become a formidable gatekeeper to repentance, standing resolutely against the raw truth of his internal turmoil. What value lay in being outwardly virtuous if the heart and soul remained in turmoil?

"Don't struggle against them," commanded the dragon, less joyfully this time. "Let go. Release yourself. You're always trying to be something better than what you actually are. You will never be good enough. Just be yourself. It's *okay.*"

Aisling, having struggled to conquer her fear, looked to see her partner succumbing to the dragon's touch. She realized now that her plan for striking a deal with the dangerous creature was ridiculous.

She berated her audacity for attempting something so reckless and stupid.

Before she could spiral into the despair of self-chastisement, she took control of her thoughts. Now was the time for action, not contemplation – especially not self-incrimination. She dug out some copying paper from her bag and hastily started writing an enchantment. With each stroke of her pen, she poured her intent and as much raw magic as she could muster into the ink.

With the enchantment complete, Aisling snatched up a large, silver goblet and hurled it directly at the dragon. Her aim was true, and she was set on freeing her companion.

The dragon let go of Phillip and turned towards Aisling. He merely laughed and said, "Don't worry, darling, I haven't forgotten about you. I'm almost done with this tasty piece of meat, and then we'll finish what we started." When he turned back to ensnare Phillip, though, he found nothing but empty air.

Although the dragon had only let Phillip go for a mere nanosecond, it was a moment enough for him to break free from the dragon's trap and teleport next to Aisling. He was on his knees now and catching his breath.

"Well, I wasn't expecting that," mused the dragon, surprised at the turn of events. "No matter, I'm not finished with you yet." He gracefully transformed into his fearsome draconic form once more and lunged towards the two students.

This time however, Aisling was prepared. She held out her enchantment and shouted, *"Escrit en piere, la plume esclere!"*

Aisling focused intensely as a copy of her inscription chiseled itself onto the dragon's chest. He roared in agony and tumbled to the ground.

"Stupid girl, you can't stop me forever!"

Before they could find out exactly what the dragon's next plans were, Phillip snatched onto Aisling's ankle and teleported them back to the academy. To his relief, the anchor worked precisely as planned. They were far removed from the deadly dragon. They were safe.

Fatigued from the hike, the pair simply laid on their backs on the grass. They took deep breaths as they listened to the shouts of other kids playing in the background. None of their schoolmates knew the perilous encounter they just had, and the contrast was significant. Aisling almost wanted to laugh at the ridiculousness of it. After a few moments of peace, Aisling decided to break the silence between them.

"Phillip," she began, but he cut her off.

"Just a few more moments please," he said. "I don't want to analyze what happened just yet."

Aisling sat up. "We're going to need to discuss it eventually. That was such a surreal experience. What are we going to tell Mr. Wells and Dean Schulz in the debriefing? Why didn't you look away from the dragon? How could you bear to look at him?"

True to her nature, Aisling opened a firehose of questions on Phillip, who just wanted to catch a break to process. He wasn't sure she would understand what he had to say since he himself didn't understand it entirely.

Phillip nevertheless sat up. His gaze was distant, unsure of where to begin. Confusion pitched his voice when he asked "Didn't *you* find him charming, too? He was beautiful – as both dragon and human. He felt hot, but in a good way kind of. Like a sauna, maybe? I don't know."

"He was consuming you," replied Aisling.

Phillip nodded in agreement. It must have been lies, everything that he had been shown. Despite his gilded scales, the snake's true nature consisted of darkness and death. That's what *it* showed Phillip.

Still grappling with the lingering effects of the encounter, Phillip couldn't help but ask Aisling about the spell she had used to defeat the dragon. "What spell did you cast that made him crumble? What kind of rune could do that to a *dragon*?"

"It wasn't actually a rune. I just wrote down the first thing that came to mind," Aisling said evasively. She seemed a little embarrassed to say what she really wrote.

"Come on," encouraged Phillip. "I'm not going to judge you."

"I wrote '*Domine Iesu Christe, miserere nobis,*'"

"Lord Jesus Christ, have mercy on us," translated Phillip. "What made you think that would work?"

"I don't know exactly. We say it a lot at church. And I was thinking of Saint George. And maybe because I've heard you say something similar from time to time, and I also added a crucifix. In any case it did work. How? I don't know. For all we know, the carving into his impenetrable scales simply hurt him. But that's all that matters to me now. Come on, we should go find Mr. Wells and Mark. They're probably waiting for us in his office."

With a shared nod of agreement, they rose to their feet, ready to confront the aftermath of their extraordinary adventure and seek the guidance of their mentor and fellow student in the safety of Mr. Wells' office.

25
CLUES AND BLUES

As the group trekked deeper into the woods, Mr. Wells found himself repeatedly admonishing Phillip and Aisling for getting too far ahead on the path. At first they were listening, but gradually they kept hiking further and further away from Mr. Wells and Mark. Even though it felt like a short time interval, Mr. Wells and Mark didn't realize how far away the other two had strayed ahead of them.

That instant, Mr. Wells called out after them, but the distance was insurmountable. He tried hollering again a few times, but it was in vain. When Mr. Wells watched his two students' figures disappear into the mists of the dense forest, he instinctively grasped onto Mark's arm. Mark, unsure what to do, stopped in his tracks.

"What do we do now?" he asked, breaking the silence. He looked eagerly at his teacher for an answer, but Mr. Wells was pensively staring in the direction (he thought) Aisling and Phillip went towards.

After a few seconds, he finally answered, "As long as Aisling and Phillip stick together, they'll be fine. Phillip can always teleport them back to his anchor if necessary. As for us..." he trailed off to take a second to look at his watch. It read twenty-nine minutes. "We should head back. The alarm's about to go off. Lead the way, Mr. Navigator."

Mark appreciated Mr. Wells pure confidence – it was a rock that he could count on. Mark took out his quartz glass, and in his other hand began raveling the Clue. Mr. Wells pivoted, following Mark's direction along the path he had set. He was concerned for the two young students, but he was sure of Phillip's capabilities and Aisling's resourcefulness.

Unfortunately, raveling the Clue was more tedious and slower than having to unravel it. Sure, he didn't have to focus on casting the spells to maintain the Clue anymore, but the mechanics of holding the quartz glass to see the Clue while raveling it simultaneously was difficult. A few times he dropped the quartz glass and swore.

The return was smooth so far, but something felt off. Mark's aptitude allowed him to see minute details in places he traveled through. A patch of moss on this stone, a broken branch at a forty-three-degree angle. He didn't think about it consciously, but added up, they were enough to tell him they weren't where they were supposed to be.

"Mr. Wells, I don't recognize going through here before."

"That doesn't surprise me, the forest can change its shape," replied Mr. Wells nonchalantly.

"Something feels off about the direction we're heading, though. I can't place my finger on it."

Mr. Wells gave him an intrigued look, as if he were taking his statement into serious consideration. He knew that much of a navigator's abilities was instinct, especially a novice. Mark felt unease at the uncertainty that swept over Mr. Wells face. However, since they had no other options, they decided to follow the Clue that Mark had diligently set beforehand.

As they kept walking, the atmosphere became thicker, almost suffocating, and an intense feeling of fear started to settle upon Mark. For a second, he thought he saw a tall man following them, but imagined it was just a tree. Later, Mark saw the same man with a wide grin on his face staring at them from several yards away. It felt like there were butterflies gnawing at the insides of his stomach, and his goosebumps were screeching at him to sprint to safety.

"Mr. Wells..." Mark cracked.

"Don't look at it. Don't make eye contact with it. Just keep walking next to me. Here, hold my hand." Mr. Wells held out his hand, and Mark awkwardly took it. He felt a bit childish doing so, but his pride was overwritten by his sense of self-preservation. Mr. Wells also took the quartz glass, so Mark didn't have to fumble with it. Although it didn't feel like they had been walking long, the sun had already started to set.

"That's not good," commented Mr. Wells, who again looked at his watch. Only forty-two minutes since they entered the woods. Thirteen minutes had gone by since they turned around.

"What isn't good?"

"The sun – it's setting. We won't have long before it reaches dark. You were right; something isn't right about where we're heading towards."

Mark had been so focused on raveling the Clue, that he hadn't noticed the sun's descent.

"This must be from the forest's impact on time length. Do you think it's the same for Phillip and Aisling? I wonder if it's random or measurable..."

Mr. Wells paid no attention to Mark's queries. Rather, he squatted down towards the wet floor. Mark glanced around to see what he was looking at, and then it struck him. He pulled on the Clue, and a loose end came towards it.

"That can't be it. Something must have cut it."

"Or somebody," murmured Mr. Wells, noticing the clean cut of the twine. The teacher was alert, but he didn't look too anxious yet, which comforted Mark. The truth was that the teacher was seriously troubled about the situation, but he didn't want to upset his young student – that would only make the situation worse. Besides, he knew that he himself could be dangerous, too, if it became necessary.

Mark took his glass back and spun around with it close to his eye to see if he could catch a trace of any of the spells that he had cast recently. Mr. Wells did the same, except he had a more advanced version of a magical omniglass. He efficiently clicked from gypsum to aquamarine to amethyst before putting it away. The sound of his knuckles cracking warned Mark to be prepared for whatever was coming – now was the time to be scared.

From ahead, they started to hear faint chirping noises. Although they weren't moving anywhere, the soft fluttering of wings was definitely moving towards them.

Mark held out his hand and incanted, "*Lixalux*" and a fluid ball of light poured into his hand. A couple of moths were attracted to the light, and one bit Mark, who swatted it away.

"Put that out," commanded Mr. Wells.

"We can't see well," Mark tried to argue.

"Listen to me, and we might *both* make it out alive."

Mark heard the seriousness and gravitas in his teacher's voice. He closed his hand into a fist and incanted, "*Exsicco.*"

"Those are *Calyptra canadensis* – the Canadian owlet, and I believe they are bringing their master with them," informed Mr. Wells.

Mark followed Mr. Wells' gaze upwards and saw a large figure with huge moths' wings and large red eyes eerily descending towards them.

Mr. Wells spoke quickly and quietly to Mark. "Close your eyes and keep a tight grip on me – as tight as you can. Don't say anything."

Mark immediately followed his teacher's orders. He didn't see the humanoid figure descend, but he heard his raspy, hissing voice.

"Fresh meat for me? How sweet. Do you know how lucky you two are? I haven't tasted the blood of humans in many decades. I shall savorrrrr this moment."

Mark cringed at the touch of a moth's wing fluttering against his cheek, and as they started to land and crawl all over his body, taking small bites. Every instinct and stimulus in his body told him to let go, to make a run for it, to start swatting or fight back, but he maintained fortitude and stillness – cool as a cucumber. The only change he made was to grip his teacher's hand harder. He heard Mr. Wells make a different sort of hissing noise and was wondering if he was casting a spell to save them.

"What is the tall one saying? Are you trying to attack me with a little magic? That won't work here, my dear one."

The Mothman rubbed a hairy finger against Mr. Wells cheek and was amazed at how easily he seemed to maintain composure. Time seemed to slow down, and then suddenly, the cry of terror stabbed the heart of everyone in the immediate area. Approximately a third of the moths dropped dead in mid-air from the chilling, cackling call.

Mark was no longer able to maintain his strength when the sound penetrated his ears. It was a mix between a snake's forked hiss and a rooster's proud cry. Mr. Wells himself felt shivers down his back at what he had summoned. Perhaps it was irresponsible of him, but that was something to worry about later. He didn't bother watching the cockatrices descend on the moths (big and small), but he couldn't help but hear the disturbing crunching noises they made.

The Mothman himself laid out a haunting shriek. *"No! My children! Come, we must go!"*

Many of the larger moths succumbed to the cockatrices in order to protect their father, and the other smaller moths fled from the midst of chaos. Mr. Wells kneeled down to his student to make sure he was okay. He put his arm around Mark and pulled him in closer to comfort him.

He whispered into Mark's ear, "It's going to be okay; trust me. Just remember: no matter what, keep your eyes closed and don't say anything until I tell you to. Do exactly what I tell you to; you're under my protection."

A large cockatrice landed before the pair, and Mr. Wells kept his gaze low as a sign of respect. He had seen the hauntingly vile creatures before and felt no need to examine who he was talking to. Mark couldn't hear the conversation that took place on the psychic plane.

"A palatable delicacy you have called us to. Is this boy the dessert?" hissed the cockatrice into Mr. Wells' head.

"No, he is under my protection, and I require your assistance."

"How unfortunately brusque you are. He does look meaty. Are you sure we can't have just a bite? A couple of fingers perhaps?"

"No, you may not. We require your assistance."

"Straight to business I see. All these years and you can't even take a second to say hello to an old friend? Ask how I've been?"

"We need help exiting the Enchanted Forest."

"I myself have been doing well by the way, not that you asked. Besides, why should we help you?"

"It is the Law. Don't make me use your true names."

"Do you even still remember that? It must have been a long time since you've had to use it."

"Would you like me to recite the statutes?"

"There won't be any need for that. You may ride on me for old time's sake, but your little friend will be carried out."

Suddenly, another cockatrice snatched Mark away from him. Hastily, Mr. Wells climbed onto the back of the cockatrice he was talking to, and they flew off in the direction of the other cockatrice.

Before Mark was snagged and carried away, all that he was able to hear was a horrific combination of crowing, crunching, and hissing. When he felt talons grab him from his back, he was so shocked that he thought the motion was his soul's ascent to heaven.

Still, he remembered Mr. Wells' words and did his best to keep his eyes shut and remain calm. He knew he had to trust his teacher. The icy wind blew through his hair, and his whole body was shivering. It didn't take long before he was carelessly dropped from the air onto his back on a soft patch of grass. The landing knocked his wind out. He was shivering more violently now from the fear and the cold and rolled into the fetal position and waited for Mr. Wells or someone else to find him.

He didn't hear Mr. Wells' footsteps approach, but he felt his hand softly touch his back. He began to speak to Mark; his voice felt warmer than usual.

"It's alright now, Mark. You can open your eyes."

Mark hesitated to open his eyes. He was still in a state of paralyzing dread. After a few seconds he opened his eyes but remained lying down. Mr. Wells held out a canteen to him.

"Here, drink some water. I also have a granola bar for you to eat. Do you like chocolate chip?"

Without saying anything, Mark gratefully took the drink and snack from Mr. Wells, who waited patiently for his student to recover. After a few minutes, Mark was finished eating.

"Mark, can you tell me where we are, right now?" asked Mr. Wells softly.

"I'm not sure," said Mark.

"We're not in the Forest anymore. Can you use your aptitude to tell where we are?"

Mark took a deep breath and looked up at the sky. Stars started to peak out in the sky's dark shade of blue, only a trace of sunlight could be seen at the end of the horizon. He looked down and closed his eyes. He felt the grass and the ground. He listened all around him and smelled the air. He let his sensory inputs process in his mind while he slowly calculated their location. Already knowing that they were somewhere deep in Appalachia helped him narrow down their location.

"We're somewhere in western West Virginia. I hear water far away. I think there might be a small town nearby also. I can smell gasoline."

"Good, good. Do you have your phone on you?"

"No, none of us took our phones with us. We didn't think we would need them. Or that we would be able to use them."

"Alright, that's okay. I brought mine. I'm going to call Dean Schulz and let him know where we are and that we're okay. Here, have another granola bar."

Mr. Wells stepped a few feet away from Mark to give him some space. He found his boss's number in his contacts and tried to give him a call. Unfortunately, the call dropped because the signal wasn't strong enough. This wasn't a problem for Mr. Wells, who was talented with physical magic, and even had a degree in physics from a normie university.

Mark told him that there was a town somewhere in the area, which meant that there were roads, which meant that there were telephone poles and cell towers. He held his phone in his left hand,

and with his right, he pointed two fingers towards the sky. He focused on making an ethereal "antenna". What mattered now was catching a signal. It didn't take long to do this, and once he received four bars, he tried to call Dean Schulz again.

Almost immediately, the dean answered. "Henry, are you alright? Is Mark with you?"

"Yes and yes, we're both alright. What about Phillip and Aisling? We got separated in the forest."

"They're alright. They returned a couple of hours ago. The three of us are in my office right now. You're on speakerphone."

"Perfect, so the anchor worked. Mark and I are all the way in West Virginia, by the Ohio River. He told me there's a town nearby, so I'm going to see if I can get a motel there."

"Do you have your wallet on you? Do you need money?"

"I'm good, I just wanted to let you know that we're okay and to make sure that Phillip and Aisling were okay."

"Hi, Mr. Wells!" called out Aisling through the phone. "We're okay; we were so worried about you guys! We have so much to tell you! Can we talk to Mark?"

"Let me see." Mr. Wells looked at Mark who was sitting cross-legged and staring at the ground. "Hey, Mark," he said softly away from the phone so the others couldn't hear. "Your friends are on the phone. Do you want to talk to them?" Mark just blinked a few times and without a word shook his head.

"You know Aisling," he said, returning to the phone. "Mark and I had a difficult time getting out of the woods on our own, and we're both pretty burnt out. How about we all talk tomorrow about our discoveries?"

"That's alright, Mr. Wells" replied Aisling, who tried to keep a positive tone.

"Hey Henry," said Dean Schulz. "I'm going to take one of the school's flying cars over to where you guys are tomorrow to pick you up. Can you send me an address once you get to where you're going?"

"Sure thing, boss. When should we expect you?"

"I'll let you know once I'm able to get some directions and get an ETA."

"Perfect. Well, I'm going to let you go now because Mark and I have some more hiking to do to get to town."

"Alright, see you tomorrow, bye."

Mr. Wells put down his hands and walked back to Mark who was merely sitting on the ground. He hadn't moved at all during the phone call.

"Hey Mark, you've done a really good job today," he said. He was trying his best to be encouraging, but he was honest. The cry of a cockatrice a mile away could throw a grown man into gut-wrenching sobs, so he was impressed that Mark kept his bearing so well. "Do you think you could lead us into the town you were telling me about?"

Mark didn't say a word, he just nodded his head and stood up. He looked at the sky to position himself with the stars and started heading northwest. He felt Mr. Wells come close to him and slide his hand into Mark's.

"I'm not getting separated from any other students again."

Mark felt his eyes on him but didn't return the look. He didn't really care right now. He couldn't care about anything right now. Something about the cry of the cockatrice had shattered his spirit. He couldn't even feel all the blood from the moth bites pouring down his body, yet somehow Mr. Wells left the forest only slightly disheveled. Mark allowed himself to have just one more thought before shutting his brain off. *Just how powerful is Mr. Wells?*

Mr. Wells was concerned about Mark's behavior. He learned over the years that most people – even most magi – won't ever have experiences half as dark as the one they shared tonight. Although he himself had been able to develop the necessary coping mechanisms to deal with the presence and experience of what some would consider "pure evil," others hadn't. The general public lived lives that were soft and easy. It was imperative that Mark see Dr. Toumi right away once they returned to school.

26
THE GIRL'S GHOST

Kalina woke up on the cold, hardwood floor of a small, dusty room. It was completely pitch black, and it had a strong smell of some sort of musty mélange. Panic quickly dominated her senses. The last thing she remembered was walking through the woods, leading Miss Dalton towards the origin of Samantha Hastings.

The back of her neck was stinging, and when she reached back she felt a bruise, meaning she was hit. *What about Ms. Dalton? Is she safe?* She was worried at first but understood there was only one obvious explanation for the events that occurred. She sighed deeply and her shoulders slumped in shame that she couldn't recognize what was happening beforehand.

Ms. Dalton had clearly been manipulating her – using her power for… That angel wasn't a real angel – it was either an illusion or a demon. Kalina wasn't sure how or why Ms. Dalton was doing this, but she must be exceptionally powerful if she could somehow evade Kalina's own precognitive abilities. *Was she a witch?* She wondered how it was possible Ms. Dalton could gain an alliance with a literal demon, and she shivered at the thought of other occult practices Ms. Dalton might be involved in.

Kalina, having been left in complete darkness, cautiously stood up and held out her right arm to feel her way around the room. Her searching hand didn't have to travel far, however. She didn't even need to extend it all the way before it reached the rough surface of what she guessed was a brick wall – the nooks and crannies grated against her skin, and she could feel the rectangular pattern of the smooth cement holding them together.

She held out her other hand in front of her as she slowly paced forward. After only a couple of paces she reached another wall. The room was smaller than she had originally perceived; it was more like a pantry, and there was no discernable exit or escape. She couldn't even feel a door.

Kalina considered trying an incantation but realized that it would be dangerous to try something in an environment where she couldn't see anything. She didn't know anything about where she was, and the spell could end up backfiring on her or worse.

With nothing else to do and no immediate solution in sight, Kalina opted to sit back down, leaning against the brick wall with her knees drawn up to her chest. Her head hung low and, and she couldn't help but succumb to fear and uncertainty, tears welling up in her eyes. There were neither binaural beats nor any intricate runes to conjure this time; it was just her and the unsettling silence and darkness that enveloped her.

Kalina slowly recalled the wisdom of the nun, taking in a deep breath. She began to recite the Jesus Prayer that Sister Maryam had advised her to use in moments of physical danger and spiritual turmoil. As she repeated the words, she could feel a growing sense of tranquility wash over her, but her mouth was becoming dry and parched with the prolonged recitation. The fight against her fear had been successful thus far, causing exhaustion to creep in. Her eyelids felt heavy, and she embraced the promise of rest.

Curling into the fetal position on the floor, Kalina cleared her mind and surrendered gladly to the pull of sleep. Her breathing drew out as she drifted into unconsciousness. The whole world around her suddenly shifted into a deep shade of blue. Startled by the change, Kalina jolted upright to examine her surroundings. She was perplexed at the mysterious bluish hue that was illuminating the room.

"Hello," said a soft voice behind her.

Startled, Kalina turned around to see another girl a few years her senior looking down on her. She looked familiar, but Kalina couldn't place where she had seen her before. Between them was Kalina's sleeping body still curled in the fetal position on the hard floor.

"Have you done this before?" asked the girl, tilting her head.

"No, I don't think so. Maybe something similar. Is this an out-of-body experience?" asked Kalina, as an explanation began to dawn on her.

The girl shrugged slyly, "It's a type of astral projection, but we don't have much time to discuss that. I'm here trying to save you."

"Who are you?"

As soon as Kalina had asked the question, the world became bright once more. She squinted her eyes as her pupils adjusted to the change in lighting and realized that she was outside again. In her left hand, she was holding an orange.

"I am Edith, and I once found myself in a situation quite akin to yours. My companions and I were approached by a certain Caroline, or Cara, as she is known amongst our social set. The diabolic ceremony she performed wholly absorbed our abilities – our mystical talents, our youth, and all the endowments we possessed. She extended a cordial invitation for me to join her party, and I accepted."

In front of Kalina stood the very same plantation mansion that had haunted many of her prior visions. It was eerily familiar, and this time, she was able to push the boundaries of time and space to enter the imposing house. She cautiously walked down the hallway, being drawn to a room from whence she heard the chilling sounds of an incantation being pronounced.

Kalina's eyes widened in revulsion when she saw the unnatural witchcraft taking place; Ms. Dalton sat at the very center of it. Four poor, pale girls lay prone around her. Although each girl was in a state of unconsciousness, they were stiff and still, resembling fallen pillars. Circles and lines and curls bound and connected the youths. Kalina recognized some of the runes and shapes as the ones Ms. Dalton had utilized to aid Kalina in drawing forth her subliminal meditations. These ones weren't made with chalk and salt, though. Rather, it was blood, hair, and nails that painted the wooden floor. If Kalina were in her corporeal body, she would have vomited at the sight and the stench.

Sensing her presence, Ms. Dalton opened her eyes and smiled at Kalina. She was speaking to her, but the sound was muffled. Kalina could tell that she was pleased about something, and she put a hand on her shoulder.

Ms. Dalton opened her cruel, snake-like eyes, which pierced Kalina's very spirit. She smiled at her, but rather than the honey-sweet face she was used to, Ms. Dalton looked like a wolf reveling in her prey. Ms. Dalton started to speak in Kalina's direction, her teeth looking like fangs, but the noise was still muffled. It wasn't Kalina she was talking to, and it wasn't Kalina who was in that room at the moment, but Edith.

"I conveyed to her my intent to align with her and her assembly, but in truth, it was a fabrication. My true purpose was to liberate my companions."

Kalina was compelled by an inexplicable impulse to extend the orange towards Ms. Dalton. It was clearly Edith's manipulative way of symbolizing alliance with the hag. However, before the plump fruit could be handed over, Kalina's hand crushed the orange, releasing a magical shockwave so powerful that its reverberations could still be felt through the memory.

The juices of the orange splattered to the wooden floor with an acidic sizzle. Mystically, the drops all gravitated towards pieces of Ms. Dalton's runic craftsmanship, incinerating them. Edith's friends, being released from their horrible bonds, each woke with a gasp.

Ms. Dalton, too, was affected by the unexpected spell, her own surprise evident as she staggered back. It was clear to Kalina that this was a form of magic unlike anything she would ever learn in school. It was clear why Ms. Dalton craved Edith's magical abilities.

"I had indeed taken her aback, granting me a brief advantage. It proved sufficient to release my friends from her grasp. However, we were all too aware that I couldn't hold her in combat for an extended duration. As the other young ladies distanced themselves, I, too, made the decision to flee. Alas, it would prove to be an ill-advised choice."

Although every instinct in Kalina told her to flee with all the other girls, her projection was forced to stay behind with Ms. Dalton.

"I beseech you to heed with the utmost gravity."

Ms. Dalton, whose visage became beet red, furiously stood up and stormed to another room. Instead of following her teacher, Kalina instead floated, pulled by an invisible string of fate. In that room, there was a large window. On the windowsill there was a painting with the precise likeness of Edith. This time, Kalina could hear Ms. Dalton clearly. She was chanting something in an ancient language that made Kalina's ethereal body shiver.

The painting started to glow green and Ms. Dalton reached out her claws to touch it. Kalina felt her body start to tremble and the world became blurry. Her vision returned to the glowing blue of the astral plane that she experienced earlier.

"So it was you that I was seeing in my visions," she addressed the girl before her.

"Yes, although it wasn't me who initiated them. Your aptitude allows me to make a connection with you that I wasn't able to make with all the other victims. You're powerful. I might actually be able to save you."

"How?"

"When the moment presents itself, place your trust in me. I shall endeavor to assist your escape to the best of my abilities."

Before Kalina could ask any further questions, the room plunged back into inky darkness, leaving Kalina once more in the chilling solitude of the void. She curled back into a ball on the cold, unyielding floor. Sleep, prayer, and patience were her only companions now, and she held onto the hope that when the time was right, Edith would return to her aid.

27

PLEASANT POINT

Dean Schulz strode towards room 16 at the Pleasant Point Valley Motel. His knuckles rapped firmly against the door, and it creaked open to reveal a ragged and bleary-eyed Mr. Wells. The dean couldn't help but feel concern for his colleague – never had he seen him in such a state (well, not since the dean found him and transformed him into a teacher). *Mein Gott,* he thought to himself, *If Henry looks like this, I can't imagine the state that Mark must be in.*

The dean's thoughts fluttered to doubt at the wisdom of encouraging this unique yet dangerous school project. Before his invading thoughts could take off, Dr. Toumi caught up to Dean Schulz and greeted Mr. Wells with a nod of understanding. Sensing his friend's inner turmoil, Dr. Toumi placed a warm hand on his shoulders, and used his empathetic abilities to help him.

Dean Schulz, having recovered from his initial shock, spoke determinately, "Good Morning, Henry. Where's Mark? How has he been since you left the forest?"

"We've been up all night," said Mr. Wells in a low voice. "It's a good thing you came, Luke. You two are the only ones who know about my history. We were in danger in the Enchanted Forest, so I had to summon for help. I would have fought, but I wasn't sure that if Mark would have been able to survive the battle."

Dean Schulz pinched the bridge of his nose, either in disappointment or frustration, and Dr. Toumi just shook his head, fearing for the potential psychological damage done to Mark. They both knew better than to ask questions at the moment, especially if there was a student within earshot. Besides, Dean Schulz would get a fuller briefing when the whole team was reunited, and an even fuller one when it was just Henry.

Inside the motel room, they found Mark lying on the bed, his eyes open but unfocused. He didn't acknowledge their presence as they entered. It was evident that he had struggled to fall asleep, plagued by persistent nightmares that had kept him awake all night. The concerned trio exchanged worried glances, recognizing the toll this extraordinary experience had taken on the young student.

"Mark," began Mr. Toumi. "I can feel fear coming off of you. Not just that, but a lot of different feelings – doubt, anger, and disgust. There is more to this, though. I can help you when we get back to school if you'll let me."

Throughout the night and into the morning, Mark remained silent, refusing to utter a single word. When he finally did speak, it was with a strange and disconcerting quality, as though the words that emerged from his lips weren't quite his own.

"What did you summon, Mr. Wells?" he asked, turning his face towards his teacher. Mr. Wells had been feeling guilty and ashamed of what he had resorted to and felt his pupil's eyes burn into his. There was a searing scrutiny in his pupil's gaze. Both Dean Schulz and Dr. Toumi held their breaths, waiting for Mr. Wells to give an answer, neither sure of how he would explain the event.

Mr. Wells considered both his options: on the one hand, he didn't want to enlighten his student with knowledge that he simply wasn't ready for. On the other hand, he felt that Mark deserved to know the truth of what he experienced.

He took a deep hesitant breath before giving an answer. "The cockatrice. It's kind of like a basilisk with wings," he explained. "That's why you're feeling the way you're feeling. They're associated with pure evil. Actually, they almost are pure evil, and as a matter of fact you've taken it rather well compared to most people."

He tried to sound encouraging at the end but was unsure how Mark would take it. Mark was a young man of duty and honor; traits he had likely inherited from his military father.

Of the three students he had been tutoring, it was Mark who had displayed the most tenacity and diligence. Mr. Wells couldn't help but wonder what the consequences might have been had Phillip or, God-forbid, Aisling been the ones accompanying him on the adventure during the summoning. The potential aftermath in either case could have been significantly more severe, and this thought weighed heavily on his mind.

Mark gave a succinct response. "Alright," he replied in a monotone cadence, acknowledging the explanation he received. "I understand where the emotions that I'm feeling are coming from. They're not my own, and the information helps a little bit, but there's still that seed..."

His voice trailed off as the three teachers listened attentively to his reflections. None were sure what to say; this had never happened to a student before, but Mark continued.

"There was something else, too. The smiling man."

"The smiling man?" inquired Dr. Toumi.

The cockatrices having taken over the spotlight, Mr. Wells overlooked the memory of the Smiling Man. His heart skipped a beat, having almost forgotten their close encounter with the demonic entity. However, this was an easier answer to give to his student.

"That wasn't a man. It was something else, just posing as a man. When you have an evil thought, do you entertain it?" Mark didn't answer, but Mr. Wells continued anyway. "That's why I told you to ignore it. It probably led us to that moth-human chimera."

"You met Mothman?" asked Dean Schulz, surprised. There were plenty of things that he did *not* know about. Nevertheless, he restrained from asking further questions or making more unnecessary comments while Mr. Wells and Mark awkwardly discussed some more.

He wasn't sure how much information to give to Mark. The intricacies of this wisdom might be too advanced for the poor kid, and it was certainly above the material taught at Cardinal Key Academy. Mr. Wells felt his heart skip a beat as Mark continued to talk, knowing exactly what Mark was trying to describe. Before they began down the rabbit hole, Dean Schulz tactfully interrupted the conversation.

"Why don't we head out before it gets too late? We can discuss all this stuff when we get back to school. I'm sure your friends are impatient to hear from you. Also, I've brought breakfast," he finished, lifting up a hand to present a big brown paper bag with a Psomira logo.

28
FRIENDS REUNITED, CONCERNS IGNITED

Phillip and Aisling impatiently sat waiting in Mr. Wells' office. They were unsure when Dean Schulz and Mr. Toumi would return with Mark and Mr. Wells, but they didn't want to risk missing their arrival.

They were bored and antsy. Aisling had suggested earlier that they could play cards while they waited, but Phillip didn't think it was an appropriate time for that.

Eventually, Aisling voiced a concern of hers. "Why do you think Dean Schulz took Dr. Toumi?" she asked. The seriousness of her face signaled that she was deeply worried about the safety of their teacher and friend.

Without missing a beat, he responded, "Probably in case Mark or Mr. Wells got injured. He's the school physician, so that must be the reason after all."

Phillip was logical and realistic, but other students, especially optimistic ones like Aisling found him to be tactless and insensitive.

"That's disconcerting," she replied

"I wouldn't be too worried," reassured Phillip when he noticed the discomfort he unintentionally caused Aisling. "When Mr. Wells was on the phone last night, he didn't seem like he was seriously concerned about anything. I am curious as to why Mark didn't want to talk to us, though."

Aisling appreciated Phillips efforts to reassure her, but she nonetheless sighed, "We'll find out soon enough."

Unfortunately for them, "soon enough" started to take too long, and the hunger in Aisling and Phillip's stomachs was beginning to outweigh their patience. They were considering heading to the mess hall for lunch, when they heard the echo of footsteps approaching from down the hall. They bolted out of the classroom, and to their delight, they saw the beautiful appearance of a completely disheveled Mark and Mr. Wells. The pair were sauntering down the hall as though nothing special had just transpired.

Both Aisling and Phillip were so excited that they raced down the hall to greet Mark with a bear hug. Their momentum was so intense that they almost tackled him to the ground. Mr. Wells observed a faint blush bloom across Mark's face, and thought he detected a subtle hint of a smile form on his lips. *Good,* he thought to himself. *It's good that he has friends to be with and who will support him.*

Once the initial excitement had passed and the pair of students joyfully greeted their teacher, Phillip asked, "What happened to Dean Schulz. Isn't he supposed to be here for our debriefing on the information we gathered from the Blue Ridge Enchanted Forest? We pretty much told him everything that happened to us already. Did you? And when do we get to hear about what happened to you guys?"

"Not quite yet," answered Mr. Wells, who expected analytical Phillip to be the first to business. "Right as we arrived, he got some important news that a student went missing last night. He's calling some investigators, and they're searching for the student right now."

As if on cue, Dean Schulz appeared out of nowhere at the end of the hall.

"Phillip," he shouted, and lightly jogged towards the group. "Your sister – have you seen your sister at all since last night when you got back? Did you see her before you guys left?"

"Well, I saw her around at lunch time yesterday. That's... it....," he replied. He drew out those last words. He could put two and two together, but he was hoping that she wasn't the missing student Mr. Wells had just told them about.

"Her roommates say she didn't come back to their dorm last night. According to them and her dorm mother, she was supposed to be having a private tutoring session with Ms. Dalton, but no one knows where she is either."

"Do you think she kidnapped her?" anxiously questioned Phillip, who started to feel worry for his sister creeping up his chest.

"We don't know the details yet, but I just got off the phone with Detective Christie, and he's on his way. If you come across any news, let me know immediately. Here's my card, and here's Detective Christie's card."

Dean Schulz sped off after the brief encounter, leaving Phillip behind in shock. Even if Phillip could materialize words from his larynx, the dean had left too quickly for Phillip to ask any more questions.

"Well team," began Mr. Wells awkwardly. "It looks like we're going to need to hold off on the debriefing for now." He put a hand on Phillip's shoulder in an effort to comfort him. "Don't worry, I'm sure they'll find your sister. For now, just sit tight, and do what you can to help. I'm sure your parents are being notified immediately. I'm going to go get something to eat and take a shower."

The three students watched their mentor walk away. Aisling thought that his reaction was a little insincere and even callous, but Phillip recognized the look of exasperation on his face and understood his good intentions. He had never seen his mentor so tired out before. After a few moments of tongue-tied silence, Aisling gasped.

"It all makes sense now," she whispered loudly.

Both Mark and Phillip turned to face her. They both internally braced themselves for whatever idea she might have. Although many kids in their grade had made fun of her for her crazy "conspiratorial" ideas, everyone knew that when her thoughts were complete, they were incredibly insightful.

"What makes sense?" pushed Phillip, hoping that she would say something that would help them find his sister.

Aisling's eyes were dancing from corner to corner, even her pupils were rapidly dilating and constricting. Phillip and Mark had seen her like this before – she was rapidly connecting the dots.

She continued, "It makes sense why there was a pattern of school girls going missing. It was her all along wasn't it? Ms. Dalton I mean. She was going from school to school all over the continent, possibly the world, changing her identity for each place she visited. We never considered the teachers to be the ones behind it! She's a *witch!*" She spat out the word with disgust. "How had she not been caught before? And that's why Samantha Hastings escaped! She must have been a victim! She didn't faint! She was put into a coma *when* she reached Ms. Dalton. Remember what Maura said? That must be why she looked so frightened!"

"That *hag,*" sneered Phillip with as much vitriol as he possibly could put out. "I'm going to kill her."

"We need to find her first," said Mark, his face becoming hotter than Hades. Normally he kept fairly calm, but this time he was letting his emotions out.

Aisling spoke up again. "I have an idea," she said in a hushed tone. "But it's not exactly 'legal.'"

"I don't care," said Phillip. "It's my younger sister. I'll do anything I can to save her."

Aisling pulled out her phone and scrolled through her photo albums. "Okay, but you definitely can't tell anyone about this." She showed her phone to her friends.

"What are we looking at?" asked Mark.

"It's a spell for tracking someone."

Mark took a closer look, and his eyes widened. "That's blood magic!"

Phillip felt his heart racing at the possibility of breaking a treasonous international law for the sake of his sister. Then he thought about all those other girls, Samantha Hastings being an exception of one who came back. They don't even know what that *harpy* did to the others. It was worth it. For Kalina.

"Shhh!" hissed Aisling.

"Where did you find this?" asked Phillip.

"I found it on the dark web, while we were researching navigation techniques. It's the best shot we have at finding your sister, especially since we can use *your* blood as you two are siblings. See here, there's a section for sibling magic."

Phillip hesitated. From a very young age, everyone in the magical community was taught that blood magic led to evil deeds and was completely illegal (except for licensed and monitored use by a mere handful of select healers and expert doctors). Even still, Kalina was more important to Phillip than any law.

"Let's do it," he said confidently.

"I'm in. I can cast the spell," answered Mark. Phillip and Aisling both cast surprised looks at their normally reserved partner.

"Well alright," said Aisling. "I'll go get the materials. Mark, you'll make the map and cast the incantations. Phillip, you'll draw the blood."

All three immediately headed in separate directions to begin their work as fast as they could.

Mark went behind Mr. Wells' desk to rummage through it. Having worked with him and Phillip, he knew that he kept some enchanted cartography paper. He just wasn't sure where.

"It's in the middle right drawer," stated Phillip, intuitively knowing what his partner was hunting for.

Mark snatched up a thick piece of paper, and carelessly swiped everything off Mr. Wells desk. A lamp broke, startling Phillip. Mark laid the piece of paper on the weathered wooden desk, and started to mark cartographical symbols on the parchment.

After he was finished, he reached to his side and took out a large knife that he took with him on the trip into the forest and motioned for Phillip to come over. Although his sister was in immediate danger, he hesitated at the sharp knife

"Well what did you think was going to happen? We don't have time to go get a syringe, and you're obviously her closest relative alive and present! It's not like I'm going to slit your throat or anything."

The urgency in Mark's voice reminded Phillip of the situation and he marched over, trusting his best friend. Phillip held out his hand and tightened up in preparation. Mark rolled his eyes at the melodrama.

"It's not like the movies, I only need a few drops," he said as he punctured Phillip's pointer finger.

Relaxed, Phillip placed his finger over the parchment while squeezing it, to produce more drops of blood. As he was doing that, Mark took out his compass and began an incantation while facing north, anchoring the map. He was reciting quickly, switching between Latin and English, but Phillip couldn't catch all of it. This was the navigator's domain of expertise, not the traveler's.

Slowly but surely, the drops of blood drew themselves into a map as if pulled by a magnet. After a while, the blood fully formed into a contoured map, but it was still in motion. Although Phillip had studied map making and navigation with Mark, the design was too complex for him to understand. However, Mark was bent over it, intensely reading and interpreting it.

"What now," asked Phillip impatiently.

"Not sure. Aisling has the rest of the spell. This was my part."

At that moment Aisling burst in with her arms full of various magical materials for the blood magic recipe.

She took one look at the map and all she said was, "Good."

She took out some copying paper first, and copied the image of the recipe onto it. Then she put down a bowl that was filled with herbs, minerals, and the like.

She crossed herself from left to right before turning to Phillip and said, "I need your blood now."

Without a second thought, Phillip held out his hand, ready for another puncture. Instead, Aisling brusquely slashed across his palm. He yelped and tried to pull back in shock, but she forcefully held his hand over the bowl. As his blood was pouring into it, she started shouting enchantments. Phillip and Mark both recognized the sing-song sounds of her Irish as she spoke.

Suddenly, her eyes started to glow. Phillip wanted to cross himself at the fear that his friend had just been possessed, but Aisling still had an iron grip on his right hand. Fortunately, she quickly returned to normal.

Robotically, she took out a vial of Mendicol® and dumped it over Phillip's palm, causing him to yell in pain. Mendicol burns like rubbing alcohol, but more intensely. Smoke rose from the slash as it closed itself together. There was a mark still there, but at least it was closed. Phillip knew that the Mendicol would take care of the scar eventually. Next, Aisling spread some soothing Vitamin E on it before finally wrapping it in bandage.

"You could have warned me," said Phillip.

Aisling merely shrugged and said, "We've got work to do. Your sister isn't getting any safer, and we don't know how much time we have left."

Aisling stood still for a while, intensely examining the contents of the bowl and the map. She was nodding her head, double-checking their progress (they all knew blood magic could be seriously danger-ous if handled improperly).

"What next?" asked Phillip impatiently.

"Bring the map," replied Aisling. "It's time for us to move outside for the next part."

29

THE RITUAL

As Kalina's body gradually awoke, she found herself on a different floor, in a large illuminated room. She tried to adjust from the discomfort of the hard wood beneath her back but was met with shivers of panic when she realized she couldn't move. Her breath became shallow and quick, and her heart pounded against her chest. A chilling, sinister yet familiar voice broke through the haze of her anxiety.

"Looks like someone's awake. You are exceptionally resistant to my potion!" She sounded frustrated yet intrigued at the same time, causing Kalina to feel like an animal being examined at the zoo. "No matter," continued Ms. Dalton. "I'll just brew another, more concentrated batch."

Kalina was as stiff as a statue, only barely able to adjust her line of eyesight, but in her peripheral vision, she could see Ms. Dalton move behind her. She could hear her former mentor humming a tune while she was chopping and crushing something. Kalina's mom liked to use a mortar and pestle, so she could recognize that sound anywhere.

"I knew I had a good feeling about you," she stated as though it was just another ordinary day for her. "You know; I think you might be the first person who's ever woken up on their own from my potion... *And* I've been improving it for almost two thousand years!"

Despite her situation, Kalina felt a small amount of pride in herself at the praise, but immediately pushed that feeling aside. She wanted to say something – anything. She was desperately trying to open her lips an inch or to bring forth any sort of noise. If only she could cast a small spell, maybe just nudge her pointer finger. But every time she tried, the action only caused her whole body to be gripped in numbness that tingled uncontrollably.

"I suppose you're wondering what exactly I mean by that," continued Ms. Dalton. "You must be feeling so many intense emotions – confusion, betrayal... anger?"

Kalina in fact had been feeling angry, but the toying way Ms. Dalton said it sounded like she wanted her to. In an act of defiance, Kalina calmed her mind and her passions to seek stillness (not that she had much choice in that matter).

Ms. Dalton paused for a brief moment, as if she were carefully selecting what to say next.

She eventually sighed, "But you must understand, darling, it's really not personal. Well, not from my perspective at the very least. I've been doing this for a very, very, long time, but you might actually have already perceived that."

Ms. Dalton was overly dramatic in her speech and gestures. She clenched her fists in excitement before she explained, "I can't quite fathom the extent of your potential, but I can sense the amount of power you carry... Oh, I can hardly wait to be rejuvenated by your youthful purity."

Ms. Dalton's sweet southern accent had vanished completely at this point. Instead, her voice adopted an eclectic blend of accents, creating an unsettling yet captivating auditory mosaic. As she worked on her mysterious potion, she recounted her extraordinary life experiences to Kalina.

""Whence to start? I came to be as Carannóg in the first century following the *supposed* incarnation of Christ, albeit His renown had not yet reached the shores of Britain. I sorely yearn for those primeval times, when our kinship with nature was an unbroken bond. I can vividly remember the coming of the Romans, who irreversibly altered our way of life. Indeed, I was but a tender maiden at their arrival. I do in fact have memories of Queen Boudicca's valiant but ill-fated revolt, yet, regrettably, our paths did not cross."

"Then arrived those Anglo-Saxon invaders, they did. I sought out to lend aid to me own kith in the ward of our lush isle, but, alas, we were overcame. And nay, no reign of King Arthur, as some may spin the tales. Although I have heard the name of a famous and puissant general who bore the selfsame moniker, I never had the chance to share words with him. I opted to take dwelling in Wales after they overran my homeland, and later fared to Brittany in Francia - the sole time I did forsake my beloved isle ere I came here. The European continent, truth be told, never held much favor in mine eyes, and I dare say the Saxons, stacked against them Gauls, began to grow on me a little bit. Their lasses proved rather fun for both the art of kidnapping and magical experiments."

Ms. Dalton loudly sighed as she reminisced of those times, and it seemed that the more she spoke, the less comprehensible she became. Kalina didn't even want to imagine what "fun" meant to the wicked woman. What did she even mean by "experiments?"

"Thereafter came the Vikings. That was a wælisc tide to be alive upon my island, and I did get to witness many a hild! Oh, dwelling by the sea did grant me such a thrill. I indeed rather looked high upon their ruthlessness, to be truthful, and I ne'er raised a finger to help the Angles. Ye ken, those Northmen did mind me of the strength and hæðengeld that my own folc had whilst we were withstanding the Romans. 'Tis a shame they forleoran it... Look upon Sweden today, forsooth. It is utterlie unwaec!"

Again, Ms. Dalton paused to collect her thoughts. Her memories were clearly bringing back emotions that she had long forgotten.

"Hmmm... then came the Normans. I was taken aback by how swiftly the English adapted to them. I had evermore boasted about how my people fiercely held our ground against our adversaries, but, perchance, the English aren't truly mine own kin. Maybe I'm simply swayed by opinion, for I held no fondness for the new court's 'Latinate manners,' if thou can indeed term them with such *politeness*.

"Then, the War of the Roses unfolded, followed by the Civil War, the Scottish Rebellions, the Seven Years War. One lesson learned: there's still another cursed war. By this hour, my sojourn in Britain had its limits, and counsel led me to distant shores. I contemplated Ireland – 'twas near my homeland, yet English folk there proved dreadfully vicious. I foresaw wars and tumults ahead, thus America called to me, a venturesome, burgeoning realm of the British. Even their wars proved diverting, especially the Civil War."

Kalina disengaged from the ceaseless ramblings of her former mentor and directed her focus towards meditation and prayer. She recalled how useful the Jesus Prayer was and brought it forth to the center of her attention. She knew it was necessary to have faith and trust that Edith would come to her aid soon.

She delved deeper and deeper within herself. It was a struggle to fight off the temptation of Ms. Dalton's words. As she continued to wage war on the intellectual realm, she felt something graceful lay upon her.

She heard the soft voice of Edith's shade inside her head, saying, "*As the final gleam of my aura dwindles, I bestow upon you my benediction.*"

A luminous, bluish-white light was sparked in the depths of Kalina's unconsciousness. With all the strength she could muster, she kindled and nurtured the ethereal light lest it wane and die. *The hour is upon us,* she urged herself.

The radiant glow grew until it enveloped her, and when she opened her eyes, her vision was saturated with the brilliant radiance. Her tense and numb muscles were finally able to relax, and she stood up to face the bewildered Ms. Dalton. The whites of her widened eyes declared her astonishment.

With all the manna in her body, Kalina began to incant in a symphony of voices,

"*At this hour I invoke God as judge!*

I call upon the might of the angels, saints, and martyrs as witnesses!

By the power of heaven, you are broken!

By the light of the sun, you are revealed!

By the whiteness of snow, you are deprived!

By the force of fire, you are branded!

By the flashing of lightning, you are struck!

By the velocity of wind, you are silenced!

By the depth of the sea, you are humbled!

By the stability of the earth, you are shaken!

By the hardness of rocks, you are shattered!"

The entire mansion trembled violently, its foundations quivering under the force of the thundering storm Kalina had summoned. Ceramic vessels shattered while windows burst in a flurry of glass shards. Ms. Dalton, overstimulated by the cacophony of chaos, struggled to maintain her footing despite her archaic power and knowledge. She attempted to cast her own counter spells, but whatever Kalina had been able to call upon was too overwhelming.

To her credit, the average witch or magus would have been utterly spellbound and destroyed by the time Kalina had completed the incantation, but that was only the beginning.

Kalina glared at the distraught Ms. Dalton, clapping her hands once, twice, then a third time. A final release of her stored mana sent the entire mansion crumbling around them. Kalina, immediately restored to her ordinary self, conjured the first spell that sprang to mind.

"Tardus Cassus!"

Her whole body was able to slow down, but the impact with the ground was still harsh and rapid. Oddly, this worked to her advantage because while Ms. Dalton was still gracefully gliding to the first floor, Kalina sprinted away, hastening her escape.

Without turning around, she yelled "*Ygron pyr theto*!"

The searing intensity of the fire nipped at her heels as she raced across the well-manicured lawn, placing more distance between herself and Ms. Dalton. In her sights lay the boundary of Ms. Dalton's own little springtime realm and the wintry winds beyond it. Right behind the oak tree that marked the boundary was a curtain of snow, and that was her target.

Although her legs were burning with exertion, she pushed forward and saw three figures emerge from the tree-line of the Enchanted Forest. *Were they part of Ms. Dalton's coven? Her underlings?* She stumbled and tripped at the sight of them. When she got up, however, she realized that one of them was sprinting to her faster than the others – it was none other Phillip! Inspired with renewed energy and determination, she sped towards him with all the strength left in her body, and then some.

30
THROUGH SMOKE AND SNOW

Aisling led her companions to a secluded spot along the school's property, nestled at the very edge of the forest. The absence of other students playing outside indicated that the news of Kalina's disappearance had spread among the faculty. Before they would complete the spell, they decided to tie themselves together with some of the leftover Clue. They didn't want to risk getting separated this time as the consequences would be far graver.

Aisling looked around her before lighting a match and gently tossing it into the contents of the bowl. Immediately when the wooden stick hit the crimson pool of blood, the whole bowl erupted into a brilliant inferno. Instinctively, all three of the students looked around nervously; their unexpected spectacle looked like they were performing pyromancy. (In reality, what they were doing was a far more serious crime).

Aisling maintained the spell, incanting in Latin, which Phillip couldn't understand at all. A fragrant smoke gradually lifted from the bowl. As Aisling chanted, the burned remnants of the bowl took on an alchemical transformation, transmuting into a shiny metallic surface. Upon the surface, it revealed a vivid image of Kalina, alive and asleep in a dark chamber. *Thank God,* thought Phillip, *at least we can scry that she's alive for now.*

Aisling changed tone as she transitioned into the final segment of the spell. She began to hymn in a different, more ecclesiastical dialect of Latin. Above the bowl, the smoke had regathered, shaping itself into a life-sized projection of Kalina, her body oriented towards the woods. As Aisling reached the spell's conclusion, the projection condensed in stature until it transformed into a gaseous ball of light.

Meanwhile, Mark had been watching the blood map, seeing how the sanguine lines rearranged themselves all over the parchment. It was difficult for him to logically discern what he was reading, but his intuition told him that it was a sort of compass.

The wispy ball of light dazzled them, gathering their attention before ebulliently dancing off into the dark, mysterious woods. Without a moment's hesitation, the trio embarked on their second journey into the woods – they had just survived the Enchanted Forest, and they can do so again.

All three hastened to follow the wisp as it gracefully twirled around the Enchanted Forest, seemingly leading them into the most illogical directions. Multiple times, it decided to take them in circles or head back the direction they came. Mark tried to comprehend and predict its whims, but its ætherial nature made it nearly impossible for him.

Nevertheless, they trusted the wispy light, and while Mark examined the map, Aisling and Phillip cast minor spells to clear a path for them, whether it be through mist or marsh. It was a matter of life or death that they didn't lose sight of their blazing beacon.

Their task grew increasingly challenging, though, as if the very Enchanted Forest was conspiring against them. The further they ventured, the colder the atmosphere became. Snowflakes started to fall, growing in size as the trio pushed onward.

They were relentlessly putting in all of their effort to rescue someone dear to them, and the mission had finally bore fruit as they approached a clearing. Though the snow fell more rapidly, beyond it lay a vibrant green lawn hosting a large mansion.

At this moment, the bubbly ball of radiance zipped away from them towards a colossal oak tree that stood at the divide of the contrasting climates. As soon as it landed, they felt an intense surge of magical energy hit them, and they saw the mansion collapse in the distance. They rapidly paced towards the boundary, although unsure of its magical qualities and what lay beyond it. Their alertness bolted at the sudden explosion of flames that attacked the ruins of the house.

From the blaze emerged a short figure, rapidly sprinting across the field towards where Phillip, Mark, and Aisling all stood hesitantly. Upon recognizing his sister, Phillip was the first to react and urgently dashed towards her, zapping himself out of the damaged Clue that barely held them together. They both headed in the direction of the oak tree that stood between them, where the winter was cut off and springtime began. Mark and Aisling ran towards Phillip, who outpaced them with iron determination to reunite with his sister before any lurking danger could separate them once more.

All of a sudden, Kalina collapsed onto all fours, right at the oak tree. Phillip imagined that she had some sort of green aura surrounding her, but it didn't seem like it belonged to her. His sister valiantly tried to crawl, and her hand started to reach the boundary. He could tell she was in immense pain and used the rest of his energy to make one final sprint. He reached out his hand in anticipation – only a few paces away. Their fingertips were a centimeter away, and for a split second they touched.

31
LIMINAL LANDS

Mark paused to catch his breath beneath the oak tree, and Aisling soon caught up with him with the damaged Clue trailing behind her. They both witnessed Phillip and Kalina before their eyes. Mark looked around, but he couldn't see a trace of where they might have gone.

"I thought I was just about to catch up to him when he teleported," he huffed between deep breaths. "Where do you think they went?"

Aisling followed him into the pleasant warmth of the springtime realm. She couldn't answer yet since she was still gasping for breath and recovering from the cold. Mark didn't wait for her to answer, but continued his stream of consciousness.

"Why did he abandon us?" he wondered aloud. "Where could he have possibly gone? His house?"

Aisling pursed her lips thoughtfully before she answered, "I don't think he would do that intentionally. Yes, we were in a stressful situation, but he probably just did it by stimulus. You know how they test us for our aptitudes, and it feels like the magic around us is heightened to two hundred percent?"

Mark nodded in agreement, understanding where she was headed with this.

"Maybe something like that happened?" she pondered. "In any case, hopefully this plantation or whatever is somewhere outside of the Enchanted Forest. We might be safe here... or at least we won't be freezing to death."

They both calmly strode towards the blazing ruins of the mansion, planning what their next course of action would be. This time they had their phones on them, but they couldn't get a signal. Mark wasn't sure whether or not they were still in the Blue Ridge Enchanted Forest. Right now, he was telling Aisling about the signal enhancement spell that Mr. Wells had used.

Half-way across the field, however, the ever-burning fire that surrounded the collapsed house began to wicker and wave. They pulled apart to reveal a dark shadowy figure rapidly floating toward them. Mark turned to run, but Aisling's limbs were chained by the terror exuding from the ghastly figure.

"Aisling, what are you waiting for?" shouted Mark, but she was too stunned to speak. He reached out to drag Aisling by the remnant of the Clue but knew that he didn't have enough time.

The woman was close enough now that they could see it was a raggedy Ms. Dalton. Mark himself wasn't waiting around to find out what she wanted from them, and he decided to make a preemptive strike.

"*Viasynitou Anemou!*"

The spell ineffectively died out. Mark grimaced as he realized he should have learned more combative spells since his duel with Mr.

Wells. Ms. Dalton didn't even seem to notice that he had cast it. It was too late now, though, as she was directly in front of them.

"You're not much for me," she said hovering in front of Aisling, inspecting her. "But I suppose you'll have to do." She didn't even acknowledge Mark's presence. Instead, she just started waving her hands and arms, causing the grass around Aisling to burn into runes that she had never witnessed in all her studies as a scribe.

Mark wasn't having any of it, he knew he couldn't take her on by himself, so he started hissing. He remembered the strange sounds his teacher had made yesterday evening – they were etched into his heart. This time, he did catch her attention.

"Don't be silly, boy," she said. "I'm not in the mood."

Ms. Dalton snapped her fingers, and Mark tumbled forwards. It felt like he just had his breath knocked out. Meanwhile, Aisling stuck a trembling hand into her pockets, the momentary distraction once again enough for her to pull one last trick up her sleeve. She hadn't given all of the fae's magical cards to Mr. Wells, and she poured her mana into the charged slip of paper.

Once it hit its threshold for magic, it burst into sparks and transformed into a magnificent hawk made of infernal light. It rushed around the three, captivating their attention. Ms. Dalton, shocked at a flavor of druidry she hadn't seen since she was a little girl, didn't even attempt a counter-spell this time. She just sped away. The hawk descended towards her, so hot that the lawn was incinerated. In its trail, burning blades of grass smoked and spun into other predatory raptors of flame, following the target of their creator.

Aisling, free from the witchcraft of the ancient hag, was able to run away with Mark to safety. Once they got to the large oak tree, they weren't sure what to do. If they left the confines of Ms. Dalton's small realm, it would essentially be out of the frying pan and into the fire. In the distance they saw the infernal tornado of predators descend upon a spot, presumably where Ms. Dalton was. *Thank God that must be the end of her then,* thought Mark.

After a few, slow minutes, Aisling asked, "Mark, do you know where we are?"

They remained at the threshold between Ms. Dalton's realm and the Enchanted Forest.

"No, actually, but we're not in the forest. It feels more liminal than that."

Aisling followed his brooding stare beyond the oak tree, but she couldn't tell what bothered him.

"That's weird," he finally stated. "The climate looks rather temperate. There was snow before."

"Enchanted Forests can have an interesting effect on time and space," responded Aisling, regurgitating what they had studied in class.

Without asking, Mark gently held onto Aisling's hand (they had lost their pieces of Clue at this point) and cautiously reached beyond the oak tree. Aisling was too tired not to have faith in who she considered a brother and gracefully followed his lead.

After several minutes of testing the boundary, Mark finally came to a decision to cross the boundary, leading Aisling with him. The climate wasn't as nice as Ms. Dalton's pristine realm, but it was significantly more temperate than that of Northern Virginia at this time of year. At first, Aisling suggested that maybe they time-traveled into the future, but Mark corrected her.

"No, we're in the South," he informed. He closed his eyes and focused his attention on his other senses, that they might pick up some more intuition.

Aisling had always kind of thought that his aptitude was rather boring, but looking at the way it was performed changed her view of him. Her aptitude was more formulaic: write these symbols, draw these runes, use these colors, etc. He, however, had to rely on his feelings and sensations to draw conclusions that the vast majority of people would have missed.

"We are *very* far away... Not coastal. Georgia, I think." Mark moved forward and sniffed, maintaining hold of Aisling. "I *feel* like this is the right direction."

He led Aisling north through the thinner woods. The trees here were different, and the climate *did* feel warmer. Eventually, they reached a tree line, beyond which lay a tan meadow.

"It must be beautiful here in the summer," commented Aisling.

"31°30'N 84°22'W about," said Mark, who surprised himself with the accuracy of his internal GPS. *That must have been from the magical surge Aisling was talking about.* "We're definitely not in the enchanted forest anymore, but we still have to figure out how to get out of here. I wish Dean Schulz gave me one of those calling cards he gave to Phillip."

Aisling gasped in excitement and started frantically reaching into her pockets. She pulled out her wallet and said, "That reminds me.

He gave my little sister Maura a card when he interrogated her about Kalina, and then she gave it to me because she thought I could help!"

After a few seconds of digging through her wallet, she triumphantly pulled out a neat card with Detective Christie's name on it, a number, address, and an incantation that triggered a sequence of numbers that would signal where the caller was in case of an emergency.

32
THE INVESTIGATOR

Detective Christie clung to his seat, his grip tight on the helicopter's armrests as the deafening roar of the blades threatened to drown out his thoughts. He couldn't help but glance sideways, trying to steal a fleeting moment to admire the picturesque landscape unfurling below. It had taken him countless years to wrestle his fear of heights into submission, and now, suspended in the sky, he could finally savor the majestic beauty from such an elevated vantage point.

As the sprawling panorama rolled beneath him, he found himself lost in thought, tracing the intricate tapestry of hills, forests, and winding rivers that crisscrossed the Georgia landscape. His journey here had been swift and driven by a mysteriously urgent call that had interrupted an otherwise unfruitful and stressful afternoon. The coordinates provided had led him to this rural corner of America, a place far removed from his usual haunts.

The question nagging at the edges of his mind was how someone from such a random area in the deep South had managed to acquire one of his calling cards. Detective Christie's memory sifted through his extensive case history, searching for a missing puzzle piece that would explain this puzzling connection. Yet, no significant case from this region stood out in his recollection.

The best working theory he could come up with was not only considered improbable, but impossible. According to the Dean of Cardinal Key Academy, the Blue Ridge Enchanted Forest had somehow become navigable to ta few students who dared to venture within. A shiver of unease coursed through him, for if the Academy's claims were true, then one who navigated its depths could emerge anywhere it was found, carrying secrets, mysteries, and perhaps, a dire message that had summoned him this distance. The Blue Ridge Enchanted Forest was, as far as he knew, connected to the wider Appalachian Enchanted Forest ecosystem.

It was the dead of night by the time the pilot spoke through the headphones that they were approaching their destination. There was a time in the past when a young Detective Christie would have felt a little queasy being on his own, in the middle of nowhere, in the middle of the night. He had since developed an innate instinct for approaching danger or any sort of trap, and he didn't feel that there was anything to worry about.

The dean's earnest request to accompany him had been met with a firm refusal from Detective Christie. The detective explained that someone needed to remain behind to keep a vigilant eye on the school, ready to take charge in case any unforeseen events occurred. Besides, this investigation was delicate, and the dean's presence would have been more of a hindrance than a help. Detective Christie couldn't afford any distractions.

The pilot's voice crackled through his headphones, announcing their imminent arrival at their secluded and mysterious destination. Despite the dark uncertainty that lay ahead, Detective Christie's gut remained untroubled. He had a good sense of foreboding and could read the telltale signs of a trap. He *knew* that he had nothing to be worried about.

And what if there were? He coyly asked himself. A wry smile curled at the corners of his lips as he contemplated the possibility. Even if it were one, he mused, he held an unshakable advantage. He was among a select few on the entire continent who possessed not just a license, but mastery of true combat magic. Not that watered-down, wishy-washy classroom dueling that some schools offered as an elective (and even those were generous descriptions). At fifty years of age, and a detective of almost thirty years, there was nothing under the sun that could truly catch him off guard.

The helicopter landed with a gentle thud onto a clear, grassy knoll, and Detective Christie was pleased to finally be on land. Almost immediately, two figures were rushing towards him. He instinctively tensed into a defensive position, but a second glance revealed to him who they were.

One of the figures sported a crimson Cardinal Key Academy hoodie, adorned with the school's distinctive crest and colors – an unmistakable identifier that these were indeed students, likely the ones the dean had mentioned.

The helicopter's rotor blades slowed to a stop, and the students, a young girl and a boy, brusquely came before the detective.

"We're so glad you were able to make it!" said the girl with the untamed ginger curls. "We were starting to lose hope that our message didn't reach you."

Detective Christie *knew* how to read people's tone and body language, and these two students were genuinely distressed. He was concerned at the heavy burden the young boy carried in his heart. It was important he escort them back to Virginia, but for now, his primary pursuit was answers.

"Alright," began Detective Christie with a matter-of-fact tone. "Let's start at the beginning. Who are you?"

"My name is Aisling," declared the girl. "I'm Maura's sister. You got to meet her twice. First, when you met her at the appearance of Samantha Hastings, then earlier today when Kalina was reported missing. That's when she gave me her extra card."

The answer seemed to please Detective Christie, who slowly nodded his head before turning to the boy.

"I'm Mark," he said tersely, with much suspicion.

Detective Christie watched Mark's eyes astutely navigate his body like he was examining him. Detective Christie didn't even bat an eye for it; years in the business had honed his ability to keep his true thoughts and emotions concealed. He couldn't help but think to himself, *with a stare like that, this kid might just have the makings of a fine detective.*

Detective Christie took a deep breath. What they said made sense, and more importantly, what they said was the truth. "And I'm assuming you ended up here because you were traversing the Appalachian Enchanted Forest?"

"Yes," said Aisling. "We've been working on researching how to travel through it this semester."

Ah, so I was right. These are *the students Dean Schulz was talking about – and he wasn't exaggerating on their success if they were actually able to get out at all.*

Aisling continued, her voice earnest, "We're friends with Phillip, Kalina's brother. That's why when we heard she was kidnapped, we thought we could navigate the Enchanted Forest again as a team to track her down, and we did!"

Detective Christie raised an intrigued eyebrow at the claim. "You mean to tell me that you were not only able to make your way through an Enchanted Forest, but you were also able to locate the exact person you were searching for?" He let his words linger for a dramatic moment before finishing. "Impressive. So, where are they now? Can you guide us back to the spot where you found Kalina?"

"Wait...," said Aisling. "Kalina and Phillip haven't shown up yet? Phillip's a traveler, he should have been able to teleport back to Cardinal Key! The anchor worked last time, and we didn't move it!"

Detective Christie put a hand on Aisling, who was speaking a mile a minute at this point. He certainly didn't want to bring the girl back to Virginia in a hysterical state. For now, he cast a strong gaze at the boy – *Mark.* He was a tough shell to crack, but Detective Christie preferred the calmer ones because their testimonies were more accurate and helpful.

Mark shook his head thoughtfully. "We *were* hoping that you would have news on where Phillip and Kalina were. As for where we found Kalina, the woman who took her – Ms. Dalton – she had somehow been able to build an estate on the boundary of the Enchanted Forest. I don't know how."

Mark intentionally left out the part where the disgraced teacher attacked them. If he had done so, they would have to explain how they escaped. The detective wouldn't be gullible enough to buy a story of them just running away or fighting her off. He would *have* to know they used combat magic, and with the stench of blood magic on Mark's and Aisling's hands, he couldn't deal with that at the moment.

While Detective Christie did believe that the students believed what they were telling him was true, there were some parts of their story that were unbelievable. Certain cracks in their retelling that just didn't add up. It was his nature to be suspicious, but he didn't want to lose their trust just yet.

"And how were you able to navigate the forest?" he asked in an exaggeratedly innocent tone.

Mark's heart skipped a beat when he heard the question. The idea that they might have been talking to a telepath scared him. Even though the magical governing authorities aren't technically legally allowed to use telepathic force to gain information, they had been known in the past to break the law.

The girl with the bright red hair struck a quick, anxious glance at her companion, who was doing a good job of remaining nonchalant. It was a micro expression, but Detective Christie only needed a fraction of a second to catch it.

"I used an advance footprint tracking spell," answered Mark, without missing a beat. He figured that he would have to come up with something eventually, and this was one of the better excuses he came up with in his head. "I have a navigation aptitude, and I retraced our steps before they faded away."

This was the first lie that the students had told him, which made him even more suspicious. The students seemed to perceive that he caught on to their lie, and the girl changed the subject.

"Would you be able to take us back to school, please, sir?"

"Yes, but we're going to need to stop on the way for gas. We'll take the helicopter back to Head Quarters, and from there we'll drive to Cardinal Key Academy. It might take a couple of days."

It would have been easy to strike anxiety and fear into them, but it was unnecessary. There were already too many questions to be answered now. Where did Kalina and Phillip go? What happened to Ms. Dalton? These two students were his best leads right now, and he didn't want to risk cutting them off.

33
REENROLLMENT

Kalina's eyesight blurred momentarily, and the world swirled in disarray as she tried to stand up, making her nauseous and bewildered. This was the first time Phillip had ever teleported her anywhere, and she was feeling the consequences. She lay belly down on a cold, marble floor for a little bit until the disorientation settled. When her eyes sharpened, she sat up and looked around. Around her was a labyrinth of books on shelves and in piles – she had never seen so many in one place before. There were even medieval looking scrolls, and ancient jewelry sprawling all over the ground, but Phillip was nowhere to be seen. *That's odd*, she thought to herself. *Phillip wouldn't have just abandoned me in some random place. Where is he? Where am I?*

Once Kalina was confident that her vertigo had completely subsided, she stood up and walked around for a little bit. She didn't want to explore too far because she was worried that if Phillip came back for her, he might not know where she had gone.

She peered through the shelves and saw many strange names for a variety of books. There seemed to be an infinite number of all sorts of them. *How Colored Pencils led to the American Great Depression, The History of Uncountable Numbers,* etc.

From a pile, she picked up a book titled *The Astrological Symbolism of Pocket Watches*, and skimmed through it before realizing that she was far too tired to read at the moment and sat back down.

After a while of waiting, she began circling the shelves again and exploring a wider area. She found desks, pens, tables, and all sorts of things, but she always circled back to where she was. Suddenly, a man came out from behind one of the bookshelves, surprising Kalina, who made a small yelp.

"Peace to you," he said. Kalina thought he was remarkably handsome, especially the way he was dressed. It looked like he had just walked out of one of the icons she was used to seeing at church. He was tall and had dark, wavy hair that reached his shoulders, green eyes, and a golden, smooth complexion. He was dressed in exquisite Byzantine robes.

"Are you an angel?" asked Kalina. "Am I dead?"

The man roared in laughter. "No, I am not an angel," he replied, trying to stifle his laughter. "My name is Athanasios, I come from Rome."

"Athanasios like the saint?"

"Yes, that's who I'm named after."

"If you're from Rome, then are you Catholic or Orthodox?"

The man gave her a confused look. "Verily, are they not one and the same? Yet, I discern that you are a newcomer here, a conclusion easily drawn given the youthful countenance you present.

"I was just in the Enchanted Forest. Where am I?"

"You're in the archive section of the void. You are not a traveler are you? How did you end up here?"

"My brother is a traveler, but I'm a clairvoyant," answered Kalina. "He had just saved me from a woman who kidnapped me. I'm trying to go home."

"And where is that?" asked Athanasios. "I might be able to direct you back to where you came from."

"I'm from Virginia."

"You're going to need to be more specific. Not only do I need to know an exact delineation of whence you came, but also from when you came."

The more Kalina conversed with the man, the more she understood what was happening. Her aptitude powered the gears in her brain, connecting them all into one smooth function. She was unsettled that she couldn't predict or discern as much as she normally could, but she attributed that to the fact that she was in what Athanasios called "the void."

"Oh, I see. You can't really help me after all, can you? I have to find my way back by myself."

"Now you see," replied the man with a smile. "I will walk with you back home just to make sure you do not lose yourself. Is that alright?"

Kalina appreciated the man's help, and she led him through a maze of bookshelves. Eventually, they came across a wall with a bronze door set in it. She turned to look at the man once more.

"One more note of importance," said Athanasios. "You have an aptitude that is not just psychic, but noetic. I will let you consider that."

"Thank you. Well, this is where I leave you," she said. "Good-bye."

"God be with you," he answered and watched as she opened the door and stepped through it.

Kalina braced herself to teleport again, but this time, the journey was a lot less chaotic. In her defense, she wasn't expecting to be teleported last time, *and* she had just escaped a black witch.

She turned around to look back at Athanasios, but she no longer saw the door. In its place was an old pine tree. She still wasn't sure where she was, but she could tell she was no longer in "the void." Her mind calmed down so that she could activate her aptitude to find her way back to school. She was still in the Blue Ridge Enchanted Forest, but it seemed as though she kept the gift that the angel –no, the *demon* – had given her, allowing her to find her way back to the academy.

She could only imagine how worried everyone must be, and she felt it important to return as fast as possible. By now, Phillip had probably teleported back to school, and she needed to let him and her parents know that she was safe.

Immediately, she could sense the capricious spirit of the Enchanted Forest, but she was able to sway it to her benefit. If there was one good thing that came out of Ms. Dalton's mentorship was the lost knowledge to communicate with the primordial entities that constituted the Blue Ridge Enchanted Forest.

Speaking of Ms. Dalton, what happened to her? wondered Kalina to herself. *Will she come back for me? Who will be her next victim?* Internally, Kalina started to make plans and use her aptitude to make predictions. However, she had to put this aside for now because she needed to focus on where she was headed.

It didn't take her too long to make her way out of the forest and find the school, but the atmosphere was different. For the first time she noticed that it was warmer. Northern Virginia weather was like this though. It would snow one day, and the next day it would be a balmy seventy degrees outside.

Although it was late afternoon on a Saturday, there were no students to be seen or heard. There was also a reinforced fence now acting as a barrier to the woods, *likely in response to what happened to me,* guessed Kalina.

She decided that her first stop would be to head to the mess hall for some well-deserved food – she was starving after almost a whole day of not having anything to eat or drink. Afterwards, she would find the dean.

When she got to the mess hall, however, the doors were locked, which was unusual. Normally the mess hall was open most of the day during the weekends. Kalina decided to change course and find the dean instead, but all the doors to the school were locked. She went to the dormitories – also locked. She walked around the school campus aimlessly looking for anyone. From all the hiking, she found herself sweating like a pig, so she took her cardigan off when finally, she heard a voice call out behind her.

"What are you doing here? Students aren't supposed to come back from break until tomorrow!"

Kalina turned around and enthusiastically ran up to the familiar woman.

"Mrs. Donna! Where is everyone? Is the school on lockdown?"

She saw her dorm mother's jaw drop and her eyebrows shoot upwards. She could see the shock in the whites of her eyes.

"Kalina! How did you get here? Are you okay? Where have you been? I have to call your parents! We have to go see the dean!" she spoke rapidly without hesitation or taking a breath.

"Ms. Dalton kidnapped me, but I'm okay. Phillip, Mark, and Aisling found me and saved me."

"We know what happened, but that was over a month ago! Where have you been since?"

Her hard words hit Kalina like a brick. If she had been missing for that long, her parents and brother probably thought she was dead. Tears began to swell in her eyes and drip down her cheeks.

"Come on honey, you must be starving. I'll take you to the kitchens and you can call your parents. We'll get Dean Schulz and Detective Christie to come while you have some supper."

The first person Mrs. Donna called was Catherine Todorova, who was crying with joy when she heard Kalina's voice. Both she and Mr. Todorova immediately got in the car and headed straight to Cardinal Key Academy.

"We thought we had lost both you and Phillip forever," she said with a shaky breath.

"Wait, what exactly do you mean 'lost both me and Phillip'?" asked Kalina, concerned

"You don't know?" replied a startled Catherine. "You *both* had disappeared over a month ago. Only Aisling and Mark were ever found."

Kalina was surprised to learn this about her brother. She had just assumed that he would have been able to teleport to safety. She closed her eyes and used her aptitude to try to pinpoint his location, but she couldn't at the moment. However, her logic was still sound: if her brother had been able to push her somewhere else – both spatially and temporally, it's possible he might have accidentally done the same to himself. Kalina's education told her this was impossible, even for magi, but recent events had just proved otherwise. She was a living example of the laws of nature and magic being broken.

"Whatever happens to him, I'm sure he'll be okay," assured Kalina, who had the utmost faith in her older brother. If he *were* dead or severely injured, she would know – she was certain of this. This was a mystery to be solved in the near future, she thought to herself. In the meantime, she would have to be strong for her parents.

34
THE EASTER RETURN

A deluge of students, teachers, and staff flooded the Cardinal Key auditorium at the behest of Dean Schulz. Although it was customary for a grand speech to unfold after break or at the end of the year, most students had the idea that there was something special about this morning. Whispers floated through the student body, carrying rumors of a student returning to school.

Kalina herself was nervous about the forthcoming announcements, since she already knew for a fact that she was going to be thrust into the limelight. She hated having too much attention, but she was glad to see all her friends were healthy. Likewise, her friends were absolutely ecstatic to see her. She couldn't yet explain to them that what was forty days for the whole school was only a matter of hours for her. She wasn't even sure that a whole day had lapsed since she ventured into the woods with Ms. Dalton.

Maura and Laurelle flanked Kalina's sides into the auditorium as they navigated through the cascade of students, protecting her from the onslaught of students trying to catch a glimpse of her. One would have thought they had seen someone rise from the dead, and for all they knew, she did.

Dean Schulz, hailing from a lineage of Prussian nobility, held an unwavering commitment to punctuality that rivaled the precision of a Swiss watch. His aristocratic bearing echoed through the halls of the school, demanding the same behavior from his staff and students. When the clock struck eight, his authoritative voice silenced the student body and began the anticipated announcement.

"Ladies and gentlemen," he commenced with a dignified air. "I understand that there have been rumors circulating with regards to a student who will be returning to school. Allow me to clarify – such speculations are misguided and false."

Murmurs and whispers rippled through the assembly. Many had already caught a glimpse of Kalina and were left puzzled by the dean's seemingly contradictory statement. A sea of perplexed faces gawked at Dean Schulz, who was waiting patiently for the students to calm down. With a hint of a smile on his face, he knew the insatiable curiosity of his students wouldn't be able to resist the allure of his words.

"As a matter of fact," he continued. "We are not welcoming *a* student back, but *two* students! Just the other day, I received news that Robert Nelson has woken up from his coma."

This time, the whole auditorium exploded in a symphony of cheers and applause – a standing ovation for the health and safety of two of their beloved classmates.

The dean waited a few minutes for the joyous applause to calm down before continuing in a firmer tone. "I would like to remind everyone that both Kalina and Robert will bear a considerable amount of stress during their return. They have a lot of catching up to do, and I am requesting that their privacy be well respected. They are *not* exhibits at a carnival to be gawked at or questioned. *Do I make myself clear?*"

The students somberly groaned, "yes" in agreement. They knew better than to make the dean angry. Afterwards, Dean Schulz continued the announcement with less exciting updates and reminders of school policies. Once he finished, the students grabbed their backpacks and headed to their first period classes.

Kalina and her friends stuck together as they headed out of the noisy auditorium. She had a lot of questions on her mind, but since none of them could hear anything amidst the roaring flood of students, they decided to save their conversation for outside.

"Who's been teaching your classes since I disappeared?" asked Kalina, who felt it strange to talk about herself in such terms. Of course she never disappeared from herself, just from everybody else. "Obviously, it hasn't been Ms. Dalton."

"Yeah, no one knows for sure what happened to her," replied Laurelle. "For now, Dean Schulz has taken the reins. He's okay, but not as much fun, though."

Laurelle tensed up when those last words slipped her lips, remembering what happened to her friend. Kalina just laughed at her friend and said, "It's fine, I know what you mean. She was skilled at her craft; that's how she was able to manipulate me and all of her other victims so effectively."

"She had us all fooled," Laurelle admitted with a trace of rueful regret.

"Not me," claimed Maura staunchly. "I knew there was something up with her from the beginning. Ever since the first day of class."

Laurelle rolled her eyes. "That's because you were convinced she had something against you."

To their surprise, Kalina answered in agreement with Maura's sentiments. "Actually, Maura was right all along. Your intuition must have kicked in after the incident with Samantha Hastings. She was a past victim of Dalton's. She kept her alive because she was doing experiments on her. You see, Samantha Hasting had a very unique aptitude: cellular regeneration, which allowed her to heal quickly and age slowly. That explains why she was so afraid when she saw Dalton. That's why when Dalton reached her, she fainted. It wasn't a mere accident."

Both Maura and Laurelle gasped with newfound understanding. The school staff and the detectives that had addressed the students only gave a partial disclosure based on what they thought the students needed to know.

"Maybe I'm a psychic!" exclaimed Maura, who was now justified. "Maybe that's how I knew about all this!"

Kalina and Laurelle chuckled at Maura despite the darkness of their discussion.

"Don't laugh! I'm being serious. At the very least, I hope I get an aptitude this year. Did you know that Aisling didn't get an aptitude until seventh grade? My parents were *not* happy about that."

As they arrived to class, the three students talked about aptitudes and who they thought was going to get one next month. Of course Kalina could know if she wanted to, but she didn't want to reveal her power level to everyone yet. She wondered what that Byzantine (Roman) man had meant by her powers being noetic and not psychic. *Is that what Sister Maryam meant by saying, "Your talents are beyond what you are aware of?"*

35
ROBERT MEETS KALINA

Kalina sat in a deep meditation against one of the tulip trees that was beginning to blossom. Her knees were against her chest and her head hung low. She looked like she was crying or upset, but she wasn't.

"I knew I'd find you here," said a deep masculine voice beside her.

Kalina stood up to greet Robert. Charismatically, she leaned against the tree. She had been waiting for him to find her, but for now she let the cards play out.

"I heard you went missing, and..." his voice trailed off, leaving an opening for her to continue for him.

"And you wanted to ask me about it. About what happened. About what you saw," she finished for him. He was clearly not expecting her knowledge and comprehension of what happened.

"How did you know? Are you a telepath also?" he asked.

Kalina shrugged before giving him a vague answer. "In a way I was in her head also," she said. "Dalton had stretched herself too thin."

Robert twisted his lips in a mix of emotions. "Her birth name was Carannóg. She and her gang... they're pure evil."

Kalina raised an eyebrow. "It looks like you might have some information that I don't."

Robert shook his head before elaborating, "I lived in her head... and she lived in mine for almost half a year. She was a tough fighter, but I'm strong. I'm more powerful than she expected."

Kalina nodded in empathy. She could understand Robert's frustration that so much time had been stolen from him. Thank God he was as powerful as he was. Everyone knew it, but Kalina's aptitude allowed her to actually sense it.

Sympathetically, she sighed, "She wasn't trying to kill you, just stop you."

"Don't be silly, she didn't care if I died, but I'm tougher than she expected. The question is: stop me from what? I know she's awful, but I never understood why me? It was just so random. Why would you attack somebody who got knocked out during a football game?"

"Don't you see?" asked Kalina. "She's the one who tampered with the wards. Everyone knows that you're the most powerful telepath the continent has seen in over two centuries. There were rumors spreading around that you were going to wake up Samantha Hastings."

"Who?"

"Haven't you spoken to Aisling or Mark yet?" wondered Kalina. *Surely, they or Dr. Toumi should have filled him in by now.*

"No...," he muttered hesitantly with a downcast gaze. "It's just been so awkward. I know she and Mark got *close* while I was in the coma, and I know how he feels about her. I don't make it a habit to poke inside people's heads, but sometimes I can't help it. I don't know what might have happened while I was gone, and I'm afraid to find out. I have no idea how she's changed, and I don't even know about the future of our relationship." He took a deep sigh, and brushed some hair back.

Kalina licked and pursed her lips. This was not the reaction she was expecting or wanted. Right here was the most popular kid in school. Football player, powerful magus, genuinely intelligent and friendly with everyone. And now he was in front of Kalina pouring his feelings out. She simply didn't know how to handle the situation.

"Well," began Kalina, hoping that the words would come to her if she just started talking. "Let's take a walk." She took off in the direction that Robert came from, and he obliged her.

"Where are we headed," he asked.

"You'll find out," she replied mysteriously.

Robert was quiet for a long moment, and Kalina felt his presence in her head.

"I thought you said you don't make it a habit to poke inside people's heads," she accused.

"I've gotten a lot stronger since dealing with that witch, but you don't have anything to worry about. Your mind is iron; I can't break through."

"I know," she replied.

"Are you a psychic like me," he asked. "I know you haven't been tested for your aptitudes yet, but I already knew mine beforehand. I was able to read people's thoughts and move things with my mind when I was six."

"It's better not to speculate on such things," answered Kalina, who wanted to keep her abilities a secret. Other magi for the most part could discern that she had some psychic abilities, which is fine. However, if the specifications of her aptitude were revealed, she would be in danger – just like she was a target of Ms. Dalton's. Instead of leaving Robert hanging though, she changed the subject. "We're going to meet Mark and Aisling because we need their help to find Phillip."

"Yeah, I heard he was missing, but I don't know where I would find him. I was planning on working with Dr. Toumi to see if he could help me set up a sensory deprivation bath so that I could do a global search for him."

"Something tells me you won't find him there," replied Kalina. When Robert gave her a confused look, she just said, "Let's go find Mark and Aisling. Many of our questions will be answered then."

Robert clearly wasn't enthused about the idea of meeting his (ex?) girlfriend and the guy who had a crush on her, but he was able to push these feelings aside for the sake of a new quest.

Kalina and Robert strolled across the field to the library. It was a weird experience for Robert, who wasn't sure about Kalina or how she knew where to find everyone. He didn't know anything about her except that they had a shared experience being targets of Dalton. To him, she was just a sixth grade kid, but she spoke and strode with the confidence of a master magus.

"So," he tried to start small talk. "Are you excited about getting your aptitude next month?"

"No," she said honestly. "I already know what I am."

"Do you think you're a physicist or a psychic?"

"I didn't say I *'think'* I know what I am. I said I *'know'* what I am."

Robert tried peering into her head again to see exactly what she meant, but she was still blocking him. This was unusual – sometimes trained magi like Dr. Toumi could keep him out, but this was an untrained twelve-year-old. He thought for a second, and then it dawned on him.

"Oh, I see, you *are* a psychic. You're a clairvoyant."

"Sure," replied Kalina, who sounded annoyed at having to have this conversation a second time and was furthermore annoyed that he actually got a piece of information out of her.

They entered the library and scanned the shelves for Aisling and Mark. Kalina didn't have to search too long. They were in their typical spot, the only atypical aspect being the absence of Phillip. Kalina strode up to the pair, mustering all her confidence – she would not be kicked out this time. Robert on the other hand seemed less sure of himself.

"Hey, Aisling... Mark," he greeted.

"Hi."

"Hey."

The whole interaction was awkward. Kalina felt awkward. The three high schoolers felt awkward, even Mark.

"Hey, Aisling. Hey, Mark," said Kalina, breaking the tense silence.

"Hi, Kalina," responded Aisling. "I'm sorry I haven't spoken to you about Phillip since you... got back. We tried searching for him for a while, but we got ordered to stand down. Besides, Mark and I have both been busy with classes."

"That's alright, and thanks for coming to rescue me from Dalton. I appreciate that." She tried her best to sound sincere. "Speaking of Phillip, that's why I'm here. We need to find him."

"Aisling and I have actually been discussing some theories, but now that you've returned most of them have gone down the drain. We thought you two would be together. Where *did* you go for over a month?" asked Mark.

"Well that's just the thing," enlightened Kalina. "I didn't go anywhere. I came straight back to school. Do you know what that means? Phillip can travel through time, and he probably sent himself to a different time period."

This was the part Kalina was most afraid of. Although Aisling had a reputation for being rather "open-minded," Kalina was still worried that she might be ridiculed for saying something they were all taught was impossible. To her delight, she took her suggestion seriously and nodded her head.

"That actually makes a lot of sense. We didn't even think to touch on that, but we exhausted pretty much all other options," replied Mark. "When do you think he went?"

"I honestly have no idea yet," responded Kalina.

They all sat in silence trying to come up with a hypothesis, but they were all drawing blanks. Even Aisling wasn't coming up with anything, and she always had theories for mysteries.

"This is racking my brain!" exclaimed Aisling loud enough to receive a glare from the librarian.

"That's okay," said Kalina in a low voice. "It will come to us when necessary."

"What about Dalton?" inserted Robert. "They never caught her. What are we going to do about her? We can't just let her get away!"

"We didn't," asserted Mark. "There's no way she could have survived."

"Well she did," countered Robert aggressively. "I can still feel her presence on the psychic plane."

"Maybe it's a ghost?" suggested Aisling, trying to ease the situation. "I cast the spell and watched her die, too."

"No," stated Kalina, who was now staring out the window with glossy eyes. "You injured her gravely, but you didn't kill her. I have a feeling we'll be seeing her again."

"Her and her friends," added Robert.

Kalina turned to look back at Robert, while Aisling and Mark exchanged looks.

"Want to share with the class?" asked Mark.

"I was able to get a lot of information while we were in each other's heads, but she's part of this old cabal. They're from different parts of the world – "

"And different times," interjected Kalina. "Dalton was over two-thousand years old."

Mark and Aisling were surprised at Kalina's information. There were certain magi known to have extended life periods (there was a dean who lived to be three centuries old), but for someone to be thousands of years old was unheard of. They returned their gazes to Robert, signaling for him to continue.

"I didn't catch all their names, but the head of the group was a woman named Dido, from some Phoenician city – Carthage, I think. Another was a man... he was Semitic, the Levant? Another was named Samuel, from Hispania. The fifth was from the Renaissance, but I didn't catch his name. The sixth is Rachel, the youngest, born in America. I know they do vile things, but I can't quite determine their goal."

"I can help with that," continued Kalina. "I met a past victim – Edith. I think that Ms. Dalton wanted her to join their cabal, but she refused. It seems as though Ms. Dalton was kidnapping us to steal our magic and our youth."

"But how come Samantha Hastings is still alive, then?" interrupted Aisling. "And how was she able to leave the forest?"

"I'm not entirely sure, but I can make a pretty good guess," answered Kalina. "Samantha Hastings was simply more useful alive. Ms. Dalton told me that she experimented on some of the girls she had kidnapped. I think Hastings might have been one of those girls."

"Cellular regeneration," remembered Aisling. "That's disgusting."

"I have some more info on that," began Robert. "When I woke up from my coma, so did she, and her mind is a mess. It's absolutely broken. They're moving her to the psychiatric wing, but Dr. Toumi is still going to check up on her. As for how she would be able to traverse the Enchanted Forest in that state is still a mystery to me."

Kalina shook her head somberly, "If I had to guess, Ms. Dalton did something to her to make her like that. I wonder if I would have become like that, too."

Kalina remembered that she herself, through Ms. Dalton's scheme, had become able to traverse the Enchanted Forest. She didn't voice her concern with the others, but she secretly wondered what this meant for her own mental state. Would she become as broken and lost as Samantha? Or maybe she would become as evil and black as Dalton. Who knew what the price of knowledge was.

36
THE RECRUITMENT

After what felt like an especially frigid winter, the spring finally warmed the gardens at the Virginia Magical Burgess, bringing it renewed life. Many of the people who worked here loved to eat outside this time of year, and the tables were enchanted to repel bugs.

Norman Poitier was one such person, who sat by himself at a table at a bench by a little stream where he watched the koi fish meander under the flowering dogwood trees. Usually, he would like to talk about politics or current events with a colleague or a close friend, but today he was rather tired from all the work he'd been receiving. He tossed a piece of bread from his sandwich to the koi and watched them race for it.

"Hello, Captain Poitier," greeted an unmistakable and unforgettable voice.

"I haven't been a captain in quite a while. How can I help you, Detective Christie?" he responded.

"Haven't you heard the news? That Kalina girl has finally showed up, and the football player has just woken up from his coma. Even more interesting, so did Hastings, even though she's been transferred to the psychiatric ward."

Although the news did surprise him, Norman Poitier turned his head deliberately to face Detective Christie, who was taking a seat across from him.

"And what about Phillip? Any news about him?"

Detective Christie looked down and shook his head.

"We're not sure where he could have gone, but we've been working globally to pick up any information. Apparently when he got tested for his aptitude, he teleported all the way to London."

"Yes, I've heard that story. He and my son are best friends."

"It's a good thing, too, otherwise we couldn't have gotten our hands on that recording they gave you. How do you think your son got himself into this?"

Mr. Poitier took a deep breath while shaking his head. Although he was impressed Mark and his friends had taken some initiative, he was worried about the potential danger and trouble his son had gotten himself into.

"I don't know. Mark isn't typically a troublemaker, but Aisling has been known to be a bit... impulsive. Still, Mark's a good kid."

"Oh absolutely," replied Detective Christie. "And I wasn't implying that he was a trouble-maker. In fact, I think he might have what it takes to become a detective for the Courts."

Norman Poitier scoffed lightly at the compliment.

"Did you come all the way here to sweet talk me about my son?" he asked sarcastically.

"No, I've been asked to assemble a team, and I want you to be a part of it because of your son and his friends. I've been combing through the information they've collected and sharing it with our friends globally and they've found similar patterns of kids being abducted. We think there might be some sort of cabal."

Mr. Poitier raised an eyebrow. *Those kids really got themselves into something this time* he thought to himself. *The best way to protect Mark now would be to join.*

"That sounds like a plan, and I'm glad my translation of the recording was useful."

"If anyone could decipher an extinct ancient language, it would be you, but it still raises more questions. Clearly Dalton was involved in some sort of group, of which she was not the senior member."

"You're right, it was the other woman – the one who was scolding her. It's good that Dalton didn't listen to her. If she had, she would be half way across the world and no one would know about her. Clearly her recklessness made her standing in the group shaky, not that it matters now."

"It does, but we'll talk about it when you come into work to meet the team next week," finished Detective Christie, who stood up to depart.

"One more thing," said Norman Poitier. "It's about my son. I don't want him to be involved in this. It sounds like it's far more dangerous than we realized at first."

Detective Christie nodded in understanding. "Of course not. No more kids need to be involved in this."

The two magi gave each other nods and a handshake at the end of the conversation and went in opposite directions. There was no need for Norman Poitier to give his boss a notice, for all the office knew, he was just moving to a different department in Richmond.

37
THE APTITUDE TEST

The rest of the year was going by swimmingly. Robert and Aisling had mutually decided to split up, but he still had his teammates to support him. Because he had practically missed more than half a school year, he was told that he would need to redo it. On the other hand, Kalina was able to catch up with her peers at lightning speed.

Kalina, despite being the youngest, took the reins on the operation of finding Phillip and Dalton, and she told everyone to stand down for now. Aisling and Mark were comforted by her return in the first place, and they trusted her opinion. She and Robert, having the shared experience of being Dalton's victims, became closer and closer, and he began to view her as a younger sister.

"Did you know we're cousins?" asked Kalina as Robert walked her to the laboratory.

"Don't change the subject. Getting tested for your aptitude is extremely important," he replied.

"I don't think I can do it, even if it's part of our grade. What if I hurt Dean Schulz?"

"I doubt it – he's tougher than he looks for all that aristocratic exterior. And you don't even need to get a result. You just have to show up!"

Kalina was shaking her head in anxiety.

"It's too dangerous. I'll have to figure something out. You're the only one I trust with this."

Robert gravely nodded his head.

"I understand," he continued sincerely. "But you're going to have to figure something out. I have to leave you now, but you can find me at the stadium when you're done."

"Thanks anyways," sighed Kalina.

She walked towards the doors to double check the time she was signed up for – 10:00 AM, another four minutes. She went to sit down on the bench across the entrance. No sooner had her dress touched the cushion did another girl, who she recognized as a seventh grader, come out with Dr. Toumi.

"I can't believe I got one this year!" exclaimed the girl ecstatically. "My parents are going to be so happy!"

"Congratulations, Agnes. Why don't you go call your parents and tell them the news?" said Dr. Toumi.

Agnes sprinted down the hallway, and before Dr. Toumi could tell her not to, she was out of the building and out of sight.

"Hello, Kalina, how are you?" he asked. Kalina had always found his Syrian accent comforting, perhaps because her own father had an Old World accent himself.

"I'm well, but I think I might have a problem."

"If it's about your aptitude test, then you should be fine. Come on in," he said. He motioned her to enter, and she couldn't really deny him. "A lot of students get nervous when it's their turn to find out what their aptitude is. But I assure you, no matter what, you'll turn out fine. Even if you don't have one."

Kalina entered the room, which had been cleared out for the tests. In one corner was a table that had various knick-knacks on it – herbs, toys, and even a caged rabbit. No one ever spoke of the aptitude test, and there were different ways to conduct one, so Kalina had no idea what to expect. The room was dark as all the curtains and blinds had been closed. Only a few candles and a lightbulb illuminated the space. Dean Schulz was sitting at a desk at the far end filling out paperwork.

"Hello, Kalina," he smiled at her. "Are you ready for your test? If you're anything like your brother, we'll be in for quite a surprise."

"Well..." began Kalina, but she wasn't sure how to explain her situation to the dean.

"I think Kalina is a little bit worried about the test," answered Dr. Toumi for her, causing Dean Schulz to cast a perplexed look.

"It's not that," said Kalina. "I can't do it. It's too dangerous and I don't want to hurt anyone."

Dr. Toumi grinned, but Dean Schulz burst out into laughter.

"I'm serious!"

"Kalina, we have been present for many students' aptitudes, and I'm still standing," stated Dean Schulz. "If I hadn't been here, Robert Nelson probably would have blown up this building! But it's still standing, and so am I. Whatever your aptitude is, everyone will be safe."

"What if I already know what it is?" challenged Kalina.

"Oh, so you're a psychic," said Dr. Toumi enthusiastically. "That's a start."

Kalina shook her head. "No, it's more than that."

"Well can you tell us?" prompted Dean Schulz, but Kalina shook her head still. "I'm sorry, Kalina, but I can't give you a passing grade unless you take the test."

Kalina stared for a moment in Dean Schulz' eyes, unsure of what to do now. She couldn't yet control her aptitude, so scaring the dean was off the table. She could see many paths that lay ahead of her – showing off her precognitive abilities, refusing plainly, even trying to bribe her way out of it. None of them ended well for anybody involved. The only path she could not decipher was one where she actually took the test, so she relented.

"Fine, but don't say I didn't warn you," she sighed heavily.

Dr. Toumi gave her an encouraging smile and led her to a chair while Dean Schulz began the spell. He didn't speak at all, but was twisting and moving his hands, occasionally muttering under his breath. Once, he had to look down at a sheet of paper, presumably there to remind him of any parts he had forgotten.

Kalina was able to decipher some of what he was doing. The room was magically sealed, and her sense of magic was heightened. Dr. Toumi stepped away to a cage and brought her a small, furry animal.

"You should have learned about these in your class," he said.

"Yes," replied Kalina. "*Sylvilagus marginialia*... They were bred in the states for experiments, right? I didn't know we used them to test for aptitudes."

"We try to keep the process hidden so that the results don't get skewed," explained Dean Schulz.

Kalina held the fuzzy creature in her lap and started caressing it. She couldn't tell the difference between the magical beast and a regular rabbit. She stroked its long ears, wondering if it had a name.

"Mmmm.... Oh yes, right there," moaned the rabbit.

Kalina shrieked and tossed the rabbit down.

"The rabbit just spoke to me!" she yelled. "What does that mean?"

"Very interesting," said Dr. Toumi while Dean Schulz was whispering notes to himself in the corner. "We haven't gotten anyone with a talking rabbit in a while. That's a psychic outcome, right?"

"Hmm," responded Dean Schulz. "I think so, but we'll have to double check the book. You can give her the elemental test now while I continue. You can resume your seat, Miss Todorova."

Kalina sat back down, and Dr. Toumi resumed the test. He brought her various random objects and asked her a few questions. Although there were no more animals, there were some plants she was asked to hold.

"Thank you for being so patient, Kalina," said Dean Schulz after about twenty minutes. "There's just one more part to the test before you can go."

He strode before her, with his hands behind his back. She thought he looked domineering and confident. Quickly, he took out a spray bottle and squirted something pungent in her face."

Kalina had already started to get frustrated with what she thought was a ridiculous trial. Now angry and in shock, Kalina shot up, and with a resonant voice demanded, **"Enough!"**

She recognized the sound, it was similar to (if not as powerful as) the voice she used when she incanted against Dalton. She wasn't sure if she would ever be able to achieve that kind of power level again, but the spell wasn't over. The curtains opened and the sunlight filled the whole room. It was splendid but terrifying, causing Dr. Toumi and Dean Schulz to collapse to their knees.

Back to her normal voice, she stated "This test is over!" and left the building.

That split second of heightened power was all she needed to perceive and discern the entire life stories of Dean Schulz and Dr. Toumi. It was brutal, and she didn't know how long it would take for them to recover. She felt like she had stripped them naked – how would she be able to look at them the same way again? She knew all their secrets and passions and desires. She knew how they were born and how they would die. She knew –

"So how did it go?" asked a voice from behind her, interrupting her thoughts. When she saw it was Robert, she gave a forced smile.

"As expected," she replied with a shrug. "I thought I was going to meet you at the stadium."

"Well, I thought that you might need some company after the test. Tell me about it while we walk?"

Kalina was glad that there was someone else who could under-stand her, especially since Phillip was gone. She had her friends, but she wasn't even sure that she could trust them. Robert was different, though, and he was powerful. He knew the burden that she was under.

38
OLD HABITS

Kalina was finally glad to be home. The last quarter of school was extremely stressful for her since she had an extra month of catching up to do. On top of that, she had finals to worry about.

Normally, the family had dinner together, but Kalina's mom just ordered some food to go. Kalina was told she could eat in the car, and her mom hadn't even ordered anything for herself. The disappearance of Phillip had really taken a toll on the both of them, and Kalina noticed that her mother looked rather emaciated.

They got home late, which was also atypical, and the first thing Kalina did was go to her room. She was tired and wanted some privacy. It had been a while since she prayed, so she went to her corner and did the Trisagion and evening troparia out of discipline.

I wonder how my friends are doing, she thought to herself. She knew Maura would be happy to tell her parents about her aptitude. *What was it again? It had something to do with sound – accents? Actress? Acoustics! That's it.* Laurelle on the other hand, would return home empty handed. *How would her parents react? Would they be angry at her? They were both only half-magi, so maybe it was expected.*

There was a way for her to check in on her friends, but it had been a while since she did it. Kalina went on YouTube and searched for

Passerelle. Yes, Sister Maryam had warned against it, but Kalina had been so young then. She was older, smarter, and more advanced in her abilities now. Now that she knew what to avoid, she felt that she could handle it. She placed her noise-canceling headphones over her head and slowly transitioned into a reverie.

Instead of blue, the world became bright and fuzzy. It hurt her eyes at first, but they adjusted. She looked around to find herself in the school library. She wanted to look out the window, but it was too glaring.

She decided to turn around and see where else she could explore. Since there was no one in the library, there was no point in sticking around. Besides, she had already tried reading the books in such a state before, and their undecipherable texts usually woke her out of the reverie.

Kalina carefully paced her way to the double doors that revealed the hallway. Instead of being illumined with overhead lights, though, there were oil lanterns flanking the doors all the way to infinity. All the doors were alike, except they each had a plaque with a name on it. Kalina could instinctively tell which door belonged to whom.

The first door to her right spelt out Catherine Todorova – mom. *No,* she said to herself, *that's not who I'm here for.* She continued down the hallway until she came across a wooden door with concentric rings engraved onto it. She double checked the plaque, which said "Maura Donovan," and she entered.

Vertigo attacked Kalina immediately as she struggled to stay balanced in the shaky dream. She tried to walk to the door, but she ended up collapsing at the edge of the bed, where Maura was crawled up, trembling. She was sobbing loudly, but even louder were the screams that came from outside the room. She couldn't quite hear the voices, but there was a woman yelling something about being angry when drunk – it was too muffled for Kalina to understand. Maura's sister, Aisling, burst in and Kalina felt a string pull her back into the infinite hallway.

That's just a dream, right? Thought Kalina. *Maura and her sister are so nice, there's no way that can be real. It's just a nightmare,* she assured herself.

Next on her list to check was Laurelle. She opened a loose and unmarked door and found herself in a warm, cozy field. Laurelle was at a table with a bunch of friends who looked like they were having a Halloween tea party. There was a fairy, a mouse, and Laurelle herself was dressed up as a candy-corn witch. Kalina smiled to herself at the cozy atmosphere. It reminded her of summers when the family liked to get together for a barbecue and build a bonfire. *Wait a second!*

Kalina looked down to see a flickering light coming from behind her. She turned around to see all of Cardinal Key Academy ablaze and screams of students in the distance. Behind her, she could hear the sound of laughter coming from the tea party. It seemed like a celebration. *There's no way she's enjoying this.* And with that thought, Kalina felt the same string pull her back into the hallway.

After witnessing her roommates' subconscious minds, she wasn't sure if she wanted to continue. *Oh look, there's Robert's!* His door was a darker hue than the others, and it was beautifully engraved with sharp Teutonic designs and weaves. It looked as though he crafted it himself. Kalina tried to open the door, but it was locked. She tried again, but it wouldn't budge. *Go figure he would have the power to block me out.*

Her mind swung like a pendulum, trying to decide whether to keep going or to wake up. As she stared into the distance, though, a figure emerged. Kalina was curious at first, but the figure was quickly growing larger and larger and she realized who it was. This time, however, the veneer of the sweet middle-aged teacher was gone. All that was left was knotted skin and bones, and it was speeding right towards her. Kalina's heart raced, and she panicked. Her legs seemed only to move in slow motion, and she feared that she wouldn't be able to get back to safety.

A door to her left opened up, and a young man pulled her in, rescuing her from the predator.

"I thought you were told to stay away from this realm," quipped the young man. His hair was all shaggy, and he desperately needed to shave.

"Who are you? And what do you want from me?" demanded Kalina.

The young man just rolled his eyes and continued his lecturing.

"I mean cheating in your classes is one thing, but snooping on your friends..." he gave Kalina an extremely judgmental look that her brother had often given her.

"Oh my God," she stated, but her lips couldn't continue.

"You shouldn't take His name in vain," replied Phillip. "Now, how are we going to get you home?"

"Wait, what do you mean? Everyone's worried about you! Where are you? Why are you old? Where can I find you?" She shot each question at her brother with rapid fire.

"Calm down," he said. "It'll all work out for the best. I just came to pop in to save you from that hag and also to let you know that I'm fine. Let everyone else know, too."

"Can't you tell me anything else?"

"Afraid not. It might mess with the spiralization."

"The what?" Kalina glared into the familiar eyes of her brother, but couldn't see anything.

"Yeah, I wouldn't waste your energy on that. I've had twenty years to figure out how to block that, and you aren't even at your peak yet!" Phillip took a deep breath before continuing tersely. "Well, enough chit-chat. Let's get you back."

Phillip outlined a glowing door frame with his finger, and before Kalina could reject, he pushed her through.

EPILOGUE

Phillip landed a few feet away from where he had put the anchor, but it wasn't anywhere in sight. It was dark outside, and his heart panicked when he realized that Kalina wasn't in sight either.

"Kalina!" he shouted, desperately looking for his sister who he had just rescued. *Maybe I didn't reach her in time. Maybe the witch got her before I did!*

All these thoughts clouded his head when he realized he could hear music in the distance. There were faint sounds of students, but who would be out this late at night? He took out a piece of rose-quartz and looked around. *Illusion magic.* He couldn't see beyond it, but maybe Kalina was there. Phillip sprinted over to the illusory bubble, and tripped when he broke through the boundary.

"Hey, man! What do you think you're doing? You've just broken the spell!" shouted a tall teen with a letterman jacket.

Phillip started uncontrollably coughing at all the smoke that permeated the atmosphere, and his ears pulsed at the high pitch of what sounded like a whistle. Shouts rippled through the partying students, each desperate to get away before they could get caught by a teacher.

Phillip himself tried to stand up and gain his bearing, when he heard a shrill woman yelling at him.

"What are you doing outside after hours!" she shrieked

Phillip tried to listen to the rest of what she was shouting, but he couldn't. His world became black, and he passed out.

***

When Phillip woke up, he found himself in Dr. Toumi's office, where there were a couple of other students he didn't recognize also laying down.

"Great job, bozo," said one of them who was awake. "Thanks to you, we got caught. Who knows what the repercussions are going to be."

Phillip recalled the previous night. There were a bunch of students having a party, which was weird. The school would have been on lockdown if Kalina was still missing, but maybe they were celebrating because she was found?

"I'm sorry, I was just looking for my sister."

"What happened to her?"

Before Phillip could respond, a woman in an old nurse's uniform walked in. Quickly, the other boy laid back in bed and pretended to be asleep.

"Looks like our mystery kid is awake," she said.

On cue, an elderly man walked in. Although Phillip didn't know who it was, he thought he looked oddly familiar.

"What's your name, sugar?" asked the nurse.

"My name's Phillip, I'm Kalina's brother."

"Is she a student here?"

The question caught Phillip off guard. *Of course she's a student here. Everybody would have been looking for.*

All he said was "Yes."

"And where do you go to school?"

Phillip looked down at his Cardinal Key hoodie and gestured to it.

"I go to Cardinal Key."

The nurse slowly nodded her head, as if thinking to herself.

"I see," she replied. However, Phillip noticed that her voice sounded like she didn't believe him. Almost how he would talk to a young child that he didn't understand. His mind, more clear, began to be more suspicious of the environment he was in.

"Who even are you? Where's Dr. Toumi?"

"Who?"

"This isn't right. This must be an illusion."

Phillip reached into his pocket to try to find his quartz-glass, but everything had been taken away from him. Quickly, his heart-beat starting to speed up, he got off the cot and went to leave. But the elderly man blocked him off.

"Why don't you sit back down, young man," he said. His voice was stern, but not aggressive. Phillip, though, having just rescued his sister from a bona fide witch who posed as her teacher, was significantly more skeptical of authority.

"I'm going to Dean Schulz, now," he answered.

He turned around and teleported himself into the dean's office, but he wasn't there. Moreover, the whole office looked different, and the typical portrait that stared students down was no longer there. However, the portrait of one of the previous deans was present. Phillip had always thought the eyes in this portrait always looked friendly. As Phillip stared the painted face down, he started shaking his head at an epiphany.

"No, no, no..." he whispered to himself.

The door opened, and the old man walked in.

"I'm glad your magic is still working," he said. "It seems as though you're feeling much better now."

Phillip opened his mouth to speak, but he was tongue tied. He stared at the man, then stared at the painting, then back at the man.

"Are you... no... you're not...."

"Don't say too much. I don't want to know, but I perceive that you're a traveler. That's interesting. I've never heard of one who could travel through time."

"It's not possible," replied Phillip, unsure of himself.

"Well, clearly it is. What year are you from, if you don't mind me asking."

"2024."

The old man – Dean Foster – had walked to the back of his desk and handed Phillip a newspaper.

"Well, Phillip, welcome to the 60s."

Phillip took the newspaper in his hand and looked at the headline:

Reported RFK 'Ultimatum' To Johnson Stirs Tempest

In the top right corner was the date: 18 March 1968.

GLOSSARY AND NOTES

- <u>Leverate:</u> a magical elevator implemented before electrical elevators were invented.

- <u>Nave:</u> the main part of the interior of a church.

- <u>VMB:</u> Virginia Magical Burgess

- <u>USDM:</u> United States Department of Magic

- <u>Psomira:</u> Magus founded breakfast and bakery popular among both the magical and normie communities.

- <u>Pylebridge:</u> Company that sells magical recipes and ingredients.

- <u>MQS:</u> Magical Quality Safety: department of the Magical Union of North America that inspects and approves of magical equipment.

- <u>Mendicol</u>®: Magical potion used to quickly heal and cleanse deep cuts with an advanced burn heal, eventually leaving no scar

- _Pratime Torbe:_ incantation used by Phillip to get his bags to follow him to the men's dorm.

- _Lixalux:_ incantation used by Mark to make a small ball of light. Made by opening the palm of the hand, into which the light flows into.

- _Exsicco_: used by Mark to put out the light. He closes his fist as he saws this.

- _Tardus Cassus:_ slows the fall of an object.

- _Teres terra:_ smooths the ground on a stoickee court.

- _Ygron pyr theto:_ Creates Greek fire; advanced magic.

- _Windows for sight, reveal the light:_ Spell used by Ms. Dalton to open the windows

- _Viasynitou Anemou_: Incantation used by Mark to send a blast of wind at Mr. Wells

- _Escrit en piere, la plume esclere :_ Enchantment spell which either copies or carves a drawing or writing from copy-paper onto the enchanter's object

<u>The Todorova Family:</u>
- Ivan Todorova: mathematician

- Catherine Todorova: physicist

- Kalina: noetic and psychic

- Phillip: teleporter and time traveler

<u>The Poitier Family:</u>
- Norman Poitier: linguist, former Signal Corps officer, VMB employee

- Marie Poitier: naturalist

- Andrew: augur

- Matthew: aeromancer

- John: zoolinguist

- Peter: navigator

- Arthur: naturalist

- Mark: navigator

<u>The Donovan Family:</u>
- David Donovan: Druidry (studied in Ireland)

- Anne Donovan: aeromancer

- Aisling: scribe

- Maura: acoustician

About the Author

Originally from Virginia, Stephen Sterling is a college student studying math, who discovered a passion for writing just over a year ago. *The Witch from the Woods* is his debut novel. Inspired by the fantasy novels of his youth, his goal was to weave together mystery, spirituality, and rich interpersonal dynamics within the enchanting setting of a magical school. Outside of writing, Stephen enjoys learning new languages—a passion that often finds its way into their stories—exercising, and hiking with his beloved dog, Poppy.

Connect with Stephen Sterling:
Instagram: @stephensterling777
X: @SSterling777
E-mail: stephensterling777@gmail.com

www.ingramcontent.com/pod-product-compliance
Lightning Source LLC
Chambersburg PA
CBHW022113310726
48972CB00007B/2011